THE LONGBOAT

NOVELS BY DENNIS VAUGHN

The Price of Revenge
The Longboat

To Sally

THE LONGBOAT

~ ~ ~

A NOVEL

*And friends. Thanks
for your support.*

BY

Dennis Vaughn

THE LONGBOAT

ISBN: 978-0-9964454-5-0

DESIGN | CURT CARPENTER

PRINTED IN THE UNITED STATES

DENLIN PRESS
www.denlinpress.com

TO TAR

Only the hand that erases can write the true thing.

MEISTER ECKHART

Prologue

TWO BOYS walked from the village to the monastery along a dusty road at the edge of the lake. The quiet was broken only by their voices and the squawks of gulls skimming over the water. One boy, dressed in jeans and a blue shirt, scratched a bamboo stick in the dirt. The other, a novice monk with shaved head and burgundy robes, threw rocks at the gulls. A late afternoon breeze caused ripples to lap quietly at the shore and lent slight relief from the oppressive humidity. The skies were clear over Inle Lake, a large body of water nestled like a jewel in the majestic Shan mountains.

Stumbling along, the boys pushed at each other's backs and shoulders, stretched their legs out to trip the other, pretended to fall, all the while jabbering and laughing.

Nyan Win, the novice, cast a stone into the air, calling out, "Be quiet, bird." He turned to his friend and said, "Why do they make so much noise?"

"They're complaining, I guess," Aun San answered.

"About what?"

"Who knows. Even they probably don't know."

After a few moments of silence, the novice said, "I'd stop complaining if you could come to live at the monastery with me."

"Me too, but my uncle won't let me. You know that."

"The abbot wants you there."

"What can I do? My uncle says no, I have to work for him."

"At the monastery we'd see each other every day, just like we did when we were at St. Paul's."

"I wish, but I'm afraid I'll never be able to leave the blacksmith's shop."

At the end of the road, on the water's edge, stood the monastery, the largest structure anywhere around. It was an old two-story, worn wooden building with a rusted tin roof, unidentifiable from the out-side as a religious residence except for the many colorful cotton robes strewn over balconies, saffron, orange and burgundy, waving in the breezes, drying in the sun, licking against the walls like flames. They approached the entrance and agreed to meet there three days later after the longboat race. Nyan Win went in. Aun San turned to walk back to the village. ∾

The older man nodded his appreciation and asked, "Do you speak English at all?"

"Yes, Sir," the boy said. The man wasn't hard to understand. He didn't have the rolling brogue of the strict Irish priests who had taught him at St. Paul's Institute in Rangoon. Nor did he sound like the stuffy British, whose words seemed to come from the depths of their throats.

"My name is Grant Jensen. What's your name?"

Aun San told him.

"Where do you live?"

The boy frowned, wondering why he would ask that question. Obviously, he lived at the lake, and he didn't know exactly how to describe his uncle's house, so he didn't answer.

"How old are you?"

"I am twelve, Sir," Aun San whispered. He wanted to put the same question back, but knew it wasn't polite to ask that of an elder.

"I'm from America." Jensen paused. "Do you know California?"

Aun San said he did. He had seen a few American tourists in the months he'd been living at the lake. They all seemed the same to him—big smiles, friendly, loud and looking for a reason to tip you. But, then they would be gone, as he imagined this visitor soon would be too.

The crew eased the longboat away from the dock. The American positioned his white tennis shoes apart on the deck and tried to imitate the rowers. Instead, he lurched forward, almost losing his oar overboard. The boy watched him, knowing he'd have to grab the beginner if he started to fall off the boat.

Earlier there had been a race between two boats, each with a crew from a different village on the lake. Now a handful of tourists mixed with oarsmen to try the art. Aun San's crew wore white shirts over light orange pants with a wrap at the waist, and sandals. The opposing boat was the same, except they had blue shirts. Jensen, who wore dark, aviator-style glasses and a broad-brimmed hat, had

ONE

The Fall

AUN SAN WATCHED as the tall, middle-aged Westerner boarded the longboat. The man glanced around and took a position on the port side next to him. He smiled at the boy, who lowered his head. The longboat, a narrow, rough, wooden racing craft fifty feet long, sat low in the water. It had no motor. A crew of forty propelled it from a standing position moving bamboo oars in a circular motion with the soles of their feet. Inle Lake was the only place where this peculiar method was used, having evolved because the reeds and floating plants on the water made it difficult to see ahead without standing.

The Western man tried twisting his left foot around an oar, then dipping the blade into the water. He broke the surface with a splash, sending spray in every direction. He shrugged.

Aun San covered his mouth, his dark, oval eyes alive. He didn't dare glance at the other young crew member, just an arms length in front of him, flicking lake water from his shirt. Aun San remembered how awkward it had been learning to row this way when he had first come to Inle Lake from Rangoon a year before. He moved toward the man and, with a shy grin, demonstrated how to brace the oar with the lower leg while leaning over the side far enough for the blade to enter the water without splashing.

been directed to join the white-shirt crew. The rest of the tourists were assigned to one crew or the other.

The race began. The boats churned through the water, the oars dipping in with near perfect synchronization. The older man and the boy, standing side by side, glanced at one another, both yelling for victory. But no words passed between them. Aun San rowed with confidence, while Jensen held tight with one hand to the boat's middle bar, trying to grip the oar with his left foot. Just then, his hand slipped from the bar and he began to fall. Aun San grabbed him by the shirt and tried to pull him back. The big body sprawled on the deck, his shirt ripped in the back and his hat and glasses hanging askew from straps around his neck. Jensen pulled himself up without acknowledging what had happened, though Aun San thought he saw a sign of real fear on the visitor's face. The man, who was no longer smiling, gripped the middle bar with both hands until the end of the race.

The boats passed the finish line in a dead heat, as always happened when tourists came onboard, and headed to the dock to drop the guests for lunch. Aun San couldn't wait to get back to the village and run to the monastery where he would tell Nyan Win about saving the old American. His best friend wasn't permitted by the abbot to take part in the races. As for Aun San, crewing in the longboat race was the only reason his uncle would let him leave work at his blacksmith shop.

Grant Jensen walked along the rickety wooden dock, then turned and looked back. The longboats were pulling away. The rough-hewn vessels were a distinct contrast to his sleek sailboat, moored in a Los Angeles marina, which was not as long but nearly triple the width. Nothing he required of his racing crew came close to the ease and elegance with which the longboat crews moved.

Jensen saw that everyone rowed, except Aun San, who stood staring at the dock. Jensen waved. The boy waved too, but the man couldn't be sure whether it was directed to him or someone else. He had an urge to have the boat stopped so he could arrange to see the lad again, to talk with him. The resemblance to his son, Peter, shocked him. No matter that they had different coloring, they had the same broad smile, the same facial expressions, the same awkward, jerky movements, the same shy yet warm quality. But it was too late. The longboats were now far offshore. Jensen signaled with both arms. The boy responded. Yes, the boy saw him. Maybe he was still smiling, he thought.

Soon he could no longer distinguish Aun San from the others who were rowing. Jensen noticed a heron strut at the edge of the water. Suddenly it took off, extending its wings, and followed the boats out into the lake. Peter had been fascinated by the great blue herons that roamed the banks of rivers they had fished together. With their long legs and neck, he always said they looked prehistoric. Jensen didn't believe in omens, but he had to wonder whether this might not be one. A shiver charged through him.

He turned and walked toward land. He had been stunned when the boy saved him from going overboard. It brought back the image he had lived with every day for the last two years—Peter, there one minute, suddenly clawing the sides of the tipping canoe, then falling into the roiling water.

He removed his hat and shook his head, running his hand through a mass of unkempt wet grey hair. The heat and humidity drained him. It must have been a hundred degrees. He felt sticky, like he was being fried despite all the sun block he had slathered on his face.

His wife, Evelyn, walked toward him from the spot on the beach where she'd viewed the longboats. She was protected from the sun and heat by a loose fitting orange blouse and a large straw hat. She had refused to join the race and had tried to discourage him. Since their son's accident, it was all she could do to board a boat with a motor, much less one without.

"New friend?" she asked. "It looked as though you were waving to someone you'd known all your life."

"No, he's a boy from my boat. I rowed next to him."

"What's his name?"

"I couldn't get it. These Burmese double-word names drive me crazy. Something like Ayn Rand."

She laughed and pushed her sunglasses up the bridge of her nose. "He probably had the same trouble with yours. Why the big attachment? Did he save you from falling in?"

"Not exactly. Well, he did grab my shirt once." He paused, wondering whether to tell her how this gesture had transported him back to Peter on the river. Instead, he said, "I wish you'd gone."

"Not a chance," she replied. "By the way, your shirt is torn."

He turned his head, his wiry eyebrows arched, and reached to find the tear. "Damn." He started to steer her toward a small café for lunch but stopped to light a Camel. The smoke circled above his head. "You're going to think I'm crazy, Evie. Maybe I am. I felt like I was, well, with Peter."

Wrinkles etched across her forehead. She glanced toward the water, then back, and asked, "How's that?"

"He was so much like him."

"What do you mean? There isn't a boy in this country with blond hair and blue eyes. There's no one like Peter."

"It's not the coloring," Grant replied. "It's his smile, his bearing. You know, that sort of head down, eyes cast upward, grinning look."

"Sounds more like Daisy," she said, her voice soft. He could see sadness in her eyes. He knew why. Their golden retriever, head down, eyes up, always made him think of Peter, too.

Trying to lighten the load, he said, "that beast"— his term of endearment for the nine-year old mutt he showered with hugs and pets and affection at every opportunity.

"Don't call Daisy a beast," she choked.

"Sorry. Bad timing." He took her hand in his. "I felt I was with him again. The boy's the same age, twelve. He's tall like Peter, and slim."

She cleared her throat. "How do you know how old he is?"

"He told me."

"So, he did talk?"

"Not really. Mostly, he didn't answer my questions."

"Well, he probably didn't understand you."

"No, he said 'my name is' and 'twelve' in English."

Her eyes widened with surprise.

"We may be in the Third World," he said, "but thanks to the Brits long ago, lots of people speak English."

At the entrance to the café, she stretched one hand to his collar, the other to the side of his face. He was over a foot taller than she was. "You know, Inle Lake is almost ethereal," she said. "The stillness, the calmness of the water, the huge mountains closing in on all this flatness."

"I know. I feel it."

"You can see how someone might get carried away by it. Particularly someone like you. So loving, and emotional, and sometimes, you know, a bit impulsive. Better not, don't you think?"

His shoulders slumped. He shook his head, not in denial, but in acceptance. Her dark brown hair was beginning to show a tinge of grey. She'd added weight despite the strain they'd lived through. No matter the changes since they met, she was still as desirable to him as the first day he'd seen her on campus at Berkeley. "Always the one with calm advice," he said. Then, his face brightened, "But I'd like to see him again. And you definitely should meet him. You won't believe it."

She frowned. "Grant, didn't we come here to get away from all that?"

He knew the reason they were here. The same thing that had impelled them to hike the Inca Trail in Peru, raft the Colorado in the Grand Canyon, and canoe the Zambezi in Botswana. Their love of tough adventure provided respites from their hectic lives and his responsibilities at the *Los Angeles Post*. The international newspaper publishers' meeting in New Delhi was a convenient excuse to carry them halfway around the world, within close range of this exotic, beautiful country they'd always wanted to visit. Grant's counterpart at the *Rangoon Times* had used his influence to obtain an extended visa and to make the difficult travel arrangements.

He patted her on the back. Their lives had been fraught with pain ever since the Botswana trip two years before. He thought of Peter constantly and re-ran their decision to take canoes out on that river. He wondered deep down if she blamed him for not saving Peter, though she never said as much. He knew that she too struggled with guilt and anguish. How stupid of them. How could they have been that irresponsible? Yes, he was emotional sometimes. And maybe a little impulsive from time to time. But this was different. Now, in the middle of nowhere, Peter was with them again. The boy with the smile. ⌁

TWO

Flame to Flame

THE NEXT MORNING, Grant and Evelyn boarded a small motorboat for the village that had manned Grant's longboat the day before. The water was calm and a slight fog, streaming randomly, rose from the marshes. Huts spotted in the reeds showed signs of life: women hanging brightly colored clothes on lines, and children playing on shaky wooden decks extending over the water. A few larger, sturdier tin buildings supported on stilts looked as though they might be unoccupied. An occasional *wat*, a small Buddhist shrine, rose above the lake's surface.

After the race, Grant had approached their Burmese guide, Kyi Kyi, about finding the boy. He said he'd been on the white shirt boat and his name sounded like Ayn Rand or Aunt Sand, or something like that. He described his age, height and weight, but his description of the boy's skin tone, black hair and dark eyes failed to distinguish him from almost all other adolescent males in the country.

Evelyn tried to talk him out of finding the boy, but he said, "We've got to. Just to talk with him. When you see him, you'll understand." Grant didn't acknowledge he was already thinking about how they might help Aun San.

She went along, reluctantly. She didn't want to get on another boat, but she was, after all, on a lake and needed to get around somehow. One operated with a motor ought to be safe enough, she tried to convince herself. She had to admit she was curious about the child. Mostly, though, she knew she would have to join her husband to counter his impulsive nature, an impulsiveness at one time she found attractive. Now it only served to distinguish him from many of his uptight peers, those titans of business who seemed so cautious about everything.

It had first manifested itself with boats, starting with a simple dinghy many years earlier, then working up to the current *Little Lady II*, named after her. It was not "little" and the name embarrassed her.

About a year ago, he saw an even larger yacht he wanted to buy. No matter that his constant crew member, Peter, was gone. Or that she wouldn't board the boat after Peter's death. Or that their teen-age daughter, Kathy, had lost interest in sailing. *What was he going to do, bob around out there in the water by himself?* Evelyn consulted a psychiatrist who said that, in addition his natural impulsiveness, her husband was probably experiencing an early mid-life crisis engendered by a disparate need to reach out and find something to hold onto in the wake of the loss of Peter. She might be comforted, the doctor suggested, that it wasn't another woman. Grant refused to see "any shrink" but he did back off the idea of the new boat. She trusted her husband and tried to be patient, but now she was apprehensive about this boy.

The boatmen shut down the motor and took up their oars. After twenty yards the boat dug into soft, dark fertile soil where the water retreated and rows of vegetables grew—floating gardens, man-made with dirt and algae pulled up from the lake. Tawny-skinned men and women wearing broad straw hats walked the narrow furrows tending their tomatoes, beans, eggplant and flowers to be sold at market. The guide explained the mystery of converting water to land as she walked with them along a path from the lake toward a small community.

In the center of the village a parade of people, young and old, men and women, carried building materials down the road, like a line of ants dragging leaves to a hill. The women, dressed in colorful traditional *longyi*, stowed their loads in straw baskets balanced on their heads. Yellow *thanaka* markings, which served both as a cosmetic and sunblock, decorated their cheeks. Men, clad in jeans or *longyi* and shirts, carried larger quantities on stretchers.

At the end of the street a wooden frame structure was under construction. As tall as a three-story building, it towered over the one-story stores with corrugated tin roofs that lined both sides of the street. From a distance, it resembled giant matchsticks tied together. Kyi Kyi explained it was to be a temple, and that all able-bodied people in the village were participating in the project, hauling dirt, stones and water from the riverbed to use in erecting the walls. The racket of nails being pounded, saws grinding through wood and sledge hammers smashing rocks rose in a roar from the site. As befit a temple, it would be the largest building in the vicinity.

Kyi Kyi went to the general store to inquire about Aun San, leaving the Jensens behind. The townspeople, walking in a loose procession, chattering and laughing, stared at Grant and Evelyn who returned the stares just as intently. From every appearance, the villagers were happy, despite their hard work. After some time, as Grant stood watching, a tall, rangy lad in jeans halted in the line returning to the river. He held one end of an empty stretcher. A young monk in robes, his head bald, held the other end. The tall boy looked at Grant who leaned down to Evelyn, pointing as he whispered, "That's him." Grant waved. The boy dropped one hand from the stretcher and waved back, grinning.

They started to walk toward him when the guide reappeared. Excited, Grant pointed and said, "That's the boy."

"You are sure, Mr. Grant?"

"Absolutely."

"Let me talk with him," she said, and moved the two boys to the side, out of the line of people doing the work of animals or machines.

With the monk watching, Kyi Kyi started a conversation. "What's your name?" she asked.

"Aun San."

"You speak English?"

"Yes."

Kyi Kyi asked where he lived and about his family. She was animated. Head bowed, his answers were brief. The monk listened.

The guide turned to Grant. "He does remember you from yesterday, Mr. Grant."

Aun San smiled.

"His English is quite good," she said. "Aun San, this is Mr. Jensen and his wife, Mrs. Jensen."

"Hello, Sir. Hello, Ma'am," Aun San whispered, reaching to grip Grant's extended hand.

"I've explained that you would like to talk with him. He is pleased. He would like you to meet his uncle whose house is down that road."

The boy's dark eyes flashed at the edges of a broad nose. His black hair stood straight up. He and Peter look nothing alike, Evelyn thought, except the smile. It was Peter's . "Tell him yes," Evelyn said.

Grant clapped his hands together once and said "Good." Not more than a hundred yards down the road they arrived at a small house made of wood and bamboo, surrounded by chickens picking in the dirt and two sore-infested dogs lying still in the sun. The shack had no front door, only a framed opening. Aun San went in and returned with a man who appeared to be about forty years old to whom Kyi Kyi spoke in Burmese. The guide introduced him as the boy's uncle. Grant tipped his head in acknowledgment. The uncle stood motionless.

"Aun San came from Rangoon to live here when his parents disappeared. It is thought they might have died after they joined the rebels against the junta, but no one is sure." Her voice dropped. "It is best not to talk about fighting against the military regime, you understand?"

The Jensens nodded.

"Aun San is shy," she added.

The boy glanced away.

Kyi Kyi continued. "He attended a very good school in Rangoon, but he does not go to school here."

Grant turned toward his wife. Her green eyes darted; her small mouth fell slightly ajar.

"Do you live here?" he asked, nodding toward the shelter.

Aun San's head moved slowly up and down. He turned toward his uncle standing at the entrance, then away.

"How long have you been here?" Grant asked.

"About a year, Sir."

"Did you like your school in Rangoon?"

"Yes, Sir."

"How many years did you go there?"

"Three, Sir."

"You don't go to school here?"

"I can't, Sir."

"Do you know where we live?" Evelyn interjected.

"He told me that on the boat, Ma'am. United States."

Grant raised his eyebrows. Black with grey, they matched his hair and seemed to jump when he spoke. "You know the United States?"

"We studied about it at St. Paul's, Sir."

"Did you learn about Hollywood? It's close to where we live," Evelyn asked

"Yes Ma'am, film," he replied, eyes wide.

The uncle stared at them as they spoke. Grant asked the guide, "Does he understand?"

"Oh, no."

Facing Kyi Kyi, Grant said, "He's lost his schooling. I wonder, is there a way we could help?"

The guide translated the idea. The boy and his uncle spoke in their language, the uncle in a stern voice, moving his arms up and down.

"I can tell he is very bright," Kyi Kyi whispered. "He cannot go to school though. He must work in the blacksmith shop. It is his uncle's business."

"Can we send him paper and pencils, maybe books, that kind of thing?" Evelyn asked.

The guide translated again. "The uncle says yes, Mrs. Evelyn." Kyi Kyi turned from Aun San and whispered to the Jensens. "The poor children in the villages, like him, need all these things. Understand, you don't know he will receive them."

Aun San said, "Thank you very much."

No one spoke. There seemed to be nothing more to say. As they turned to leave, Grant bent down and held out his large, strong hand to envelop the boy's. The return handshake was weak.

"We hope to see you again," Grant said.

The boy smiled, then looked away.

Aun San's situation preoccupied Grant and Evelyn as they prepared for bed in the modest inn that had been recommended to them.

"It's terrible what that man's doing, won't let him go to school, makes him work in that boiling place." Evelyn said, "What kind of an uncle is that?"

"The per capita income here isn't even a dollar a day," Grant said. "They have to put food on the table."

"But didn't Kyi Kyi say the uncle has six other children. That's practically an army."

"It sounds like you're more fired up about the kid than I am."

"No. I feel sorry for him. Here he is, speaking English, bright, but having to drag rocks and sand through town and work as a blacksmith. He's only twelve."

Their room and its trappings reflected the tropics: thatched ceiling and bamboo floor, bare of rugs. Candles and vases of orchids on the bedside tables lent a feeling of warmth.

"And, what about," his voice dropped, "Peter?"

"Honestly, yes, I do see him—a bit, that is. The facial expressions, the slight body, the sparkle of the eyes." She squinted as if trying to picture Peter again. "You know, Grant, the smile is yours. Like Peter's was yours."

Grant swallowed, then spoke. "So, now, who's the one affected by the ethereal quality of Inle Lake?" She didn't answer. "I was thinking about something more than paper, pencils and books, Evie."

"Such as?"

"Seeing that he goes to a good school."

"What?"

"I haven't been able to get him off my mind. We could do so much for this young boy, not forever mind you, for just a year. It's the most valuable thing we could give him. It would be a tribute to Peter, too."

"Where would he go?"

"I guess, Broadmoor, and live with us."

"We don't even know him, Grant. What would Kathy say about a stranger coming to live with us? Fifteen is a difficult time and with the loss of Peter..."

"She could handle it, I think. At least, we'd see what she thinks of it."

"Well, who can say he'd be better off after a year in school in America than staying right here living the life that is part of his culture?"

He handed her a cigarette which she waved away, telling him they shouldn't smoke in a thatched house. She permitted herself two cigarettes a day. He, two packs. At her suggestion, they went outside for him to smoke where they found Kyi Kyi sitting on the porch. Kyi Kyi, a short woman about forty-five years old, was dressed, as she always was, in light weight Western clothes. During daylight hours she invariably added a yellow floppy hat so she could be easily seen.

"We will be leaving at nine in the morning for Mandalay, Mr. Grant, Mrs. Evelyn," the guide said. "You should have everything ready about an hour before."

Grant placed his hand on Evelyn's. "I'm not sure we should leave yet, before we know more about Aun San."

"We know about all there is to know," Evelyn answered. "We can arrange for school supplies, but that's all, really." She paused, "Will you help us, Kyi Kyi?"

"But . . . ," Grant started.

Evelyn interrupted, "But, we have reservations, Grant."

"I'd like to see if there might be some way we could have him come to the United States to school. For just one year."

Evelyn turned to Kyi Kyi. "That's Mr. Jensen's idea. It is not mine."

"Yes. I'd like to explore it," he said.

"I imagine that is impossible anyway, Mr. Grant. His uncle needs him to work."

Grant had already anticipated this hurdle. "It would be one less mouth to feed. Perhaps we could make it up to the uncle. A small stipend as if Aun San were still here contributing to the family."

Kyi Kyi looked first at Grant, then at Evelyn, a bit bewildered. "I do not know what the rules are for this type of thing."

"I work for a newspaper in the States. Our lawyers can get involved, make arrangements there and find a lawyer for us in Rangoon." He faced his wife. "You know, I'm talking about possibilities. We'll have to think this out."

"We certainly will. And Kyi Kyi shouldn't have to be in the middle of it." Evelyn was irritated but not totally surprised by her husband's suggestion that Aun San come with them. She saw it as vintage Grant— spontaneous, generous, bold, sometimes maddening.

"I agree. But, Kyi Kyi, if we were to decide that we want to meet with Aun San one more time, tomorrow, can you rearrange things in Mandalay and Bagan to give us an extra day or two here?"

"Of course, Mr. Grant." The guide hesitated. "I will try if you want."

The next morning, they walked again through the beehive of construction activity in the village and down the road to find Aun San. He was with two monks by a dilapidated fence across the dirt road from his uncle's house. One appeared to be the novice who had been with him working in the village the day before. With identical robes wrapped over the left shoulder and heads shaved to a black stubble, it was hard to distinguish one monk from another, but the other was older and larger. Both carried alms bowls and were barefoot.

Aun San crossed the road to greet his visitors. His uncle glared at them from the doorway. The boy pointed toward the monks and said, "I told them you might be able to find some pencils, papers and books for the monastery. Would you like to go there, Ma'am, Sir? It is not far."

Grant and Evelyn glanced at each other. They had not reached a decision the night before on how they would approach the conversation this morning. She hadn't really wanted to see the boy again, though she hadn't gone so far as to refuse her husband's request. He knew she could stand her ground, so he interpreted her failure to refuse as indicating at least some interest in talking with him.

Grant answered, "Of course we would." He had to hide his excitement. If there were some way to bring the boy home with them, it might make all the difference, he thought. Not that anyone, anything could replace Peter. But with a focus on Aun San and the future, maybe the love and warmth that filled their home before the tragedy could be found again.

The group started down the dusty road, Kyi Kyi and Aun San in the lead chatting in Burmese, followed by Grant and Evelyn. The monk and the novice took up the rear. People in the fields stopped work to look as the group passed by. After five minutes, they arrived at the monastery. The older monk walked quickly ahead to the entrance of the building. He acted as a person of authority—the abbot undoubtedly—welcoming his guests in English, placing the fingers of both hands together at his chin, bowing slightly. He removed his sandals. The others followed his lead. They entered a room that smelled of the moldy bamboo that formed its floor, walls and ceiling. A modest Buddha image occupied a central position on one wall. The abbot dismissed a group of young monks who had been sitting on the matted floor, but turned to one novice, Aun San's good friend, Nyan Win, and directed him to stay.

The abbot introduced himself as U Tha Din and invited his visitors to sit on the floor. Kyi Kyi introduced the Jensens. After tea was served, the cleric proceeded to explain life in the monastery, the *kyoung* as he called it. Novitiates are young men between the ages of ten and twenty who take up temporary residence in the monastery, a common expectation in Burmese society. They spend long hours studying and walking in the community with their alms bowls begging for food. The abbot said he hoped someday Aun San's uncle would let him come to the monastery to live with his friend. Nyan Win stood by the wall, head bowed, embarrassed to hear his name. He was slightly shorter than Aun San, but appeared to be about the same age. The abbot asked the Jensens questions about their life in the United States, explaining he had attended school there for five years. He looked to be in his mid-thirties though it was hard to tell. He knew of Los Angeles where he had spent a month in a monastery and where he had seen the *Los Angeles Post*. "You are here on a story?"

Grant smiled and said he wasn't.

"About our rulers? You have freedom of the press. We have none. "

"I know that. It is too bad."

"Are you a reporter?"

"No." Grant hesitated before adding, "I'm the publisher."

The abbot turned to Kyi Kyi and spoke in Burmese. She used the word "publisher." The abbot, pursing his lips, said, "I see."

"My wife and I are going to New Delhi for a meeting and decided to vacation here. We met Aun San and hoped we might be able to help him."

"Everyone here needs help, Mr. Jensen. There is no democracy. The military junta decides everything. People barely survive. You see how they live in the villages."

Grant nodded. Aun San stared at the floor. Nyan Win appeared to be uncomfortable as he edged a foot or two toward a hallway.

The conversation turned to the kinds of school supplies the Jensens might provide the monks. Eventually, a gong sounded outside the room. The abbot got up, thanked his guests for coming and asked Nyan Win to show them the building and grounds. The abbot bowed, his fingers pressed together at his chin, and left the room. The gesture, called *Namaste*, symbolized sending energy from the Buddha in one person to the Buddha in another.

Nyan Win led the tour, giving brief descriptions in English of the rooms and their uses. Bed mats, with the monks' few possessions beside them, lined the floors. The monks, robes removed, torso bare, bathed outdoors using a bucket and a hose. Young ones bent over others, shaving their heads, sometimes removing lice. Evelyn looked away revolted by the lice scene.

The monks ate at long tables outdoors, set under a balcony to avoid the rain. In the adjacent kitchen, vats boiled over open fires with soups and a variety of rice concoctions that were stirred with wooden instruments practically the size of shovels. A typical meal consisted of fish paste, beans and rice. Lines formed to fill bowls.

The tour complete, Kyi Kyi, the Jensens and Aun San headed back to town. The abbot and Nyan Win remained behind.

When they arrived back at the uncle's house, Grant stopped. "Thank you for taking us to the monastery, Aun San," he said. "It was interesting to see how life is lived there."

"You are welcome, Sir."

"We'd be happy to get some things for the monks," Evelyn offered. "Kyi Kyi said she can help us with that."

"Of course, Mrs. Evelyn."

Grant turned to Aun San. "But what we really want to do is to help you." Choosing his words carefully, as much for his wife's benefit as for the boy's, he asked, "Have you thought of continuing your schooling in the United States? You could get a fine education there." He hadn't come fully intending to say that, but there it was.

Evelyn stood rigid, her jaws clenched.

The boy appeared startled by the suggestion, but didn't respond. "You're not going to get it here, that's clear," Grant added, pointing to the lake and waving his arm in a half-circle.

Aun San hesitated for a long time before he spoke. "Probably, that is true, Sir," he shrugged. "My cousins, they don't go to school. They work, some with me in the blacksmith shop. One cousin works in a gold leaf factory."

"I can talk to your uncle. I could make up for the work he'll lose," Grant said.

"Could Nyan Win come too, Sir?" the boy asked.

"No, no, that would not be possible," Grant answered.

"Then I could not go, Sir," Aun San lowered his voice and glanced at his uncle standing in the doorway. "I could not leave Nyan Win. He is my best friend. I see him a lot, even though I cannot be in the monastery with him."

"How do you know him so well?" Kyi Kyi asked.

"He came here about the same time I did, also from Rangoon. We were at St. Paul's together. His mother died and his father sent him to live with his grandmother down the road. She had him go to the *kyoung*."

Kyi Kyi said, "Aun San, this could be a wonderful opportunity. You don't know when your parents will return to take you back to Rangoon."

"My parents will not return. Some people say they are rebels still fighting in the mountains. But they are trying to make me feel better. I am sure they were killed by the soldiers."

"I'm sorry." Grant waited before going on. "If that's the case though, all the more reason for you to come to the United States."

"I understand, Sir. I would like to come. I want to go back to school. I don't want to be a blacksmith." He took a deep breath. "But I could not leave Nyan Win. I am sorry. You are generous. I like you. But I cannot think only of myself. I must think of my friend."

Grant and Evelyn stood—silent. Grant was frustrated, not knowing where to turn. He lit a Camel. Smoke swirled about him. Evelyn stared.

"I understand what Aun San means," the guide said. "Buddhism places great importance on loyalty, on thinking of others, on treating others as you would have them treat you. Aun San would not want to see Nyan Win leave, even if leaving were the best thing for Nyan Win to do for himself."

Evelyn faced Grant. A sign of relief passed her face. "Well, that settles that. It's impossible."

Aun San whispered to Kyi Kyi. She turned to Grant and Evelyn. "He doesn't understand why you want him to come with you. You don't know him."

Grant felt that being completely honest was the only possible way to convince the boy he should come. "Aun San, you remind us so much of our son, Peter. You look like him, your face, your expression, the way you hold yourself. Most of all, your smile." He paused and added, "He died two years ago. At your age." Grant turned to hide the deep blue eyes that he knew were clouding.

"Why did he die, Sir?"

"An accident. A very bad accident." He didn't go on to explain that he drowned or how it happened. "He was smart. You're smart. You need to be in a good school. You aren't able to go back to the school in Rangoon. You aren't even being permitted to go into the monastery. This could change your life." Grant said nothing about the concerns Evelyn had mentioned the night before: the impact on their daughter, Kathy, and whether this might raise unrealistic expectations when Aun San actually would be better off staying in his own environment.

Aun San pushed the sole of his sandal against the dirt. "You think his flame has lighted mine?"

"What does that mean?" Evelyn asked, her eyebrows arched in anticipation of the answer. Her vision of Peter too often was her last: crouched in the raised canoe, waiving a paddle in the air, screaming, his face contorted with terror.

Kyi Kyi tried to explain the Buddhist belief—that with the death of one personality, a new one comes into being, or, as it is said, the flame from a dying candle can serve to light the flame of another.

"You mean reincarnation?" Evelyn asked.

"Many Westerners think of it this way, Mrs. Evelyn, but it is not," Kyi Kyi answered. "It is called transmigration in English, I believe.

Each flame is causally connected to the one that came before. It is not the same flame though."

Aun San rubbed the back of his wrist on his nose. "I am sorry, Sir."

Grant strained to retain his composure. He looked at Evelyn who turned away. He had no choice but to relent. He said to the guide. "Kyi Kyi, please tell him we hope we will see him again."

Without need for translation, Aun San replied, "I also hope I see you again, Sir, Ma'am. Maybe someday you will come back to Inle Lake."

Grant, Evelyn and Kyi Kyi walked down the road back toward the boat. Grant saw tears welling in Evelyn's eyes. He knew why. Not because she wanted Aun San to come with them. Everyone already thought they were crazy for taking the kids canoeing in Africa, as she had blurted out when they were going to bed the night before. To come back from this trip with a twelve year old from Burma would be a living reminder of the tragedy and what a horrible mistake they had made. No, her tears were for Peter, and they were for Grant. Was it all to end right there?

Trying to find words, Evelyn asked, "What did he mean when he referred to his cousin working in a factory having something to do with gold?"

Kyi Kyi answered, lips spread and tight. "Gold leaf. They make all the gold leaf you see everywhere here. It is very, very hard work." Then she brightened. "But, there is easier work, too. Let me take you, Mrs. Evelyn, to a silk weaving workshop. You may find something you like and the price will be very good." ∽

THREE

Inhumane Labor

GRANT AND EVELYN left Inle Lake with Kyi Kyi and their driver, headed for Mandalay. Travel was slow, through picturesque countryside with farmers on wooden plows behind water buffalo or driving horse carts laden with crops. Late in the day they reached Mandalay, a metropolis by comparison to the lush peacefulness they had left.

Immediately on arrival, Grant wired the newspaper's general counsel and asked him to do two things: investigate what the rules are in the U.S. governing a student visa for a Burmese child, and arrange an appointment with a lawyer in Rangoon who could advise them on the subject under Burmese law. He decided not to discuss this with Evelyn at this point. There could be no harm in a simple inquiry.

They became sightseers in this exotic city, Kyi Kyi leading the way into temples, pagodas, monasteries, bazaars, and factories that sold the wares they made. Monks, in saffron or blood red robes, some wearing sandals, some barefoot, walked the dusty, rough streets singly and in groups, alms bowls in hand. Many had indecipherable tattoos on their chests, shoulders or arms.

Evelyn asked to see a gold leaf factory, and the building where the driver stopped looked like a traditional Burmese retail store. Glass-topped cabinets contained gold jewelry and packages of gold leaf. Kyi

Kyi explained that men purchased the gold leaf to apply to Buddha images as an act of piety or for good luck. Women were not allowed to do this for fear of harming the Buddha's potency.

In the back of the shop, against a wall, three young men, stripped to the waist, sinewy muscles rippling under their sweat, heaved huge mallets from above their shoulders down to to the floor to crush bits of gold. Each hit produced a loud thud. Kyi Kyi explained this was the process for creating the gilt used on the Buddhas and temple domes throughout the country. Evelyn gasped watching these automatons steadily hammering up and down, up and down, not even able to pause to wipe a dripping brow. They were permitted to break only after all of the water in a half-coconut on the floor mercifully drained through a small opening in the shell. A reed basket on the floor held the meager tips for which they slaved, to which Evelyn added a few *kyats* from her wallet.

As they stepped into the street to find their driver, Evelyn turned to Kyi Kyi. "Is this the kind of factory where Aun San said his cousin works?"

"Yes, Mrs. Evelyn. I told you it was hard work. Now you see."

"Which job does his cousin have?" Evelyn asked, backing away as if she didn't want the answer.

"I know. I asked Aun San."

"Which?"

"The one with a mallet."

Evelyn's body shuddered.

Grant lit a cigarette. "I've never seen such relentless physical work anywhere in my life. It makes our guys in the pressroom look like they're floating on clouds."

"It's inhuman. They never stop," Evelyn said.

"Eventually they get to rest, Mrs. Evelyn, but it is not often, as you could see," Kyi Kyi added.

"There's gold everywhere in this country." Evelyn almost snorted. "Every Buddha, every temple, and there are thousands of them, is covered in gilt. I can't imagine how many people must be doing this work."

"They are all young men, like those you saw, even boys," Kyi Kyi answered. "No one else could do it."

"What happens when they can't anymore?" This time the question came from Grant.

"They go to the Irrawaddy River and load and unload the barges, Mr. Grant. Not that work on the barges is easy. But at least the body does not have to be in motion every second. We will see tomorrow when we board the boat for Bagan."

That night at their hotel, over dessert, Evelyn and Grant returned to the subject that had come to dominate their trip. Flames from the candles on the table flickered, swaying back and forth as words passed between them. His hand covered hers on the table.

"You know, Grant, I'd dismissed the idea of being able to do anything for Aun San, take him home, that is. It seemed," she hesitated, "too much, and actually impossible when he brought Nyan Win into the picture."

"Doesn't it still?" he asked.

"Yes. But I can't erase the gold leaf factory from my mind. If the uncle has a son doing that awful work, imagine where Aun San might end up."

"I don't have to imagine to come up with that answer."

She remembered the nights when she would awaken and not find Grant next to her in bed. She would go to the head of the stairs where she heard sobs, only partially muffled by the closed door to the den. The first few times she went to him, but she couldn't seem to find a way to help. Nothing she said could convince him that he had dived long enough, or deep enough, to find his boy. And how, he'd almost choke, had he ever let anyone in his family go on that river in a canoe? She felt her husband had been more emotionally damaged than anyone, not only because of his feelings of responsibility, but because Peter had been so like him.

"So, I agree," she said, "Aun San should come for one year. But, we have to decide how this might impact Kathy. In a difficult period of adolescence, and still mourning her brother, I'm not sure she'd go along."

"She would have to agree, of course. We should see a lawyer when we get to Rangoon. Who knows? The whole thing may be academic. Maybe we can't get a student visa for him. We sure as hell can't sneak him out."

The next morning, they walked the sandy beaches along the Irrawaddy before departing by river boat to Bagan. The shore was crowded with lines of workers passing bags of sand one to another up the beach to the road. Others unloaded huge earthenware jars from the barges. Young women labored alongside men. As they toiled, their children played and hid among the jars. Kyi Kyi was right. Work on the river was hard too, but nothing like the gold leaf pounders.

Their small ship, the Pandaw, was luxurious, particularly by comparison to what they were seeing ashore. The crew dressed in starched whites. Staterooms were paneled in rich teak. The river boat rang of another era, the British colonial period. The contrast between the privileged and the poor in this otherwise beguiling country was stark and continually evident as they cruised south. Poverty seemed to exist everywhere. Monks apparently were spared by begging food from people who didn't look like they had enough to feed themselves.

Two nights on the river brought them to the golden city of Bagan where 2000 or so temples and pagodas from the eleventh and twelfth centuries survived, dotting the flat countryside. Each had a distinct personality. Kyi Kyi dragged them into what seemed like twenty of them, but the Jensens had lost interest in temples, Buddhas, hotels and meals. They went round and round about Aun San without resolution.

≈　≈　≈

After a week in New Delhi for the publishers' meeting, Evelyn and Grant returned to Rangoon. They stayed again at the Strand, the city's oldest hotel. It was a relic of British colonialism with wood paneling, high ceilings, whooshing fans, and friendly, uniformed staff. Once a stopping place for the likes of Rudyard Kipling and Somerset Maugham, its luster had passed, the furnishings now musty and threadbare. The elaborate wrought-iron lift was essentially unusable because, the porters warned, the fickle electrical supply could leave occupants trapped for hours.

The morning after their arrival Kyi Kyi, with a driver, showed them the sights of Rangoon in an aged but brightly polished black Buick sedan. The street scene was frantic with people walking, riding bikes, peddling rickshaws and trishaws, and hanging precariously three deep off the backs of green, white and red buses that spewed smoke into the air. Small stores faced the streets with hawkers in front on the sidewalks selling nuts, vegetables, fish, meats, local fried delicacies, wooden carvings, whatever their wares might be. Evelyn looked, wide-eyed and smiling. She liked nothing better than a street market and this was one in motion.

Buildings were in a state of deterioration, including the once elegant, old colonial homes, plaster cracking and paint peeling from their walls. In some, laundry hung from upper floor windows, partially masking the faces that peered down to survey the street scene below. Chaotic electrical wiring above street level defied the possibility that electricity and telephones were operable here.

Their appointment was scheduled with a lawyer found by the *Post's* general counsel. Evelyn had finally acceded to Grant's request to pursue the idea of bringing Aun San to Los Angeles. He emphasized they were simply fact finding and no decision would be made without her approval—her enthusiastic approval, he said.

Kyi Kyi gave the driver the address on Pansodan Road, which was located in an area populated by tea shops and bookstalls. The car pulled up in front of a three-story, faded cream-colored building.

Evelyn and Grant got out and walked to the entrance, leaving Kyi Kyi to wait in the car. Next to the door they found a wall plaque with the name of the lawyer to whom they'd been referred: "Saw Maung, Barrister at Law, 300."

The building having no elevator, they climbed the stairs to the third floor and opened the door to the office bearing the lawyer's name. A young Burmese woman greeted them in English and asked them to sit down in the cramped, but comfortably appointed, reception room. Momentarily a man appeared and introduced himself. He was short, bald and wore glasses with black frames. Though clearly Burmese, his accent and Western dress were straight from London. He led them to his office which was furnished with dark, heavy antiques, a large upholstered couch and chairs on a deep beige carpet. Grant glanced at the credentials hanging prominently on the wall above the couch. So, he attended Oxford. That will do, he thought.

"Thank you for seeing us, U Saw Maung," Grant opened. He'd learned that the "U" was a honorific, a sign of respect, used in Burma in addressing a distinguished adult male.

"I am happy to. How do you like our country so far?"

"We've had a wonderful time."

"It sounds like you are angels of mercy, the two of you."

"Hardly," Evelyn replied.

"Your general counsel has explained the background to me. I am terribly sorry about your son."

Grant nodded. Evelyn looked down.

"I understand there is a boy, presumably an orphan, at Inle Lake whom you would like to take back to the States and see educated."

"Is that possible?" Grant asked.

"Yes, but there are several hurdles you would have to clear. The first is securing a student visa from the U.S. Embassy. You would also need to have permission from the authorities here. They can be difficult."

Grant could see the legal hours building up, but he was used to that with the many lawyers the newspaper managed to keep busy.

"How would we proceed?" Grant asked, his chin lifted slightly as he posed the question.

"There is an uncle, I'm told."

"Yes," Evelyn said. Nervous, she fiddled with the handbag on her lap. "He makes the child work in his blacksmith shop. He's only twelve and he's not in school." She continued without pausing. "And the uncle has a son who works in a gold leaf factory. I'm sure I don't need to tell you about those places."

Grant loved to see Evelyn excited. To him, she was at her most beautiful when a subject sparked her passion. While her greying hair and crows-feet were premature, they added character to the sparkly personality that had attracted him more than twenty years before. Trying to redirect the conversation, he said, "The boy went to St. Paul's Institute here before his parents died and he was sent to his uncle."

"It is excellent."

"His English is quite good," Evelyn added.

"It should be. The Irish priests teach in English all the academic courses you would expect in a good school in your country. But, with the Irish influence, the boys seem to pick up a trace of a brogue, not a British accent. Now, with the school nationalized by the regime, we will see."

Grant had thought Aun San's accent was different but assumed it was the natural result of a Burmese speaking English. He hadn't considered an Irish element.

Saw Maung stood at the window facing a small gold-domed temple across the street. It was tiny by comparison to the enormous illuminated gold dome of the Shwedagon Pagoda they saw looming high above the city the night before. Grant couldn't help but focus on the similarity between the lawyer's bald head and the gold dome beyond. The fact was that in this country of so many shaven heads, Grant had come to feel slightly self-conscious with the thick mop atop his own head.

"Do you know the parents are dead?" Saw Maung asked.

"That's what Aun San believes. He feels people try to protect him by saying they are fighting with the rebels in the north."

The lawyer offered a Pall Mall from a dark wooden cigarette box on his desk and took one himself. Evelyn waved it off. He lighted Grant's and then his own from a silver table lighter. "You can expect the government will require evidence that the parents are in fact dead. If that is the case, then the uncle would presumably have to approve the arrangement. From what I've heard, I would be surprised if he didn't want some, shall we say, consideration for the transaction, something for losing the boy's labor in the shop."

"So long as it's not illegal, it wouldn't be a problem for us," Grant replied. Evelyn edged forward on her chair as if she were about to disagree, but said nothing.

"Your general counsel mentioned something about a second boy as well." An electric fan buzzed from a corner spreading smoke throughout the room.

"Yes, Aun San says he won't come without his best friend, whose name is Nyan Win. He lives in a monastery now, but the two went to the Institute together." Grant hesitated. "We aren't at all decided in his case."

"Or, actually, in Aun San's either," Evelyn interjected. "You see, we have a teenage daughter at home who must be considered. She knows nothing about this."

"We're exploring alternatives at this point." Grant paused. "We are told Nyan Win's father is a mid-level officer in the military. His mother died of TB, and the boy was sent to Inle Lake to live with his grandmother."

"If his father is part of the regime, it could complicate the matter," Saw Maung said. "You would, of course, have to have his approval. Why would he agree?"

"Because he doesn't care enough about the boy to keep him, I guess," Grant answered.

Saw Maung stopped, looked up at the ceiling as though reaching for the words he would use, and said, "There may be a way you could make all this more attractive to the authorities to gain approval. A price is usually required when you deal with the regime."

"What's that?" Grant asked.

The lawyer returned to the chair behind his desk. "Let me put it this way. You are the publisher of an influential newspaper in the United States. It is possible," he wagged his index finger toward the ceiling, "that the way would be easier with the government if your editorial policy were more, rather than less, favorable to our country. You understand?"

"I can't dictate editorial policy for the newspaper."

"Dictate? No. Influence is another matter, isn't it? The junta would like the world to believe that it is taking the steps necessary to establish a lasting and stable democracy in Burma."

Evelyn and Grant looked at each other. Did he really believe this, Grant thought, or is it the party line? He hadn't heard this from any reliable source so far. It was a military dictatorship pure and simple.

"We have an editorial board. I serve on it, but there are other people who have a vote. Burma hasn't been high on our agenda. But, as things are being squeezed by the regime, what's going on is likely to achieve a higher profile in the States."

The lawyer replied. "Perhaps it would be merely a matter of saying less, not more. Take the King Dragon operation as an example—mass arrests and torture by the government ran 250,000 Muslims out of the country. That could have been a news story or the subject of a prominent editorial. I've checked. You chose the former. The Post showed no outrage."

"Let me ask you, U Saw Maung. How do you view the government?"

The lawyer lowered his voice, peered over his glasses at Grant, then Evelyn, and said "We have lost our freedoms. The ruthless actions of the military deny the democracy they mouth. When we were under British rule, we had democracy, of sorts. Now, this." He threw up his hands.

Grant asked if he might have another cigarette. "We'd like you to explore the ins and outs of the situation and see what can be done legally and practically," he said. "In the meantime, we'll sort out what we can do," Evelyn added.

"Mrs. Jensen thinks it would be more of a burden than I do. I respect her feelings. In a sense, she would probably have more responsibility than I would. But we aren't talking about an adoption here. It would be a student visa to study abroad for a year."

Saw Maung pulled out a file and a legal-size yellow pad from his desk drawer and started to write. "What is the school in which Aun San would be enrolled?"

"The Broadmoor School in Los Angeles. A private boy's secondary school. It has a very good reputation. Our son went there. So did I."

"How do you know the school will accept the boy?"

"We had no plan for anything like this when we came here, of course, so we haven't discussed it with the headmaster. But I don't think there would be a problem." Grant answered.

Evelyn interjected, "My husband is on the board of trustees."

"Let me suggest this way of proceeding," San Maung offered. "I will first have to go to Inle Lake and speak with Aun San and his uncle. If Aun San will not come alone, then I will talk to Nyan Win and his father. Obviously, no commitments will be made to anyone on your behalf."

"Absolutely," Grant replied.

"I will investigate Aun San's parents and take care of the paperwork, contact the appropriate U.S. officials, as well as the Burmese government office. There will have to be a physical examination for the U.S. visa, but that should not be a problem. The one issue would be TB. Your statement of net worth will be required to assure you are capable of providing support."

"That will not be a problem," Grant said.

"What's the time frame?" Evelyn asked in a flat voice.

"I can't predict. There could be many issues. Two months would be expected, possibly as long as four. The red tape in these kinds of matters can be never ending."

Grant and Evelyn left the next day for Los Angeles. They had plenty of time to talk in flight. Adjusting to Aun San would be challenge enough. Nyan Win presented a bigger problem. He would double the responsibility, and neither Grant nor Evelyn responded to the boy the way they did to Aun San. There didn't seem any way they could handle two new lives, strangers from a distant country. And, what about Kathy? Being invaded by a Burmese brother or two might be too much for their increasingly tender teenage daughter. Kathy was not on the trip because she couldn't be taken out of school, but she hadn't wanted to come anyway. Evelyn's sister stayed with her while they travelled. Kathy had become withdrawn over the last two years. She was abrupt, seldom laughed, seemed to find any excuse she could not to be around. Her grades at the Bel Air School for girls had slipped. Grant and Evelyn learned she had smoked marijuana and were suspicious there were pills. At first they had thought this a typical adolescent phase. But they began to fear the cause was that she blamed them for what happened to Peter. She couldn't talk about him without leaving the room angry. How would she take the possibility of two Burmese boys sharing her shattered family and home? How would they approach her? ∿

FOUR

Inseparable Friends

NYAN WIN was excited. Aun San's uncle had agreed he could spend a night at the monastery. U Tha Din made no secret of his hope that one day Nyan Win's friend would also come to live there. So far the abbot had not been successful in convincing Aun San's uncle to go along with the idea. The old man insisted he needed his nephew in the blacksmith shop, and he would only permit Aun San to stay at the monastery on rare occasions.

After Aun San finished work, he met Nyan Win in the village, and the two boys walked on a dirt road along the lake shore. They laughed together, then were silent for another hundred yards when Nyan Win said, "I saw a man go into your house yesterday. Who was he?"

"Oh, nobody."

"That's not true. I've never seen a man dressed in a suit at Inle Lake before. Really, why was he there?"

"You remember the American man and woman who went to the monastery with us a few weeks ago?" Aun San asked, head down, fingering a large leaf he had snapped off a bush.

"The tall man with the short wife?" Nyan Win replied.

"Yes. And they had a guide?"

"I remember."

"Well," Aun San hesitated, "I wasn't going to talk about it, but they want me to go to the United States to live with them and go to school—for one year. The man yesterday, a lawyer, came to talk to me and my uncle about it."

A long silence passed, then Nyan Win asked in a quiet voice, "So, you said yes?"

"I said no."

"Why?"

"I don't want to go, that's all." Aun San turned toward the water's edge. "Come, let me beat you skipping rocks—again." It was their usual routine, competing to see who could get the most bounces and the most distance skimming rocks over the water.

Nyan Win followed. "You have to go," he said as he bent to pick up the flattest stones he could find. He turned his head, fearing his lip was quivering. He didn't want his friend to see that. "Talk to U Tha Din. He can tell you. He went to school in America."

Aun San flung the first rock over the water, getting five bounces in twelve meters.

Nyan Win felt Aun San was treated like a slave by his uncle. He worked hard in the blacksmith shop. For that, he got a roof over his head, a place to sleep, and barely enough to eat. Even Nyan Win's food from the street was better. If only the uncle had been willing to let Aun San come to the monastery.

They took turns tossing rocks, occasionally flinging one into the air at a screeching gull. Aun San had become so good at the game that Nyan Win thought he must be practicing secretly. Yet Nyan Win was the one who lived next to the water.

"I don't really know why they want me. They say I remind them of their son. He died two years ago in a bad accident. I don't know what. Besides . . ."

"Besides what?"

"Nothing."

"No, what?" Nyan Win pressed.

"I don't want to leave you. You're my best friend, the closest I have to family now." Aun San had told Nyan Win about the night in Rangoon when the soldiers came to their house and yelled at his mother to tell them where his father was. When she wouldn't, or couldn't, they told her to say goodbye to her son. She did, then hugged and kissed him, and, sobbing, whispered for him to be brave. The soldiers marched her out into the street where, after what seemed like a long time, a single shot was fired. He never saw his mother, or his father, again.

Nyan Win shrugged his shoulders. "Maybe you could be part of the American family."

"I'm afraid to go." Aun San paused. "It was funny, the lawyer asked questions about you, too. He knew who you were."

"Me? What questions?"

"Oh, about your father, the monastery, our friendship."

"Why?"

"He didn't say."

"What did he ask about my father?"

"Why you didn't live with him. What he did. I said I wasn't sure." Aun San had never asked Nyan Win about the rumor that the uncle was an officer in the military. If true, he didn't want to know it.

Finally, Nyan Win said, "I want you to go. You'd get so rich, you could come back and get me."

They smiled, but their joy was forced. They continued skipping stones over the water. Aun San set a new record at nine. Nyan Win stopped picking up rocks and stepped away to hide his sadness.

"Where do they live?" he asked.

"California, in Hollywood."

"So, when I come," Nyan Win tried to grin, "you can introduce me to all the movie stars."

That night at the monastery they slept next to each other on the dusty floor of an upstairs dormitory. From his breathing, it was apparent Aun San dropped off quickly. Nyan Win lay on his back, watching the gauze-like curtains blow into the room. Thoughts and questions raced through his head. Aun San had known about this for weeks; it was brand new to Nyan Win. When they got to the monastery that afternoon, they talked with the abbot about it.

"You mean the publisher and his wife who were here with a guide?" the abbot said.

"Yes, but what exactly is a publisher?" Aun San asked.

U Tha Din answered. "A very important person in the United States. He could help you. It's a great opportunity, like one I had."

"I don't want to leave."

"Leave your uncle?" the abbot asked.

"No." He turned to his friend, "Leave him."

The abbot smiled. "Nyan Win might want to see you have the chance. He would still be here when you got back."

"How long would you be gone?" Nyan Win asked.

"They said for a year."

"Then, maybe," U Tha Din said, "you have nothing to lose, Aun San."

Nyan Win knew in his heart the abbot was right, but the thought of his friend leaving made him feel sick. He wanted Aun San to do the best he could for himself, but he couldn't picture life without their meetings. He was afraid he might never see him again. And why was the lawyer asking questions about him?

Nyan Win tried to stop the twisting ideas the way he usually did—by thinking about the next drawings he would make. He'd had two art classes at St. Paul's and the abbot let him bring drawing materials to the monastery. What came to his mind was a boy at a prayer wheel. It could be a boy in robes, a novice like himself. Or maybe it could be Aun San throwing a rock at a gull. He could give it to him before he left, as a reminder, so he wouldn't forget. He would start in the morning. He turned on his right side, his hand brushing Aun San. He rested the hand gently against his friend's back and fell asleep. ∽

FIVE

Into the Zambizi

T HE MORNING LIGHT slid through the blinds, leaving rectangular patches of warm sun on the bedroom carpet. Evelyn always kept the blinds open in Peter's room. Entering there in darkness was something she couldn't do, even though more than two years had passed since their son's death.

She had left the room largely untouched, not because she intended it to be a shrine, but because she couldn't bring herself to deal with his possessions. A metal toy soldier army marched across a table in one corner of the room—a collection Peter started when he was about five. Her finger traced a path through the dust on the table top. In another corner she saw his Jack Kramer tennis racket, gripped in a wooden press. The walls were plastered with posters of athletic heroes, UCLA basketball star Bill Walton, Rams quarterback Pat Haden, and triangular pennants and other sports paraphernalia from both local teams. Trophies and balls competed with school books for space on the bookshelves. The World Book Encyclopedia occupied one entire shelf.

Evelyn opened a window, wondering how long it had been since there had been any fresh air in the room. Her eye caught the 1976 Broadmoor *Sentinel*, Peter's school year book, the last one in which he would appear. She sat down at the desk and flipped through the pages to the Seventh Grade class section. She found his name and fixed on the photo. Blue blazer, white shirt, striped tie, hair slicked back and a big smile. She caught her breath. He was so much like his father, almost a clone, nothing like her family. His classmates were posed exactly the same way. The boys, eighty or so of them, were white except for two African-Americans and one Asian. The latter evoked a rush. She had met the boy but didn't know him or his family, nor was she sure which Asian country he was from. She feared he'd been an outsider in the school community. His page said little. It was different for Peter. Much of the white space on his page was filled with writing by classmates: "To Peter, the best 7th grade class president. Your friend, Bill." "To a great buddy. Watch out for the girls! Chuck." "Pete —You're a swell guy. Keep it up. John."

Part of her said she should rummage through his things, keep him alive in her mind. She was already having trouble remembering some events. What did they do for his last birthday party? Not having an immediate answer made her feel guilty. The other part of her knew she shouldn't—couldn't—live in the past. She dabbed a handkerchief to her nose as she shut the yearbook. She'd read in books about grief that mourning usually lasted eighteen months. She should have gotten through it by now, but the smallest things brought him to mind, and she still found herself crying more days than not. She was sure Grant did too, but he didn't show that any longer to her. His depression was most evident from the fact he'd only sailed his beloved boat a handful of times since they returned from Africa.

Evelyn went to the closet and pushed the hangers with shirts and jackets, Levis and other pants against one another. She thought she smelled Peter's scent, yet told herself it was impossible this much later. It was time for the clothes to go. Grant had urged her to clear the room and use it as a guest room. *But why? They already had a guest room. There were too many rooms in this rambling house, too many unused spaces in need of a purpose.*

Here she was in Peter's bedroom with another boy in mind, Aun

San. There were so many similarities between them that went well beyond height, weight, smile and facial structure. Their manner of looking up shyly from a downcast head was startling. So, too, was their way of moving with loose limbs and jerky motions. The only differences—for which she was thankful—were in Aun San's coloring. Otherwise, the resemblance would have been eerie. These differences made her think of the Asian student in the yearbook and wonder what kind of difficulties Aun San might face trying to fit in here.

She walked to the dresser and opened each of its four drawers in order. Her first thought was to organize the sweaters, T-shirts, shorts and socks. But she knew the drawers should be emptied and their contents packed in boxes in the attic, or given away altogether.

She had not favored Aun San coming to live with them, but Grant pushed so hard for it she had a difficult time keeping the boy out of her mind. What her husband didn't fully understand was that the burden of an addition to the family would fall largely on her—arranging car pools, tutors, doctors' appointments, attending school events, and the like. He was so busy with his responsibilities at the *Post*. She knew, in some vague way, her husband saw Aun San as Peter, but he focused on what a great opportunity this would be for a young blacksmith from a rural village in a Third World country. She didn't see it that way. How could anybody, anything replace their son? No more than they could ever replace Aun San's parents. She returned to the contents of the closet, pushing hangers along the poles, rearranging the shirts so that long-sleeve ones were grouped together, then polo shirts and short sleeve-shirts. She stepped back, nodded with approval, and started on the pants. *Would he ever wear Peter's clothes? Could she stand seeing him walk around in what Peter had worn?* As it was now, they were stowed in the closet where she didn't have to see them. She tried to concentrate on Aun San's size versus Peter's, but couldn't be sure about either; she knew they were close. Surely, he wouldn't arrive with much in the way of clothes, at least outfits that would be appropriate for a new life. What would be there waiting for him would probably be better than anything he'd ever worn. No. *Aun San should have a fresh start.*

She glanced back into the room and shivered when she saw the African spear hanging on the wall above the bed. They had given it to Peter on his last birthday to commemorate their planned trip to Africa. Made of steel, it measured six feet long. She had found it in an African artifacts store on Melrose Avenue. The spear immediately brought her back to the memories she had tried time and time again to force out of her mind. *If only they could have foreseen what was to happen.*

Evelyn, Grant, Peter and Kathy were at breakfast in the outdoor dining area of the luxurious camp they'd selected in Botswana, joking about Peter's rumpled morning hair and discussing the plan for that day's canoe trip up the Zambezi River from Osprey Camp to Heron Camp. Evelyn had been on safari long enough to appreciate the dangers posed by the wildlife: lions, leopards, elephants, poisonous snakes. Even though the broad, slow moving river hadn't presented extreme danger in her mind, she felt uneasy about the canoe trip and tried to talk her husband out of it. Predictably, he wanted to go, and the children insisted, pleading to be in a canoe together. Knowing how boisterous they could get, Evelyn said no. She didn't want to row with Grant anyway—they always ended up arguing in small boats over who was supposed to do what and when. She assigned Peter to Grant's canoe and relegated Kathy to her own. Another boat had gone ahead earlier with their luggage. Two guides, James and William, placed their canoes at the front of the procession. Evelyn and Kathy next. Grant and Peter last. It hadn't occurred to her to ask why one of the guides didn't bring up the rear.

Animals were everywhere along the river. Hippos wallowed in the shallow water near the bank on their right, bellowing, snorting, splashing. Scores of water buffalo herded close to the river's edge on their left, watching closely as the canoes passed. An occasional crocodile sunned itself on a sandy bank; more were half-submerged, the tops of their scaly, brown heads above water, eyes barely open. On this warm, sunny day, birds swooped toward the river and the trees overhanging its bank.

After paddling a long while in the shallows close to the water's edge, the canoes made their way toward the middle of the river. The guides waved them ahead, toward an island for a picnic lunch. Suddenly, there was a scream from the last canoe. Evelyn stopped paddling and turned to see that canoe's bow shooting into the air on the back of a greyish brown, rubbery hunk emerging from the water. The animal's eyes and ears were tiny compared to its head. Tusks protruded from its gaping mouth. Grant, in the stern of his boat, hollered to Peter "Paddle! Paddle!" but the bow was so far above the waterline that the boy's oar didn't come close to hitting the water. Even from a distance, Evelyn could see Peter's face drained of color, his eyes bulging. With a high-pitched voice he pleaded "Help! Help, Dad!" The canoe moved like a teeter-totter, balancing on the hippo's huge back, tipping first to one side, then the other. Seconds passed, but to her it seemed like minutes. The canoe shuddered, thrust forward and Peter and Grant fell into the murky, churning water.

Kathy yelled "Peter! Dad!" Evelyn paddled hard, trying to turn, shouting to her daughter to change direction. The guides in the first two canoes spun around and pulled against their paddles, moving full speed toward the empty boat. Grant's lower legs and feet alternated with his head above the water as he dove and then returned to gasp for air. The water bubbled and churned, whirlpools swirled downward. Grant screamed at the guides. "My boy is gone. Dive for him! Dive, goddamn it, dive!"

Grant disappeared underwater. When he came up, James, the lead guide, ordered "Get out of the water. Now, Sir! In your canoe." The other boats came close. Grant told Evelyn and Kathy to stay away. He refused to get out of the water. He dove: down, up, down, up alongside the guide. They found nothing. No hippo. No crocodile. No beast of any kind. No Peter. The water returned to a calmer, slow movement. Evelyn bent over, shaking and crying. Kathy, tried to give comfort while pleading with her mother not to dump them over the side, too. Eventually, James helped Grant, red-faced and gasping for air, back into the canoe, then climbed into his own boat.

James took charge. "Two canoes will continue to search in this area, mine and Mr. Jensen's. Mrs. Jensen, Miss Jensen, stay close to William and scan the bank as you paddle down river back to Osprey Camp."

"I'm not going anywhere," Evelyn sobbed. "I'm staying right here, Grant, until we find him."

"We need to cover more territory, Evelyn. Go with the other boat, scout the bank."

"But . . ."

"You'll probably find he's been carried by the current downstream and is on the riverbank close by. We'll be along."

Evelyn and Kathy moved out with the other canoe, gliding with the current, circling and watching the bank. Two hours passed. Dusk approached when they finally arrived at camp. Evelyn pounded her fists against her knees. Tears fell from her cheeks. Kathy yelled at William to "do something, anything, just find him." The guide went to get the camp's general manager who returned and tried to comfort them. Grant and James arrived an hour later, Grant looking shocked, bewildered. His eyes didn't seem to focus. He called for a cigarette and pulled at it voraciously.

He exploded at the manager, "Why the hell wasn't one of the guides in the back? They were both up front, together! And why weren't there any fuckin' life vests?"

Evelyn, now hysterical, clung to Grant. Kathy threw her arms around both of them, saying "we'll find him, it'll be okay." The manager made no attempt to answer Grant's questions and began commandeering a search party, consisting of himself, the two guides, and two other locals.

"Undoubtedly," he said, "the hippo was coming up for air. Terrible luck his being right there under the canoe. I can't tell you how sorry we are." He turned and started to walk toward the river, saying, "Let's go, men."

"They're not carnivores, are they?" Kathy called out in a wavering voice.

The manager stopped. "No, it's very rare they eat meat." He didn't add that more accidents happen with hippos than any other animal in Africa. Many tribesmen didn't know how to swim, and when their boats were capsized by a hippo, they drowned. The manager exchanged glances with the guides. "You have to realize hippos are giant creatures that can weigh tons and be as long as three meters." Again, he stopped short of saying that despite their funny looking, tiny eyes and ears on a monstrous head, hippos can be vicious animals. Peter could have been trapped under one, unable to free himself and swim to the surface. The manager turned and continued toward the boats. "We're going to find him."

Evelyn clutched Grant, wanting to hit him at the same time. It was his fault. Typical impetuous Grant Jensen. Go for the excitement. No matter the risk. She had to blame someone, but she knew he was not alone to blame. She could have stopped it, too. What had they been thinking? The guides came from the camp. No one had warned the family about hippos. "Stay with the guides" was their only warning. Other guests had canoed on the river. The hippos were in the water by the opposite bank, at least ninty meters away, nowhere close to them. Peter was so excited he couldn't have been kept from the excursion had they tried.

That night, they couldn't eat, and Kathy went to her tent early. Grant and Evelyn sat on the deck outside theirs. Candlelight broke the darkness. She drank almost an entire bottle of Chardonnay. He downed two Beefeater martinis straight-up and smoked half a pack of

Camels. Evelyn couldn't get out of her mind what a guide had told her a couple of days before about how a crocodile traps its prey in its huge jaws and slaps the victim from side to side in the water until there is no life left. That couldn't be, she repeated to herself over and over. She didn't mention the grotesque image to her husband. They could hardly speak to one another. Their voices kept cracking into sobs.

The rescue party returned to report it hadn't found a trace of Peter. Grant refused to believe he couldn't be found. Evelyn cried. Escorted by a guard armed with an AK 47 and a torch to light the way, Grant and Evelyn went to Kathy to break the news and to have her join them in their tent. At every camp where they'd stayed, they had been accompanied at night by a guard with a weapon. At first, they thought it a ploy to excite the guests about the wilds of Africa, but they learned that beasts sometimes did wander into camp. As they walked, they heard elephants trumpeting in the bush and, in the far distance, a lion roaring. It was the sound of the hippos bellowing in the water close by that caused Evelyn to collapse into her husband's arms.

Theirs was a tent, but only because it had a canvas roof. It was large and luxurious and with a daybed across the room for Kathy. They cried, holding each other in a knot of arms. A flickering lantern flame cast shadows on the walls. They tried to reassure one another that Peter would be found in the morning by patrols that would go up and down the river with the first light of dawn. They hugged and kissed and, finally, climbed into their beds. Grant moved to extinguish the lantern, but Evelyn asked him not to, saying she couldn't bear to be in the dark.

Time passed. Grant, sprawled fully clothed on the bed next to Evelyn, snored lightly. The gin was working its magic. There was not a sound from Kathy. Evelyn buried her face in the damp pillow. She tried not to rock the bed with her weeping. She conjured a picture of Peter: He had hit his head and was found by three natives, clothes torn, lying unconscious on the riverbank; they carried him back to their village to minister to his wounds with red and black leaves, ancient herbal medicines; a small fire burned outside a round thatch hut's opening, revealing a dark costumed man in a deer head mask shaking a gourd over the unconscious body. Nothing could put Peter down. It was just a matter of finding him in the morning and evacuating him by bush plane to the closest decent hospital. She forced herself to return to that picture. She got up and paced the room, but was afraid to go outside.

The search continued for two days. Police from the nearest town conducted an investigation. They were polite, but ineffectual. Evelyn spent the daylight hours walking around the boat landing waiting for one of the outboards to return with Peter. When the boats arrived back without him, she dropped to the ground, head resting on her arms, and howled. Grant wanted to stay and hold her, but he broke down too. One afternoon, Evelyn tried to sneak a boat out on her own and had to be restrained. Unlike herself, she screeched at the boatmen, the police, everyone they were "fucking incompetents." Grant was told she couldn't be permitted any longer near the river on her own and had to remain with him or their daughter, preferably in their tent, away from the action.

On the fourth day, the manager and a police captain gathered the family together and informed them that not having located Peter, they would have to call off the formal search, but they would keep their eyes wide open for any signs of the boy. They didn't go into details; at that point, Evelyn didn't want them. It was enough of a horror to imagine their son struggling underwater with a six-thousand pound giant, than to picture what might have preyed on him afterward.

They left Botswana on a small plane from a grass runway in the jungle to connect to flights back to the States. Evelyn was beyond consolation. Grant overflowed with guilt, asking time and time again why it had been Peter and not himself. Kathy, in her effort to chat, struggled for normalcy. Yet she was often grim as well. Evelyn was sure their daughter blamed them for the accident.

For months, Evelyn clung to the hope that her camp fantasy

might miraculously come true, that Peter was alive. She had always heard there was nothing worse than losing a child, and she felt it full force. It was so out of order. A parent wasn't supposed to have to prepare for that. Weeks passed before they were compelled to acknowledge reality. Hope was gone. A memorial service was held at St. Joseph's Episcopal Church in Beverly Hills, followed by a reception at their home. Almost all of Peter's classmates were there. Everybody, it seemed, had loved Peter Jensen. A lot of boys were trying to be men, to hide their emotions, while many men, and more women, wept openly. Grant wanted to speak but Evelyn feared he wouldn't be able to get through it without falling apart. In her case, she didn't fear, she knew she wouldn't be able to get up before a standing room only crowd. Imagine having to beg forgiveness at your twelve-year son's funeral for a decision that led to his death?

As Evelyn pulled the pants from Peter's closet one by one to inspect their condition, she noticed a large roll of paper on the floor under some unused hangers, partly obscured by boxes of games. A brittle rubber band at one end was all that held the roll closed. Another band that had apparently circled the other end lay broken on the carpet. She opened the roll and found a poster of Farrah Fawcett in a red swim suit. Evelyn's right hand moved to her mouth to cover a gasp. She felt an immediate, direct contact with Peter. She hadn't known he was already interested in girls. She wished she had.

She looked again around the bedroom. She decided she would keep the clothes, because they represented a link to her son, not because Aun San might actually wear them. She would pack them in boxes for the attic. The toy soldiers and other possessions scattered around might as well stay. The posters would have to go—all of them. Aun San should have the walls free for his own idols. Maybe one would be an image of a golden Buddha.

She heard a noise and turned. Kathy was standing in the doorway.

"What's going on, Mom?"

"Oh, nothing, straightening things up a bit," she stumbled as she dabbed a handkerchief to her eyes. "By the way, would you like to have the encyclopedia set moved to your room?"

"No, it's fine here."

Evelyn sighed as she closed the door and stepped into the hall. How would she handle her husband? They had not really dealt with what it would mean to them, to their relationship together, to bring Aun San here. Kathy hadn't been approached yet. If the boy were to come to live with them for a year, it wouldn't, couldn't be with any idea that he was a substitute for Peter. Worse than ridiculous, a thought like that was disloyal. ∼

SIX

Red Tape

E VELYN WAS WORRIED, even fearful, as she drove to Grant's office for a conference call with U Saw Maung. She had grown obsessed by the idea of Aun San coming to live with them. She hid this feeling from her husband whom she knew was apt to interpret it as a signal of complete approval. The more time she spent at home in Peter's surroundings with his photos and possessions, the more she felt his absence. It was a huge hole, a small part of which, she was beginning to feel, Aun San might be able to fill. Her reaction to Nyan Win was not the same. It was Aun San who was the catalyst. If he hadn't reminded them so much of Peter, they wouldn't even be thinking about bringing a Burmese child into their home.

Evelyn pulled into the entrance to the garage under the *Post* building and took the elevator up three floors to Grant's office. At one end of the room was a large desk overburdened by files and loose business papers where Grant was sitting, phone in hand. He rose and squeezed her around the shoulder, as he barked into the phone that they needed further verification for a story on the U.S. response to the uprising against the Shah of Iran. To the side of his desk, the day's newspapers were segregated and hung from poles slotted in the wall as they are in a library. The *Post's* latest edition occupied a space separate from the other newspapers. Next to it was the *Los Angeles Sun*, its larger local competitor. Further down the line hung the *New York Times* and the *Wall Street Journal*.

Clyde Thomas, the family's long-time personal lawyer, and John Haley, the newspaper's relatively new general counsel, sat at a spacious conference table at the opposite end of the room. Grant and Evelyn joined them. At precisely 10 am the speaker phone rang. U Saw Maung was on the line and, in his impeccable Oxbridge accent, began his report from half the world away.

"We have completed all of the necessary inquiries with respect to Aun San's situation. His parents were killed by the regime, his mother in Rangoon and his father while fighting with the rebels in the mountains. His uncle is willing to let him go to the States but, as we discussed, he wants funds to make up for the fact that the boy will no longer be there to work in the shop."

"Counsel, this is Clyde Thomas. That sounds a bit like the Jensens would be buying the boy, doesn't it?"

"Mr. Thomas, they would be making the uncle whole. It is not a problem under our laws. You would have to determine that under U.S. law."

Evelyn knew from discussions with Grant that the lawyers had already concluded it would be all right, and she decided that she would not pursue the point further.

Saw Maung continued. "The U.S. Embassy is ready to provide a student visa for the lad and the Burmese authorities will issue the necessary passport and other papers for a period of one year. Of course, adoption was not discussed at all."

The slightest thought of adoption made Evelyn resist, so much so that she and Grant never discussed it. It was a long step beyond anything she had in mind. She could never remove from her thoughts the question: would they be considered too irresponsible to adopt, given what had happened in Africa? She knew some of their friends, while sympathetic about the tragedy, thought the couple had been out of their minds to take the kids on the Zambezi in canoes. Everyone knows how tippy they can be. She never heard this directly, of course, but she could interpret the pauses, the silence on the subject, the looks of bewilderment as conveying disbelief of what they had done.

"That's the good news. But Aun San still insists he will not leave Nyan Win. He wants to be with you; he realizes what an opportunity it is, but to him the friendship is the most important consideration."

Grant slumped slightly, but with his rangy frame even a small movement seemed outsized. Evelyn lowered her eyes. The only sound was a mild hum, always present in these offices, from the pressroom in the basement of the building. An almost undetectable vibration accompanied the noise.

"We have approached Nyan Win's father on a hypothetical basis; that is, that this is a possibility, that there are no guarantees. By the way, he was educated in Australia."

"How was that?" Evelyn asked.

"I don't know the circumstances in his case, but sometimes boys here, even in middle class families, are sent abroad to school if they are lucky," the lawyer answered. "While the father doesn't seem that interested in his son, he claims to care about his welfare and his education. He would want to meet you first and has made it clear that if adoption is the idea, he would not consent. I don't think it is lost on him that yours is, shall we say, a prominent family in the States."

Grant nodded; it never seemed to be lost on anybody. He said, "If we should decide to include Nyan Win, how, where do we meet his father?"

"In Rangoon, when you come to pick up Aun San. It would take only a short time after that for the paperwork to be processed for Nyan Win."

"Would Aun San come back with us while that's being done?" asked Evelyn.

"I think so, as long as he knows his friend will be coming."

"Is Nyan Win willing?" Evelyn asked. "We're not saying we have decided to have him, or to have Aun San either for that matter."

"He seems willing as long as he is with Aun San," the lawyer answered.

"We would take our daughter with us when we return," Grant said. "She would have to meet them before they actually came here."

"Of course."

"Tell me, was there anything said about the point you made when we met in your office, that is, the *Post's* editorial policy regarding Burma?" Grant asked.

"Not expressly. But you should be prepared for some reference to the importance of the policy toward the regime being on the 'friendly' side."

"Sir, this is John Haley. I am house counsel at the *Post*."

"Yes, sir."

"It's not possible for the paper's editorial policy to be influenced in that way. There is a process here. People in important positions with the paper weigh in on issues. Mr. Jensen does not control editorial policy even though he is the publisher."

"I understand. Maybe a better way to put it would be that the paper would be patient with the government as it follows its road to democracy."

Grant turned to the others and shrugged as if to ask whether there was anything more. No one offered a comment. He crushed out his cigarette in an ashtray brimming with stubs. "U Saw Maung. Thank you very much. We'll make a decision and let you know. The biggest issue is, as you expected, the involvement of Nyan Win. He is a nice young man but his presence, obviously, doubles the complications presented."

"Yes. I will await your decision."

The telephone conference over, the lawyers walked out the door, leaving Grant and Evelyn alone. "Well, I guess it's neither or both." She hesitated. "We've discussed it enough. I can't say no, so I guess it's both."

Grant held her in his arms and snuggled his face against her head. It had been a long time without the affection they used to show for one another. "We won't be sorry, Evie."

"There are three conditions though," she said. "One is that we treat the boys equally. Aun San gets no preference."

"Yes."

"Next, it's only for one year." As she spoke the words, she realized the futility. They both knew if one year worked, more could follow.

"Third, Kathy has to be in agreement."

"I don't relish approaching her about this," Grant said, pacing the office.

"I don't know that she'll support the idea, given how negative she's become about everything."

"Maybe it's the age, Evie. Aren't they all that way at fifteen, almost sixteen?"

"I guess so. I think she blames us for what happened," Evelyn said.

"She's never said that to me."

"Me either, but I can tell that's the way she feels," Evelyn added. "Let's talk later tonight about Kathy. I have to be off to the art museum. Another board fight about how far we'll go in prostituting ourselves to get Gertrude King's collection."

"I thought you'd decided 'no, enough, we're through with her demands,'" Grant said, chest spread, head high, in his pretend command voice.

She laughed. "We did, but we're wavering—again."

"Don't, she'll just keep pushing. Next, she'll want the city renamed after her."

As she moved toward the door, Evelyn studied the bookcases that filled one side of the room. She liked the sort of hoary tradition of the publisher's suite which she had tried, with only minor success, to update some years before. She had arranged the bookcases with memorabilia from Grant's time in the office, as well as from his father's tenure in the position before him. One photograph was of Grant's father standing with Dwight Eisenhower, another of Grant shaking hands with Richard Nixon.

She had assumed someday Peter's face would appear in that bookcase, along with those of his father and grandfather. Maybe not quite dynastic, still it was a comfortable thought and logical enough given the family's history. Would Grant have been there to see it? Would she?

Those questions were academic now. She looked. For a fleeting second, she saw Aun San's picture in the bookcase. She shook her head to rid herself of the image.

They decided to talk to Kathy at dinner a couple of nights later. They sat at a game table in the wood paneled den, a fire burning in the fireplace. When Peter had been with them, they usually had dinner in the dining room. Without him, and feeling the need for a warmer atmosphere, they now ate dinner at a game table in the den most nights. Daisy, as usual, was curled in front of the fire. For a short while, they ate in silence, cutting into flank steak and dipping their forks into baked potatoes loaded with sour cream.

Grant cleared his throat, a sure sign he was about to approach a serious subject. "Kathy, you know the Burmese . . ."

"Boy," she interrupted. "Of course, the one who reminds you so much of Peter."

"There is a similarity," Grant continued, "but we've been talking about the possibility of bringing him here with a friend for a year to go to school. It would be a wonderful opportunity for them. What would you think?"

Kathy stared at her father, then her mother, but didn't speak. It was typical of the state of withdrawal into which she had retreated. Evelyn often wondered whether Kathy blamed herself for what happened to Peter. What might she have done to save him that she didn't?

"What we want to know is how you would feel about sharing the house with a couple of boys you've never met?" Evelyn said. "I know it would require a lot of adjusting for all of us."

"So, why do it?" Without waiting for a reply, Kathy added, "Actually I think it's sick. Replacing Peter? Because someone looks or acts like him?" She threw her napkin on the table as though she were about to get up and leave, but she didn't.

She slouched in her chair, letting her short shirt reveal her thighs. These days her outfits, typical of Los Angeles teenagers, made Evelyn cringe, but she said little at the risk of ruffling Kathy's prickly feathers.

Turning to Kathy, Evelyn asked, "Wouldn't you want to meet them before you decide?"

"Will it really make a difference? I know what'll happen, the two of you will make the decision."

"You have an equal vote," Grant said. "Any one of the three of us can veto the idea."

"I'm not for it, not at all," Kathy said. "But as long as you understand that's how I feel, I'll at least agree to meet them."

"We're not talking about adopting them, you know. We're talking about them coming here to go to school for a year, that's all," Grant said.

"Dad, it's going to be embarrassing. People already think we're weird. Now, with two geeks . . ."

"They're not geeks," Evelyn replied.

"Gooks then."

"Kathy, stop."

Grant stoked a couple of logs, bringing the flames back from a slumbering glow. He lit a cigarette.

"Where are they going to go to school," Kathy asked. "Broadmoor, I assume?"

"If they can get in."

"Oh, that'll be a big challenge, Dad."

"You'll be able to introduce them to the girls at Bel Air, darling," Evelyn said, smiling.

"Sure Mom. They're a little young for my group, don't you think?"

"Well, don't you know some seventh-graders at school?"

Kathy ignored the question. Impatient, lips pursed, she asked, "Speaking of introductions, what would we call them? No one could pronounce the names they use in that country."

"We'll figure that out," Grant said. "We'd convert the names to more familiar ones. If they agree."

"What about bedrooms? Are they going to share one?"

"We need to talk about that," Evelyn said. "If you want to move into Peter's room, you can. It's bigger."

"It's Peter's room. No one else's, including mine. Anyway, I didn't want it before. Why would I now? I'd rather stay with the view of the garden and pool, not the tennis court."

"I wanted to be sure. Then, I had thought of Aun San going into Peter's room if you didn't want it," Evelyn said as if she hadn't gotten Kathy's blast that the room should Peter's only.

"That's sick," Kathy snapped.

"And," Evelyn continued, "Nyan Win could take the guest room."

"With the chintz bedspread and matching curtains? Perfect Mom."

"No, no, we'd redo it. Make it more masculine. Peter's room, too, in order to give Aun San a fresh start."

"While I've been trying to get mine redone for years," Kathy said, "with something more mature. How long has it been that I've had the clown wallpaper?"

"Whatever you'd like, honey," Grant answered. "We'll redo 'em all." He turned to Evelyn for approval.

She nodded.

Evelyn busied herself chasing down tutors to prepare the boys for entry the following fall to Broadmoor. Grant had been all but assured the boys would be admitted. Evelyn found a teacher who would spend several hours a day during the summer with them. While both boys handled conversational English, she was unsure of the depth of their knowledge of grammar or other subjects they would have to understand to succeed in such a competitive atmosphere, particularly math and science. St. Paul's Institute had a good reputation from all they had heard, but could it equal an education at Broadmoor? No matter, they couldn't lose with the extra help.

Evelyn visited Desmond's in nearby Westwood Village to find a couple of outfits for the boys to wear on the trip home, pants and polo shirts, and cotton sweaters for the plane. She doubted they had anything appropriate. More clothes would be necessary once they got here.

They made arrangements for Kathy to be released from school for one week to fly with them to Rangoon on May 1. It would be hot, but at least they would beat the monsoons. ◈

SEVEN

Adventure Ahead

ALMOST EVERYTHING AUN SAN encountered, from setting foot on the Burma Airlines plane for the short flight from Rangoon to Bangkok until he fell asleep in his new bedroom in California many hours later, felt disorienting. He'd never been on an airplane, and he hadn't seen many over Inle Lake. He had watched them fly overhead in Rangoon, but until now he hadn't realized how big they were. How did they stay up? The 747 he connected to in Bangkok even had stairs, which he climbed to find his seat.

Mr. Grant motioned for him to sit by the window next to him so he could look out. Mrs. Evelyn and Miss Kathy sat across the aisle. Aun San wondered if he had taken Mrs. Evelyn's seat and how she felt about it. He wore jeans and a blue cotton sweater. They were new, different from the clothes he'd worn before. All he had left were his sandals and a little more that came in the suitcase they'd bought at an open air market at Inle Lake. Mrs. Evelyn suggested he wait until he got to Los Angeles to see if he would wear his old clothes or new ones they would purchase for him. It was pretty clear to him what her choice would be, and he knew he'd have to go along with what she wanted.

He had been confused about what he should call these new people in his life. At the beginning, he'd said sir and ma'am but they shook their heads. They didn't like that. When he'd tried Mr. and Mrs. Jensen, they told him to call them by their first names. He found he couldn't do that without it coming out as Mr. Grant and Mrs. Evelyn, so most of the time he didn't use their names at all. Katherine said to call her Kathy, and he tried Miss Kathy. With a tone of mild disgust, she suggested that he forget that. So, he didn't call her anything either. For their part, they addressed him by name almost every other sentence. It seemed they enjoyed being able to say Aun San.

The engines thundered as they struggled to lift the giant machine into the air. Aun San's heart pounded as the plane shuddered. He glanced at Mr. Grant who didn't seem at all afraid. Then he heard a loud, groaning sound. Mr. Grant must have seen him grab the arm rests because he smiled and said, "Don't worry. It's the landing gear retracting." He had to explain how the wheels that run along the ground are pulled up under the wings until they are used again on landing.

A short time into the flight, a woman dressed in a greyish-blue uniform came to their seats. She was older than Miss Kathy, and she was beautiful. He couldn't say that about Miss Kathy really, because he wasn't used to blond hair and blue eyes, or girls as tall as she was. Maybe she was beautiful, and he just didn't know it. The stewardess, as Mr. Grant referred to her, looked Burmese. Aun San noticed other passengers opening trays over their laps, and he fumbled trying to do the same. The woman placed a small white cloth on the tray and set down eating utensils, glasses and a cloth napkin in a round ring. Smells of food that weren't familiar to him were strong. Soon the stewardess started delivering the meal. He was hungry. He'd never eaten on a white cloth before and wondered why it was there. He was aware from St. Paul's what the metal forks, knives and spoons were for, but he had never seen so many. In his uncle's house, they ate with their hands or with bamboo utensils. The meal on the plane, served by the attendant, consisted of raw shrimp in a red sauce, which he devoured, followed by a piece of meat, which he had seldom had at St. Paul's. He missed the rice and noodles and salads with fish and chicken that were his regular diet. Dessert was vanilla ice cream with chocolate sauce, something of a rarity for him, and he loved the taste.

After a while, Mrs. Evelyn switched seats with Mr. Grant and began explaining what to expect in the United States: Los Angeles, the weather, their home, the school he would go to, their friends, the friends he would have, the newspaper. He'd been with the Jensens only a few days and already wondered if he'd made a mistake. Not that they weren't nice. Maybe they were too nice. It felt like their total focus was on him, and the attention made him uncomfortable. This added to the fears he had about new people, and places, and customs. Whether he could fit in? Whether he could do the schoolwork? Whether the other students would be nice to him? How Miss Kathy would treat him? The decision to accept the Jensens' offer had been hard. But his option was to continue sweating in his uncle's boiling blacksmith shop forging steel. U Tha Din's influence was important, and, when he learned the Jensens would accept Nyan Win, it seemed too late to turn back.

Mrs. Evelyn told him he could watch the movie, *Superman*. She helped him adjust the headset and find the audio channel. She explained the story was about a man wearing a tight blue costume, with an S on the chest, and a red cape and flying over tall buildings like a bird. Aun San had seen a comic book at St. Paul's about Superman, but he didn't believe it was true that a man, even in the United States, could fly.

"Mrs. Evelyn, why is he called Superman?"

"Because he can fly."

"Not really though?"

"No, not really. But they'd like you to think so."

When the movie ended, she helped him arrange his pillow and blanket and then pushed her own in place. She told him he should sleep. He tried, but couldn't. It was stuffy and the motors made so much noise. He would have felt a lot more at ease if Nyan Win had been able to come with him, but Mr. Grant had promised that his friend would follow as soon as his paperwork was completed. Aun San thought the Jensens and Miss Kathy had gotten along well enough with Nyan Win during their two days together at Inle Lake. He knew a meeting had taken place in Rangoon between the Jensens and Nyan Win's father before the Jensens returned to Inle Lake for Aun San. It seemed strange that Nyan Win's father required a meeting because he hadn't shown any interest in his son since he was shipped off to live with his grandmother. He never once visited him at the monastery. How much did he care? Aun San didn't have a father anymore, but he would rather have the good memories of growing up with his parents in Rangoon than have a father like Nyan Win's. Why did his parents have to die? He had loved them so much. No one, nothing, could ever take their places.

Ultimately, Aun San fell asleep. When he awoke, Miss Kathy was sitting next to him. She hadn't talked to him much during the short time they'd been together. Had her mother forced her to trade seats?

"How do you feel?" she asked.

"I'm hungry again."

"I think they'll serve breakfast in a few minutes."

Aun San didn't know what to say so he slid past her to go to the bathroom, a tiny space with devices he didn't recognize. When he hit a metal button and the toilet flushed, there was a whoosh that made him feel he was going to be sucked down into it. The water didn't run out of the sink; he had to push another lever to make that happen. When he returned to the cabin, he found Kathy sitting in his seat next to the window. He said nothing.

"Aun San. You have to call me something, you know. Make it Kathy, all right?"

"Yes. I will try—Kathy." There, he said her name, but it didn't make her seem any more friendly.

"Do you want to see a picture of Peter?" Without an answer, she opened her bag and removed a worn and soiled photo. She handed it to him.

Aun San studied the picture. He couldn't see how he resembled Peter, whose hair was thick, curly and blond. Besides, the photograph showed Peter's blue eyes. He remembered there was suppos-edly something similar about the smile. Maybe he could see that, a bit.

"Doesn't look like you, does he?"

"No."

"My parents think he does. I know his hair and eyes and skin are different, but there is something. They say it's the smile, along with the way you glance up when your head is lowered. The way you stand, the way you move." She paused. "You'll never be able to take his place, you know. So don't try. I agreed on one year, no more than that."

Aun San turned toward the aisle. No words were spoken for several minutes. Then he said, "Your father told me there was an accident."

"It was terrible." Kathy launched into the story, not sparing the gory details, nor the guilt her parents felt about it. She said it could have been different if they had let her be in the canoe with her brother. She told the story in a way that made him think she had told it many times.

When she finished, he asked, "Are there hippos in Los Angeles?"

She appeared startled. "No, none, thank God."

"I don't think there are in my country either. I feel very sorry for him. For all of you."

She didn't comment.

Aun San wasn't sure what this family expected of him. It had some-thing to do with Peter, but what exactly?

When they arrived at the airport in Los Angeles, Aun San was happy to get off the plane, but scared what would happen next. Mr. Grant said he would join him in the nonresident immigration line in order to help with all of the paperwork. The immigration officer studied Aun San's papers, stamped them and then handed them back with a grunt. No smile, no welcome. Aun San hoped not everyone was so mean here. They proceeded to the baggage area where they met Mrs. Evelyn and Kathy and retrieved their luggage. Outside, a man with a gleaming grey car was waiting for them.

"Jerry, this is Aun San. He's the young man from Burma we've talked about so much. And Aun San, Jerry helps us at the house."

"Welcome," Jerry said. He had a heavy accent and bowed awkwardly. Aun San thought he might be Chinese, but he knew he wasn't Burmese. Besides, nobody was named Jerry in Burma.

Within five minutes from the airport, Jerry turned north on what they referred to as a freeway. Aun San had never seen a six lane road like this. Not one bike or rickshaw or trishaw was there, not one person or dog walked on the side of the road. With cars hardly moving, he wondered why they called it "free." They continued slowly on this road until the mountains started to rise from the flatlands of the city. They exited at Sunset Blvd. and drove on until they turned again through a massive arched gateway on which the words Bel Air were emblazed. The buildings they passed were surrounded by walls of stone or wood or tall green hedges, with steel gates. The metalwork was elaborate, not like anything he'd seen in the blacksmith's shop. They turned again at St. Cloud Road and soon slowed as gates swung open before them. Aun San saw a large building as they passed through the open gate. The only structures he had ever seen like this were the embassies in Rangoon he walked by with his mother on muggy afternoons and the Governor's Residence hotel which he peeked his head in. *Was this an embassy? The Burmese Embassy maybe? Was there more paperwork to be done? Or, was it a hotel?* He didn't ask.

The car stopped in front of double doors to the building, a two-story high structure, beige-colored and red-roofed, surrounded by trees, lawn and dense plantings. Jerry carried the luggage to the door and moved the car around a circle into a separate smaller building. A dog bounded up to them, tennis ball in mouth, singing her greeting as much, it seemed, to the stranger as to the others.

After petting, then introducing Daisy, Mrs. Evelyn said, "Welcome home, Aun San."

"We're very glad you're here with us," Mr. Grant added.

"You'll need a nap. Later we'll eat and give you a tour," Mrs. Evelyn added.

As they took him to his bedroom, he was stunned by what he saw. *Home? This is where you live? Where I'm going to live?* The area they had entered, where the front door and the bottom of a staircase met, was as big as his uncle's whole house and almost as big as his family's home in Rangoon. The floor was wooden, though it didn't look like the floors at home. The wood here was darker and shiny, and had a different smell, not the moldy one he was used to. They climbed stairs to the second floor. The long, wide upstairs hall floor was not wood; it was not covered by mats, but by a soft, green rug.

They followed the hall to the end. Mrs. Evelyn opened a door. "This is...your bedroom, Aun San." He felt she had almost said "Peter's." Kathy had told him about the room, that it had been Peter's. It had a fresh scent, almost metallic. "Don't bother to unpack," Mrs. Evelyn said. "Pull down the bed covers, like this, and sleep awhile, not too long or you won't be able to sleep tonight. When you wake up, come downstairs."

Aun San fell on the bed. It was so soft and springy compared to what he was used to. He wanted to sleep but couldn't. He got up and inspected the room, the closet, then what he knew from St. Paul's to be a dresser and a desk, both of them dark and polished. He had wondered what it would be like to be in this room, whether some-how, someway Peter would still be there. But he sensed nothing. Everything felt new. From a window on one side of the room he saw a tennis court. He went in the bathroom and stared into the shower. He turned a dial to the right and water came out. He turned it off right away. He wanted to use it and thought he could figure out how, but he wasn't sure he should; they hadn't said anything about it. He had little to unpack, but he took one thing from his bag, a small photograph of his parents in a crude, wooden frame. His father held him as a baby, with his mother looking proud. He stared at it until it made him too sad. Although everyone here said he resembled Peter, he knew he had his mother's features. He held the picture to his lips, then slid it in the back of the drawer of the table next to his bed. Finally he was able to sleep for about an hour.

After his nap, he went downstairs and wandered until he found Mrs. Evelyn. She was in a white, glistening room, obviously a kitchen, but different than those he'd seen. There was no open fire, no huge kettle steaming. Everything was so clean.

Mrs. Evelyn greeted him. "I'll show you the rest." He walked behind her through the house, wanting to run away rather than follow her. When they passed through what she described as the living room, large photographs in sparkling metal frames on a piano caught his attention. One picture was of Peter. He didn't ask about it. He knew Peter's face from the photograph he'd seen on the plane. Was this his last picture, he wondered? They entered a rectangular room she called a dining room with a long wooden table and lots of chairs lined up around the sides and ends. The houses in which he had lived had simple tables for eating in the living space. The smallest room in his new home, the den was the word she used, was the one that felt the best to him. It had wood walls with spaces in them: a fire pit in one, shelves in another on which glasses and amber colored bottles sparkled, and a television in still another. Rows of books occupied what wall space remained.

They walked out to the garden, where Daisy came running, and joined Mr. Grant who bent down by the pool to read the temperature gauge. "Good, eighty-four degrees. You can swim anytime."

"You do swim?" Mrs. Evelyn asked.

"Yes, Ma'am."

"I assumed you must, living at the lake." She stopped, then started again. "But, you know, it's odd. There are some places in the world where people live near water but never learn to swim."

"And this is a tennis court," Mr. Grant said. "Have you played?"

"I have, at school. I am not very good, Sir."

"You're the perfect age. We'll get an instructor. Remember, Aun San, you don't need to say Sir and Ma'am anymore."

It was nearly dark as they returned to the house and sat down for dinner in the dining room. Aun San didn't feel well and asked to go to his room. Mrs. Evelyn accompanied him and gave him a kiss on the cheek. It was the second time she had. The first was when she greeted him on their return to Inle Lake. She smelled different than his mother had, more like flowers. Kathy, who had followed them upstairs, half-waved at him as she left the room.

He sank into the bed, feeling as though he was disappearing in the soft, thick blankets. He took the photo of his mother and father from the drawer and put it under his pillow. He felt alone and wished Daisy could sleep in his room. The one thing he wanted was not to wake up, startled and clammy, to the sound of a single gunshot, as he had so often since the night the soldiers came. Maybe that would go away here in America.

The next morning over breakfast in a small sun-filled breakfast room next to the kitchen, Mrs. Evelyn said, "There are so many places we want to take you, the zoo, the theater, sporting events and all. But we really should wait for Nyan Win, don't you think?"

"Yes." He wanted to do everything with his friend.

"Yet, we can't wait until then to get you some clothes."

Mrs. Evelyn drove him to Westwood Village where they visited a large store that she said sold the right kind of clothes for a young man. The Village didn't look like one to him. It was much bigger than his village and bordered what he was told was a huge university called UCLA. The buildings were strong, made of brick with arches. There was no gold anywhere on the buildings. There were no barefoot monks begging with alms bowls. No one wore robes. No dogs ran loose in the streets, no open fires, no noisy roosters crowing. The roads were paved, not dirt and dusty. Women's clothes were dark, not colorful. The closest thing he could find to his country were the young people, probably students from the university, riding bicycles. No one pumped rickshaws or trishaws with side seats. And all the people rode inside the buses, instead of some hanging off the back.

In the store, he tried on what Mrs. Evelyn called sports coats, shirts, ties, trousers and shoes. He didn't understand what the dark blue coat had to do with sports, but he didn't ask. The shoes were stiff compared to his sandals. She said he had to have collared shirts for school. The coats and ties were for social occasions, whatever that meant. When the salesman tried to show him how to tie a tie, he almost choked.

"Will Nyan Win wear these, too?"

"Yes. But they won't be identical. There will be different colors and patterns. So you won't look like twins," she smiled, adding, "Not that you do, of course. The only clothes that will be the same are coats. You have to have a blue blazer, and, oh yes, the shoes, because every boy wears penny loafers."

As the days went by, Aun San felt more and more disoriented and strange. He knew he would be a lot happier when Nyan Win got here. He could return to Burma if he wanted. Mr. Grant had told him that. But he wanted to make the most of what U Tha Din said was this opportunity to get an education and learn about a different world. And, what did he really have to return to? The blacksmith shop? His uncle? ∾

EIGHT

The Bond

SEVERAL WEEKS LATER Nyan Win arrived, accompanied by Mr. Grant and welcomed at LAX by Mrs. Evelyn, Kathy, Aun San, and Jerry. He was given the tour of the house as Aun San had been, and he struggled to stay awake for the roast chicken and asparagus dinner Mrs. Evelyn prepared. When he and Aun San used Burmese words at the dinner table, Mr. Grant suggested they always speak in English, even to one another, to improve their command of the language. After dinner, Nyan Win asked to be excused from the table, saying he was tired from the long trip. He went upstairs, turned on the lamp next to his bed, and gazed around the large room. With the heavy blankets and curtains, the deep rug and the dark wood, it wasn't like any place he'd ever lived before, and he felt more than uncomfortable. All he could think of was he shouldn't have let Aun San talk him into coming. But he knew he couldn't decide to go back home on his very first night in America. U Tha Din would be upset; he had been so in favor of him taking advantage of the Jensens' offer. He knew he couldn't count on his father for anything, even coming to Inle Lake to visit him once in a while. His grandmother had been mildly opposed to his leaving, but she would tell him he had to stick it out more than one day.

After a couple of hours inspecting his room and bathroom, he put on a robe that he found at the foot of his bed, walked to the bedroom door and peaked out. There was a dim light at the end of the long hall. He didn't see or hear anybody. He stepped as quietly as he could down the hallway to Aun San's door. They hadn't been able to talk together alone since his arrival. He was afraid to knock, so he opened the door a crack.

Aun San stirred. "Who is it?"

"It's me," he whispered.

"What are you doing?"

"I can't sleep."

"Are you scared?" Aun San turned on the light next to the bed and propped himself up on an elbow.

"No."

"Then, what?"

"I haven't slept alone for a long time. Usually, there are all these bodies strewn along the floor, snoring, whispering, farting. It's so quiet here."

"Farting?" Aun San put his mouth to his forearm to make a fluttering noise, then his hand to his mouth to gag a giggle. "You told me monks don't fart."

"I never said that," Nyan Win blurted out.

"Liar."

"No. Monks are the worst. It must be what we eat on the streets."

Aun San rubbed his eyes. "I had a hard time sleeping at the beginning. We didn't have as many people at my uncle's as at the *kyoung*, but there were a lot for a small space."

"It's so stuffy in my room, like it is in here," Nyan Win said, sitting down on the bed. "The windows are all covered. There aren't any breezes."

"You'll get used to it."

Nyan Win didn't answer. Then he said, "Can I stay here in your room tonight?"

Aun San hesitated, "You can't tell Mrs. Evelyn or Mr. Grant."

"Okay."

"Where will I sleep?"

"On that bed," Aun San answered, pointing to an adjoining twin bed. "But don't mess it up."

Nyan Win wondered how he could get in the bed without messing it up. He slid carefully under the blankets, figuring he'd straighten them out in the morning.

"Aun San?"

"Yes."

"I missed you very much. All those weeks waiting . . ."

"I know. I missed you, too."

"Did you ever worry I wouldn't come?"

"Maybe, sometimes. But Mr. Grant promised."

"I was afraid my father might change his mind, but I made a promise to you. You're the reason I'm here. I know you wouldn't have come without me. I couldn't let you down."

"They like you. Even Kathy does. They told me so. They're glad you're here."

Nyan Win shrugged. "But you're the one who is Peter. I am not."

Aun San sounded surprised. "I am not Peter. I don't want to be Peter. Anyway, we have to wait and see how everything works out."

"He said we could go home in a year."

Aun San changed the subject. "Wait until tomorrow."

"Why?"

"You'll get a full tour like I did and see how big the house is."

"I wasn't even sure it was a house when we drove in."

Aun San continued. "You'll have breakfast. The breakfasts are good—lots of eggs and a thing called a waffle with butter and sweet syrup. Afterward, Mrs. Evelyn will take you outside where I might be having my tennis lesson. Then, I think, she'll take us to a store and buy you some funny looking clothes."

"Like what?"

Aun San listed his new acquisitions.

Nyan Win frowned. "When we went to that big hotel in Rangoon,

Mr. Grant had a suitcase for me with some new clothes. He didn't want me to wear my robes on the plane," Nyan Win said.

"They gave me new clothes for the trip, too."

"But I kept on my sandals," Nyan Win said.

"So did I."

"We had a big discussion about who was going to meet you in Rangoon. I wanted to go with them, I wanted to see you so much, but they said it was too far for a few days. They wouldn't let Kathy go for the same reason. Mr. Grant was busy at the newspaper, but the decision was for him to go and for Mrs. Evelyn to stay home to take care of Kathy and me."

Nyan Win shrugged. "I'm glad someone came to meet me. I would have been afraid to get on the plane by myself."

Aun San said, "Tomorrow afternoon you'll meet the tutor. He's nice, but hard. He's a teacher at the school we'll attend. Later, Mr. Grant comes home for dinner, and we sit around and talk a lot and make plans."

Nyan Win covered his head with a pillow. Half-groaning, half-laughing, he said, "Maybe I am scared."

Aun San giggled. "At least you won't have to wander around with a shaved head, in robes with no shoes, begging for food anymore."

"Do you think?"

"Yes. You'll never be hungry here." Aun San scanned his friend's face carefully. "You know, people are going to think we're twins."

"Why?" Nyan Win asked.

"We do look alike, except I don't have all those spaces between my teeth like you do," Aun San answered. "And you don't have this dent in your chin. And you're shorter, and . . ."

"And," Nyan Win interrupted, "I'm the handsome one."

Aun San landed on Nyan Win's bed and pummeled him on the shoulders and stomach. They tumbled around, wrestling, trying to stifle their glee, until they rolled off the bed and hit the floor with a thud.

"Shhh, Nyan Win. We'll wake them up."

"You started it."

They climbed back in their beds and were silent for a while. Then Aun San said, "We do have the same eyes, the same color, same skin, except you're a darker, same hair. At least they will think were brothers."

"Well, we are —in a way —aren't we?"

"Yes, we are." They were quiet until Aun San said, "Wait until you see Westwood Village tomorrow. Where we'll go to the store."

"Why?"

"It is so different. I think it's like being on the moon."

There was no pledge between them. There didn't need to be. It was part of their lives—an impenetrable bond. No one, certainly not Aun San or Nyan Win, could ever have imagined the distance between them the future would bring. ⌁

NINE

Struggles

WEEKS OF TUTORING passed, the teacher pressuring the boys with Grant's encouragement. They were ready when the fall term came, and they entered Broadmoor as Sanford Jensen and Winton Jensen, the names shortened to San and Win. The change was not their idea, but done at the urging of Grant and Evelyn who felt it might make it easier for them to fit in. On opening day, they were assigned to the same homeroom. This followed some behind the scenes manipulation by Grant to achieve the boys' desire that they be allowed to be together. It was clear that they were afraid in this new environment and they wanted to face it shoulder to shoulder.

Mr. Crowell, their homeroom and math teacher, acknowledged all the students on day one, announcing where they'd spent the sixth grade. The teacher came to San and Win and asked them to stand together. "And we're particularly lucky to have two boys from halfway around the world with us this semester." They bowed their heads, embarrassed to be singled out. "San Jensen and Win Jensen are here from Burma. What school did you attend there?" They answered "St. Paul's" almost simultaneously, without mentioning the last year had actually been spent in a blacksmith's shop and a Buddhist monastery. A muffled grunt caused Mr. Crowell to stop and gaze around the room. Then he continued. "Now, who can tell us where Burma is?"

"By Japan," one boy answered.

"Not really, James. Closer to Japan than it is to us, but still a long way from that country." The teacher pointed to a world map on the wall. "Here it is, by Vietnam. It's bordered by China, India, Thailand, Laos and Bangladesh. You've heard of the Burma Road? It was used by the British to supply war materiel to China before the Japanese overran Burma early in World War II." He paused, as if waiting for questions and then said, "You can sit down now, boys. We are happy you're here at Broadmoor."

But that was not everyone's view. On several occasions as San walked down a more or less deserted hall, someone coming in the opposite direction would thrust a shoulder into his, whispering "Gook." The same thing happened at Pop Warner Football which, at Grant's urging, he started to play along with a number of his classmates. In blocking practice, they'd hit and say, "take that, Gook." San hit back as hard as he could, but said nothing.

Win experienced trouble in the halls, too, though not on the football field, as he decided not to play despite Grant's arguments in support of a team sport experience. Sometimes students passed him squealing "Gook," or "Jap" or "Chink" and, holding their arms at shoulder height, pretended to dance. Win tried to ignore the taunts.

Most students commonly assumed they were brothers, sometimes twins, both being from Burma, the same age, the same name, and living in the same home. Reactions from some classmates ranged from bullying to hazing to mean-spirited name calling, while others simply ignored them.

The boys were well aware that the Burmese hated the Japanese because of the atrocities they committed in World War II. Having studied about Pearl Harbor, they thought Americans must feel the same way. What they found was confusion about Asian ethnicity despite all the years that had passed since World War II, as reflected by the epithets thrown at them. When they asked Grant about it, they learned about the Japanese being interned during the war. "The Japanese killed a lot of our sailors at Pearl Harbor," Grant said, "but most of the people interned were completely innocent U.S. citizens, gardeners, truck farmers, some of whom had to give up their property a few miles from here where they grew vegetables and berries. Now that is very valuable land. Interning these families in prison camps was dead wrong, a position I'm proud to say the *Post's* editorials took, but people didn't think so then."

While playing HORSE, one day at the basketball hoop and backboard at the far end of the tennis court, the boys talked about the names they were being called.

"They aren't very smart," Win said. "We don't look anything like the Vietnamese or the Japanese. Their eyes are different than ours." He posed with the basketball for a couple of seconds, then arched it upward and out with his right hand, making a clean basket. "HO" he said, meaning he had made two baskets and was closer to winning the game by spelling HORSE. San only had an "H."

"Yeah, and I bet the ones calling me Jap don't know anything about the Japanese taking over Burma during the war," San said. The next turn was his. Left foot forward, he shot with his left hand; it bounced off the rim. Daisy rolled on the hot cement nearby, scratching her back while watching the game upside down.

"Still just H, huh," Win said, unable to suppress a smile. He was seldom ahead of San in any kind of athletic effort, no matter how minor or fleeting.

San said, "I bet they wouldn't have known where to go on a map to find Burma if Mr. Crowell hadn't shown them." Swish. "HO, we're even."

Kathy had told them the basketball hoop and backboard had been installed for Peter. San said he felt every time he turned around there was something Peter had done or said or his face staring out from a silver picture frame. He increasingly felt that he was expected to fill the shoes of another boy who was dead. Not that this was ever said in so many words, but he sensed it. He didn't understand how they could expect it or how he could accomplish it.

Win ached to tell San what had happened a couple of days before at school, but he was too embarrassed. As he was walking from one building to another, Jimmy Taylor and John Hall blocked him off the path onto the lawn, repeating "faggot" in high-pitched tones as they circled around him, their arms outstretched like they had on flowing clothes. Giggling "you wear dresses, like the girls," they danced off before Win could react, not that he knew what to say anyway. He figured they must have heard about his robes, but the only ones who knew about his life in the monastery were San and the Jensens.

Win's turn with the ball came next. He positioned himself beyond the key and pushed the ball up. It bounced on the backboard, then spun around the rim only to jump out.

With another swish from the side court, San said "HOR," then added, "If they keep calling us names, I guess we'll have to fight them."

The boys were isolated. Only a few Asians attended the school. Not many students there were from foreign countries. San and Win wore the same clothes as the others kids, khakis or cords, button-down shirts, and always spoke English to each other, as the Jensens had suggested. Evelyn tried to plan parties and create social situations where the boys could mingle but she had limited success. Some of their classmates wouldn't show up or, if they did, would be grumpy because their parents had forced them to be nice to the boys from Burma. "How would you feel if you were here from a foreign country?" their parents probably said. "With no friends? And without your mother and father?" San and Win tried to dampen Evelyn's efforts, worrying that pressure on their classmates could make relationships even more difficult. The one thing they said a firm "no" to was Cotillion where they were supposed to learn to dance. Four lessons were three too many. Getting dressed up and parading around a dance floor—where they felt that girls shied away from them when they touched—wasn't for them.

Early on San showed he could do well in English and math. Win's forte was in languages and art. He had arrived from Burma with a small, tattered portfolio case of his artwork, painted in acrylic on paper or watercolor. Most were abstract views of monks standing, sitting, playing flutes. A watercolor of a boy at a prayer wheel, which he had painted for San to bring to the United States, hung in San's bedroom. Evelyn hadn't appreciated Win's artistic talents based on their abbreviated discussions in Burma. When she did, she purchased an easel and paints and urged him to take all the art instruction available at school.

Every new day at Broadmoor was an uncomfortable challenge. Increasingly, the boys wondered whether they had made the right decision coming to the United States. But they felt they had no choice other than to stay for the full year. Then they'd know what to do. ⌁

TEN

One Year to Two

T HE YEAR AT Broadmoor approached end with no one assuming the boys would return right then to their country. Grant urged Evelyn to agree to a visa extension when he saw how much more lively and happy their home had become. Laughter could actually be heard there again. Evelyn went along, seemingly having forgotten her initial insistence on a one year limit. So did Kathy, enjoying the association with her "exotic brothers" that so interested her friends. For their part, Win would have liked to return to Burma, but he couldn't persuade San.

San's and Win's issues with assimilation had abated, though hardly disappeared. It was easier for San because he was the more gregarious of the two. He was a natural athlete. The skills he developed on the football field playing tight end and his ability in tennis, particularly in doubles, helped him win acceptance.

Win, on the other hand, pretty much gave up on sports, with the exception of volleyball, which was relatively easy for him since he had played *chinlon*, a Burmese soccer-style game where players use heads, legs and feet to propel a light bamboo ball over a net. But volleyball wasn't an "in" sport among his classmates at Broadmoor. Win was basically a loner, spending lots of time in the school's art studio, often with no one else around.

Some boys had taken to calling Win "Whinny," often accompanied by a lame imitation of a horse doing just that. Win's assimilation wasn't made easier by the rumors about wearing dresses in Burma. He didn't try to explain his life as a novice, but San did. One day San found Jimmy Taylor snarling "faggot" as he circled and tormented Win. San saw no one else around so he went for Taylor, downing him with a tackle and pounding his fists into his face and upper body as he yelled, "He was a monk, idiot—something you could never be." Win pulled at San's shoulder and shouted, "Get off, I can take care of myself." San answered, "No way, we're together."

The headmaster found out and suspended both Taylor and San for one week. San and Win tried to dampen the Jensen's desire to intervene with the headmaster. Win just wanted the whole thing to go away. It wasn't clear to him whether they were trying more to protect San from the suspension or to protect Win from bullying. Whatever, the incident changed the playing field at school so that the Burma boys were now seen as a team, to be taken on lightly.

Evelyn paved the way for the boys where she could. Grant didn't, saying they had to stand on their own two feet in life and they'd better learn to do that now. Kathy didn't have to do anything to help. Her friends were clearly envious, constantly asking questions about what San and Win were like, did they laugh, did they speak English to each other, how did they eat, did they have girlfriends. Kathy luxuriated in being the center of attention.

"You can't believe what happens around our house," she'd say, which, of course, provoked more questions. "Tell me, tell me," her best friend and fellow Bel Air classmate, Joan Tinsdale, pleaded one day when they were talking in Kathy's bedroom.

"First, try eating with chopsticks."

"You do?"

"Not all the time, but for some meals. Stir-fry is one and we have it *all* the time. You know what I mean? Chicken and fish, sometimes meat, fried with vegetables, served over rice. We drown in rice and noodles."

"We have it, but not often, and not with chopsticks, thank God."

"It's hard but I'm getting better. Actually, it was Mom's idea of a compromise. In Burma, people eat with their fingers, usually the right hand, and she wouldn't buy that."

"Gross. But we eat hamburgers with our hands, I guess."

Kathy put a Judy Collins album on the record player she was given when her room was redone along with San's and Win's. She had taken full advantage of their arrival to get what she wanted for her room.

"We don't have hamburgers much anymore. *They* don't like them."

"What? Everybody likes hamburgers," Joan said.

"Not them. Too thick or something. It's their 'Burmese palate,' as Mother says in that stuffy way she sometimes uses." Kathy raised her nose.

"Have you ever kissed them?" Joan asked.

"Sure, the way you kiss your little brother."

"I didn't mean that. They're not your brothers. You could kiss them, really kiss them if you wanted to."

"Mom and Dad would kill me. They're so protective of them. I'm older and supposed to 'set an example.' God."

"I wouldn't mind kissing them, a good, passionate kiss, right on the mouth," Joan said.

"Which one?"

"I don't care. Either, both. Win is better looking, I think, but I would die for a tan like San's—no more baby oil with iodine for me."

"They're only fourteen, you know. Maybe if you keep up your volleyball at the club with Win, you can lure him into something one day."

Joan had asked Kathy to arrange for her to play volleyball with Win at Sand & Sea, a private club on the beach in Santa Monica where the Jensens and Joan's family were members. Joan and Win had started playing occasional games at first, then being matched in mixed doubles tournaments. They became winners in their age group much of the time, he having grown quickly to five-feet ten inches, and Joan almost as tall. She paid more attention to Win than anyone else did, tried to draw him out, get him involved with her friends. He talked to her about his relationships with San, with Kathy and with the Jensens who, he explained, saw San as Peter. He felt he didn't fit into the family dynamic, and he was thinking about returning to Burma in the near future.

Slowly, his feelings for Joan turned toward adoration. It was as if there was something exploding in him that had to get out. He would gaze at her and unconsciously release a quiet, deep breath as if he didn't know what to do next. When his feelings got too strong, he'd jump up and run into the surf to catch a couple of waves.

Joan became an increasing fixture on St. Cloud Road, spending Friday or Saturday night with Kathy almost every other weekend. In fact, Joan accompanied the family on a couple of vacations, one at a rented home on Kauai, the other during the winter at the family's Aspen vacation home. The Jensens told the kids they could each bring a friend. Kathy jumped at the chance, but as the days passed in Hawaii, it seemed Joan was more interested in being with the boys than with Kathy. Joan was always on the beach playing volleyball with Win or on the sand talking with San. Neither boy invited anyone. Their excuse was, "We don't need to bring friends." The truth was there weren't really any friends to invite. The trip to Aspen wasn't a total success. The boys had a hard time getting used to the cold and the snow. They tried ski lessons but neither one was excited about making it his sport.

Unlike Aspen, Kauai felt a bit like home to the boys. The heat and humidity, the tropical breezes, the plant life, the water, all reminded them of their roots, though the people, the buildings and the streets were completely different. They were in the water one afternoon trying to surf when there was a lull in the waves, and Win started to sing, "I wanna go back to my little grass shack in . . . .

San said, "Me too."

"No, I'm serious. It's been almost two years now and it's time."

"Oh, yeah, me to be a blacksmith and you to have your head shaved and beg for food. No. We're spoiled now."

The ocean was a pleasant retreat from the blazing hot sun. A three-foot wave approached. San managed to catch it and ride to shore, but Win didn't connect, leaving him to try the next wave. San swam back to join him and they started talking again.

"I could do it. Maybe my father would let me come to Rangoon and live with him."

"Like he writes you all the time?"

"Well, maybe it would work," Win said, having no confidence it would. The man had written him twice in two years, despite Win's having sent him at least ten letters.

"The girls aren't as good looking there," San said.

Win chuckled. "All you talk about is girls."

"All you do is talk *to* girls," San replied.

"What do you mean?"

"Joan."

"We play volleyball together. I have to talk to her."

"It's not *have* to. You like her, I can tell."

"Let's get this one," Win cried, as he swam to catch a wave. San was inches behind.

They came out of the water and ran across the burning sand, their feet frying, to the shade of a palm tree, short of where Grant, Evelyn, Kathy and Joan sat on beach chairs under an umbrella, playing dominos.

"Have you caught anything from her yet?" San asked, his eyes widening. "Come on, tell me."

"You've got to be kidding."

"No. Like, second base, third base?"

"No way." Win asked, "Have you?"

"Sure, doesn't everybody?" San answered.

"If you believe them, yeah, but all those idiots at school lie. And so do you—I think."

"I'll tell you more about it later," San said, smiling, his eyebrows arched, as they ran to join the others. ❧

ELEVEN

Folk Heroes

S AN AND WIN had been relatively trouble-free as fifteen year olds go, not nearly as difficult as Kathy had been at the same age when she argued about nearly everything and would have preferred, it seemed, not to associate with her parents at all. The boys didn't mind being seen with Grant and Evelyn at the Village Theatre in Westwood where they saw films popular with their age group, like *Raiders of the Lost Arc* and *Chariots of Fire*. Most of Grant and Evelyn's concerns about the boys were based on their reluctance to be involved in activities with family friends, and occasional reports from school about San being late for class or Win not concentrating on his work. That changed, however, one day when Evelyn received a call from the Police Department telling her the boys had been arrested. She immediately called Grant.

"What do you mean, they're at the police station?" he asked. "What for?"

"I don't have the details. Something about trespassing at the Mitchells. I'm headed for the station right now. You'll meet me there?"

"It's probably some damn fool prank. It won't hurt to let them sit and stew awhile."

"Well, I don't know what they did, but when the police are involved, it's important."

"Everyone knows not to go around Old Lady Mitchell's house. She's a nut."

"How soon can you get there, Grant?"

"Couple of hours, I guess. I'm with the editorial board."

"I'm leaving now. Please come as soon as you can."

"Wait. Which station?"

"The one on Butler below Santa Monica Boulevard," she paused, "where you had an experience once yourself, as I recall the story." The phone clicked.

Grant returned to the meeting, but couldn't concentrate on the discussion. He debated whether to call their lawyer, but decided it was premature. Thomas wouldn't know anything about criminal trespass law anyway. The boys would probably just get a slap on the wrist. Showing up with a high-powered lawyer might undermine the lesson to be learned and simply reinforce the idea that Big Daddy would always be around to bail them out of tough situations. That's the way his father had handled a police matter with him, letting him sit it out in the Butler jail for a few hours.

Grant found Evelyn in the station, steaming. "I've been here for almost two hours waiting to meet with the officers. And, waiting for you."

"I came as soon as the meeting was over. It was an important one. You'll understand when you see the editorial tomorrow."

The place was busy: people walking the halls, most in uniform, joking, sometimes in serious conversation. Men and women behind desks in small offices and cubicles looked up as they passed. They probably didn't often see a woman dressed in a suit and high heels here. Despite the lapse of thirty years, Grant remembered the place well, as he did the details of the evening that brought him there.

In a few minutes, Grant and Evelyn were called by the desk sergeant and ushered into a small, grey, windowless room. A grey metal table and chairs stood in the middle of the room. A wall clock clicked off the seconds. Almost immediately, there was a knock at the door. Two large policemen in blue uniforms, with badge, gun, billy club, handcuffs and radio transmitters, strutted into the room and introduced themselves. Following close behind were San and Win, their heads bowed. Sergeant Boyce started. "Your sons . . ."

Grant felt like correcting the relationship but said nothing.

". . . were found at the home of Mildred Mitchell this morning. They entered without permission."

"The boys wouldn't go in someone's home without being invited." Evelyn added, "That's not like them."

"It wasn't the house they entered. It was the garden. Specifically, the swimming pool."

Grant asked, "They have their own pool, why would they go there to swim?"

"It wasn't to swim," the sergeant replied. "There's no water in the Mitchell pool."

Grant chuckled to himself, thinking he'd one-upped the officer. "Then, all the more reason they wouldn't go there."

"You must be mistaken," Evelyn said.

The policeman turned to the boys. "You want to tell 'em?"

San started: "We were with Charlie Black skateboarding on the street and saw the side gate to the Mitchells was open. We'd been wondering about all the noise from over there in the last couple of weeks, so we decided to investigate." His head dropped.

"We thought we should be sure nothing was wrong because that gate is never open," Win added, nodding his head to underscore the importance of the information he'd supplied.

"And?" the officer asked.

"We decided to go skateboarding," San responded.

"Tell them where?" the man continued.

"*In* the pool," San answered, a limp grin passing his face.

"In the pool?" Grant's eyes bugged.

"Yes, it's being fixed, that's why the water is out, so we decided we could skateboard in it." San shrugged his shoulders as if to say, *wouldn't anybody?* "We didn't think anyone was home."

"But Mrs. Mitchell appeared with a rifle . . .," the officer started.

Win interrupted. "She pointed it right at us, called us 'goddamned juvenile delinquents.' She said our 'daddy was a big shot.' Kept saying it over and over. Then she shuffled around the pool, raising and lowering the rifle, but always pointing it right at us. She made some remarks about Orientals that weren't very nice. I thought she was going to shoot us for sure, but then she said she was going to call the police and we were to stay right there in the pool. She wouldn't even let us come up and sit on the lawn."

"We didn't think we were hurting anything," San added.

"The boys could probably be charged with trespass and malicious mischief as well," Sergeant Boyce said. The other officer stared with a frown at the two boys, but added nothing. He looked as though he might be having a hard time keeping a straight face.

Grant glowered at the boys.

The sergeant said, "Mrs. Mitchell says she won't press charges if you'll resurface the pool. The skateboards left markings on the gunnite."

"Bull...oney," Grant answered. "I thought she was resurfacing the pool anyway. That's why there isn't any water in it, right? I'm not going to give her a free ride."

Grant leaned over to Evelyn and whispered, "What an asshole." Immediately realizing his whisper had been audible and its intended reference unclear, he said: "That's Mrs. Mitchell, you understand. She's the neighbor from hell. And what about pointing a rifle at kids on skateboards? Isn't that a violation of some law? What kind of rifle?"

"A semi-automatic. The kind you can't own without permits," Boyce said. "All I can say is she's had a trip down here."

"Where is Charlie Black?" Evelyn asked.

"His parents are on their way."

"Can we have some time with the boys alone?" Grant said.

The policemen left the room.

Grant started walking back and forth, puffing on a cigarette. He wondered if the cops knew who he was. And, if they did, would that work for or against them? The *Post* had run editorials that were pretty critical of the chief and of the department as a whole. On the other hand, when compliments were warranted, the paper was usually the first to hand them out. "Goddamn it, boys." What he wanted to say was *way to go with that old bitch.* But instead what came out was, "This may be about the dumbest thing I've ever heard of."

Win said, "It wasn't Aun San's fault. It was my idea. I'm sorry."

"Not true. It was my idea, not his. Really, it was Charlie Black's idea."

"It's such a stupid notion I wonder why anyone would claim it," Grant said. "Jesus Christ."

"And, now, to get you off we have to resurface the woman's pool," Evelyn said.

"I'm not agreeing to that," Grant interjected. "It's a holdup."

"It's okay, we can stay here," San said.

"That's ridiculous"

"We can help pay for the pool," San offered.

"With what?" Grant extended his arms, his palms turned upward.

"With the allowance we've saved," Win interjected.

Grant's eyes popped as he said to Evelyn, "I didn't know we gave them that much."

"We don't."

"Then we'll get jobs and save the money," San suggested. "At the paper."

"Oh, great. You don't think maybe you're a tad young, do you? Age fifteen going on twelve?" Grant had visions of his own first employment at the *Post* sitting in the back of a pickup tossing bundled packages of papers on the sidewalk in front of restaurants, liquor stores, markets. He had to get up in the middle of the night to make the early Sunday morning deliveries, and he was sure that was exactly why his father had given him that assignment. Grant paused, then said wistfully, "Someday, maybe." No one spoke for a long period, the only noise being the clock ticking. Then Grant added: "Your Moth . . . we'll decide how long you'll be grounded for this."

Evelyn and Grant talked at length in their bedroom sitting room after dinner that night.

"This is the first serious thing they've done, Grant. Actually, I could hardly keep from laughing a couple of times."

"Well, it's a lamebrain stunt."

"They didn't plan it," she replied. "It just happened. It's not like someone was thinking it out."

"Well, at some point in your life, don't you have to start thinking?"

"They're boys. Don't be too tough on them." Evelyn said. "They've had such a hard time being *in* at school. They probably let Charlie talk them into it."

"That's a great influence. And I don't get why they're both covering for the other," Grant said.

"Loyalty. I see it every day. They're closer and more loyal than two brothers would be."

Grant sat on the edge of the bed to remove his shoes. He thought about his relationship with his half-brother, which could hardly be categorized in that way, and they had common blood. In fact, he felt Terry Jensen took every opportunity to undermine his leadership of the *Post*. The long ash at the end of his cigarette dipped, ready to fall and hit the bedspread. Normally the bedroom was off limits to smoking, but she said nothing because he was so agitated. "Evie, do you think we made the right decision to bring them here? Both of them? I mean, maybe without a co-conspirator, this kind of thing wouldn't happen."

"There's no way I could have left San there to work in that factory with his cousin for the next ten years. And Win was part of the package. He's become an equal part."

"You're right, of course."

"By the way, as I recall it, Mr. Jensen, there's a story you've only hinted about where you spent a night in that jail over something a lot more serious than this."

"That was crazy. It happened when Jack Eddy's parents came home from Europe a night early as we were having an unauthorized graduation blowout in their backyard. It was an instinctive reaction to get rid of the evidence by heaving the bottles, cans, glasses, food, everything over the back garden hedge. How could we know that Governor Earl Warren and his wife were getting out of their limo at the bottom of the cliff and all this stuff would come raining down on them?"

"And there was something about a headline?"

"Yeah." He smiled. "'Attempted Assassination of Governor.'" Dad had the story killed after the morning edition."

"And you were actually in jail, weren't you?"

"For eighteen hours. It didn't do me any harm either." He nodded, remembering his father's stern reaction to the events of that night.

"Anyway," Evelyn said, dropping the subject, "I think it's been the best for all of us that they're here together. It could have been pretty lonely for San without Win, particularly at the beginning when Kathy's arms were not exactly extended in welcome. I wasn't sure for a long time, but I am now."

It wasn't until the middle of the night that it struck Grant that Peter's name hadn't surfaced once in their discussion after dinner. Never was it said "Peter wouldn't have done that." Peter's memory was still very much there for him, but it didn't carry the same sting. Was it that San was establishing himself as an independent entity in their lives? And what about Win? Was it that his existence in their family no longer was dependent on San?

Unlike his own father in the Warren caper, Grant decided to help the boys this one time, to have lawyers take care of whatever was necessary. The reminder of the governor had softened him, making him focus on his teenage years and compare them to San's and Win's. He had to admit that they weren't into as much stuff as he had been at the same age. He was already smoking at fifteen; they did not. He drank some at parties, but as far as he knew, they didn't drink. And sex? At fifteen, he was just coming into it, dealing with forces that seemed irresistible, unable to think of much else, envious of all the guys who seemed to be so much better with the girls than he was. He had stayed away from the sex subject with the boys, as his father had with him. He couldn't face it, and it was not a role Evelyn assumed. Who knew what they thought or what they had experienced?

A couple of nights later, Grant raised the skateboard incident over dinner. "You know, boys, your antics didn't reflect a lot of smarts," he said, pointing to his brain, "I'm sure you agree." He paused waiting for confirmation. None came. He continued: "Each of you tried to take responsibility, saying it was your idea, not the other's. So, what was it?"

San glanced at Win, then replied, "Really, what we were trying to say was that it was both of our ideas. Neither one of us had to talk the other into it."

"And neither of us tried to stop it either. It just sort of happened," Win added.

"Loyalty is an admirable quality," Grant said, "But you can't be so loyal that you lie—under any circumstances."

San raised his head, "I know."

Win nodded in agreement.

The boys were grounded for two weeks. The swimming pool affair served to elevate them to the status of folk heroes at Broadmoor. They were now more like the regular guys, no matter how different their appearance and their accent. Classmates sat with them at lunch, tried to be next to them in class, waved and smiled as they passed in the halls, stopped brutalizing San in football practice, and were actually nice to Win, even though, unlike most of them, he was an artist, not a sports fanatic. It had taken three years and a jail visit to be accepted by their peers. The acceptance tasted good, particularly to Win who had faced tougher challenges to get there. No longer was the idea of returning to Burma so urgent for him. ～

TWELVE

An Estate Plan

THE STUDENT visas had been renewed for a second and a third year when Grant and Evelyn met with Clyde Thomas about their estate plan. The lawyer had been pestering them about this ever since Peter's death. They had avoided it, not wanting to think about the wills and trusts that had anticipated Peter surviving them. Complicating the matter was that they had discussed the possibility of adopting San. He had mentioned recently that he'd like to stay in the United States indefinitely. If he were to be adopted, they had to get moving as the process was cumbersome and had to be completed by age sixteen. Win talked of returning to Burma to spend time with his father, meaning his adoption was still not a possibility.

The three met in Grant's office, gathered around his conference table. He always had guests sit at the table rather than line up in front of his desk on guest chairs. The lineup conveyed a sense of class or place he didn't like. Thomas was trusted and respected within the Los Angeles Post company, his law firm having represented the family and the *Post* for decades. He was a loyal retainer and looked the part with short grey hair, rimless glasses and dressed in a dark blue suit.

"The time has come—is overdue I would say—when you have to review your estate plan," Thomas said.

"I know, we've been dragging our feet on this," Grant said.

"You're not alone." Thomas smiled and shook his head.

"No one wants to face mortality, huh?" Grant asked.

"That's part of it, but you have special problems. For you Grant, everything has to be sewed up tight because other members of the family might have designs for control of the *Post* . . ."

Grant interrupted, "I don't need to be dead for them to try that." He chuckled. Evelyn rolled her eyes toward the ceiling.

"Seriously, as we've discussed, I may end up in a conflict position and have to withdraw entirely from representing the family, but that isn't for today, is it?" Thomas rummaged through files he had placed on the table. "The first question is the one of adoption and then, whether you adopt or not, will there be provision for the boys in your estate? As it stands now, Kathy is the sole beneficiary."

"We'd like to adopt them both," Evelyn said. "Not that we had that in mind at the beginning, but we have come around to feeling that way. In San's case, there's no one to stand in the way. But Win's father, we're told, will never agree."

"Yes, but even with there being no parent to object in San's case, it's extremely hard to adopt a Burmese child. Grant, you might have to pull out all the stops with your State Department contacts to make it happen."

"I'm willing to do that. I do know people in high positions there," Grant said. He stood, then circled the table, "but we have to think about the problem with Kathy, how she's going to take it."

"What do you anticipate?" the lawyer asked.

"She's been protective of her status when it comes to the boys," Grant said.

"Oh, I think she's mostly over that, Grant." Evelyn waved her hand. "She and the boys have become closer, and a number of her friends have become friends of theirs as well."

"What about the division of the estate?" Thomas asked.

"I don't think we can decide how to divvy up everything up until we know for sure if San can be adopted," Grant said.

"But what will we do about Win?" Evelyn asked.

"In this case I'd say see how things develop, then decide," the lawyer suggested. "This is a particularly fluid situation. An estate plan, as you know, has to be reviewed and adjusted from time to time."

Grant walked to his desk and perused a thin file, then said, "In the meantime, Evie, how about a half million dollars to each boy, with the residue continuing to go to Kathy?"

Evelyn cocked her head to the side and frowned.

"If we were knocked off tomorrow that would give them enough to complete their educations, plus a nest egg for the future, wherever they may end up," Grant said.

"And there would still be plenty for Kathy?" Evelyn asked.

"Easily," Thomas answered, "in excess of five million."

It was agreed that Thomas would contact the Burmese lawyer, U Saw Maung, and arrange what was necessary with the Burmese authorities to have San's adoption approved. Thomas would take care of the U.S. legalities and review everything to be sure they had the most effective testamentary scheme possible to preserve the Grant Jensen family's stock ownership position in the *Post*. Above all, Grant didn't want the other members of his family controlling the direction of the paper, especially his arch conservative, older half-brother Terry, who had always felt he'd been screwed out of the publisher's job, and his eccentric, outspoken, never satisfied sister Jane White. Efforts had been made to patch together a friendly extended family picture, principally through an annual holiday dinner at the University Club in mid-December, but Jane usually had too much to drink and insulted most everyone in Grant's family with her tirades about the paper's support for this or that and by her less than diplomatic comments about "Orientals." She was fond of saying something or other didn't have a "Chinaman's chance" of working. Evelyn saw this as deliberate, not an inadvertent slip in front of the boys, and complained to Grant, who dodged the issue by claiming he had too many battles to fight with his sister than to take this one on. Craig, Jane's son, and

Michelle, Terry's daughter, who were also in their mid-teens, would do their best to divert attention at these gatherings, sometimes finding reasons to leave the table with Kathy, San and Win.

But the inheritance issue was not so easily solved. While on vacation in Aspen Grant and Evelyn met Burton Isaacs, a family wealth advisor, who lived there part-time. Isaacs's clientele was confidential, but Grant had heard through other sources that he represented the Kilpatrick family in Shreveport, Louisiana, owners of the *Shreveport Record*.

Grant decided to retain him and spent considerable time so that he would understand the dynamics of their family, their wealth, and the *Post*. Both lawyer and psychologist, Isaacs didn't seem daunted by the complexity of their situation. He advised that they should treat San equally with Kathy if San became their adopted son. Win's case was harder and Isaacs asked probing questions: Should it matter that he couldn't be adopted if he meant as much to them as San did? The boys were being raised with Kathy as brothers and sister, and shouldn't they be treated as such? His advice was they should; otherwise, bitter resentments between the children were bound to arise.

Grant and Evelyn had difficulty acting on what they heard. The linchpin still seemed to be whether San could be adopted or not, and that had not been resolved. Lethargy prevailed, and nothing was done to provide for the boys, leaving Kathy, for the time, the sole individual beneficiary of most of the family's assets. ∿

THIRTEEN

The Split

SAN AWAKENED as a body crawled into his bed. Despite the fog of deep sleep, he knew immediately who it was. Joan. She and Kathy and he and Win had been talking in the den earlier, playing Joni Mitchell and James Taylor records, and smoking pot. The Jensens were out of town for the weekend, and Kathy, home from college, had invited Joan to spend the night.

Joan caressed San's chest, stomach and thighs through his pajamas. He lay motionless, not knowing what to do. He did know he shouldn't be doing this, not because the Jensens would disapprove, which they would, but because of Win. He had been crazy about Joan almost from their first meeting, if only from afar, to San's knowledge. But thinking was not exactly what he was up to under the circumstances. All he knew was that he might finally be on the verge of experiencing what other guys talked about so knowingly.

Her hand moved under his pajamas, stroking him lightly and slowly. It was as though butterflies were dancing and flicking their wings over a thousand pulsating nerve endings. She pulled at his pajama bottoms and lifted her nightgown. He positioned himself on his knees and began to thrust, but he couldn't come anywhere close to the target.

"You've never done this before, have you?" she whispered.

"Sure I have," he said in a raspy adolescent voice.

"Kathy told me you hadn't."

"What does she know?"

"I can't anyway." She reached for him. He exploded, his arms falling back with a thud on the bed. Neither spoke for some time.

"I can get Kathy to invite me over more, you know, if you'd like me to?"

What he wanted to say was, *Are you kidding? I don't want to do anything else but this the rest of my life.* What he said was, "No one can find out."

"Don't worry. It has to be the same with my parents. They would kill me if I got pregnant."

"Because the baby might look like me?"

"You're very good-looking. All the girls think so." She pressed her finger to his chin. "I like that dimple, right there. No, I couldn't tell my parents I need an abortion."

"But, what about Win? I thought . . ."

"We're just good friends. He's had his chance. He's not interested."

"That's not what I see."

"He isn't. I guarantee."

San wondered when and how Win had passed up the opportunity. "How do you know that?" he asked.

"I'm not going to say."

San and Win had talked about sex for the last couple of years, with little more than rumor, desire and frustration to support their words. Now, San had actually experienced it, unfortunately with the girl Win worshiped. *Should I not see Joan anymore? Can I give up what I have just found?* Suddenly, his talks with Win about the mysteries of sex ended. San couldn't participate with the secret he kept. There was no one else with whom he could have any kind of real discussion about it. Joking and kidding with classmates was not the same thing.

One afternoon after her last class at UCLA, Joan came by and watched San's tennis lesson. When the instructor left, they went into the pool house, which had become their safe retreat because no one used the court or the pool on weekday afternoons. The plain central room contained two single beds with bolsters pushed together in a corner, a game table and four chairs. There were small bathrooms at each end, one for men, one for women. San dropped his tennis shorts and jock. Joan took off her skirt and blouse. They moved toward the bed, caressing one another, then rolling urgently on the bedspread they didn't find time to remove. They hadn't been there two minutes when, suddenly, the door flew open. Win stood, mouth open but speechless, then turned, slammed the door and ran toward the house.

San didn't know what to do. He felt guilty even though Joan had started it, and he had tried to make her understand how important she was to Win. But he couldn't help himself. At the same time he was furious Win had come in unannounced. The more San thought about how cold Win had been towards him the past few weeks, he concluded his friend must have been suspicious and had no thought of knocking at the pool house door.

San told Joan to leave. He was mad, but afraid, as he made his way back to the house and up to Win's bedroom. He wasn't sure what he was going to say. He knocked on the door. No answer. He tried the door handle and found it locked. He called and could hear Win only vaguely, as though he were yelling into a pillow. "Go away. Go away." San said, as quietly as he could, "She said you'd had your chance. That you didn't want to. What was I supposed to do?" The last words he heard before he walked down the hall sounded like, "I don't care. I hate you. Both of you."

For several weeks, the two boys hardly spoke to one another. When they did, the words were caustic, often sarcastic. When the split between them became apparent to the family, Grant and Evelyn decided to sit down after dinner in the den, the usual spot for family conferences, and talk about whatever the problem was. "It's obvious you guys aren't talking to one another," Grant said. "You were as close as any two people could be, so something's happened. What is it?"

"Nothing," San answered first, the position he regularly assumed—to speak before, and sometimes for, Win.

"That's right. There's nothing," Win added.

"Kathy, is that true?" Evelyn asked. Kathy began to cry.

"We're going to sit here until we get to the bottom of it," Grant said, "so let's go."

"I invited Joan over for the weekend," Kathy said, "and after we went to bed, she got up—I didn't know it was happening, believe me—and went in San's bedroom. And you can figure out what happened after that."

"How did you learn about it?" Grant asked.

"Win told me he was suspicious, but wasn't certain until a couple of weeks later when he found them together. I confronted Joan and San about it."

"She was my volleyball partner. That wasn't right."

"But I didn't start it, she came to me," San protested.

"Yeah, but you kept on doing it, down in the pool house, didn't you."

Steely looks flew from Evelyn's eyes. "It's hard for me to believe," she said. "Kathy, what kind of friends to do you have? Joan has been given free run of the house, Aspen, the vacation place in the Islands, and here's what happens. San is years younger."

Grant fumed. "This kind of thing was going on right under our noses. What if she gets pregnant?"

"The Tinsdales are good friends. What will they say?" Evelyn chimed in. "Do they know?"

Kathy responded, "I doubt it."

"I think we have to tell them," Grant said.

"No, Dad, you can't do that to Joan."

San's head swiveled from one to another as the conversation went on. Win stared at the rug.

"I'll tell you this," Grant said. "San, I'm talking to you. This has got to stop. Your relationship with Win is enough of a reason, but if it isn't, then consider she's older and obviously more experienced than you are. She's Kathy's good friend. Her parents are our friends. You're playing with fire. A mistake could change your entire life. Do you understand?

"Yes, I do."

Rather than stopping, San's meetings with Joan moved elsewhere. They graduated to full-fledged sex with the protection of rubbers. He was hooked. Sometimes he could think of little else, often finding himself in an obvious state of agitation toward the end of a class when he knew he would soon have to stand and walk to the next classroom. A jacket, tied at the waist, became his camouflage. Win fumed about San and Joan. He stopped being her volleyball partner, in fact stopped going to the club altogether. He moved down the beach to play on the public courts at Sorrento. Meals on St. Cloud Road were stilted. Conversation was hard to produce. And Joan was never invited back.

Over the years he'd been with the Jensens, San questioned more and more whether his role was to be Peter's replacement or whether he had value as himself? *Had he actually become Peter to them?* Win alluded to it often enough, usually sarcastically, but always, San thought, with what appeared to be envy. Peter, now dead nearly six years, was not often mentioned in the household anymore. *Was it because I am here?* But Peter was very much there. His framed photographs stared at San who rarely passed one without comparing himself and wondering, *What do I have to do to be Peter? Who was Peter anyway? What would he be if he had lived? Do I want to be him?* He couldn't help comparing his life in America with the life he had led in his homeland. When something set him off, smells, tastes, sights, whatever, what he remembered of his prior life was not Inle Lake nor his cousins and uncle. They were memories of the years with his parents before they were killed. He was glad he had his own room so that he could take their photo from the drawer and hold it when these thoughts surfaced, as they often did when he climbed in bed.

Win's anxieties were severe, too. He felt second rate in everything—in school, in athletics, in studies, in friendships and, not unexpectedly, in appeal to girls. But it was right there in the Jensens' home he felt it most. He was not and never could be San, much less Peter. The idea of returning to Burma was again on his agenda. His father was beginning to reach out, sending an occasional letter. He expressed more of an interest about school, encouraging his son to study hard and take advantage of his opportunities. He also made mention of his expanding business relationships in the States, but said nothing about their nature. He slammed American newspapers and their misinformation about the ruling regime in Burma, what he called their anti-Burma positions, though he never referenced the *Post*. But he didn't go so far as to ask his son to come home. This sporadic correspondence wasn't enough to dull the overwhelming sense of abandonment Win had felt for a long time. Many things about his life in Burma, even the *kyoung* and the abbot, felt familiar, comfortable. Little in his new life had grown to feel that way, even after four years. Win knew if he did leave, it would be without San, but that would be all right now. After all, he'd been abandoned by San as well. ~

FOURTEEN

The Junta Issue

A FTER REACHING SIXTEEN, Sam and Win started working at the *Post* during summer vacations. Grant had done the same as a teenager and thought members of the family should learn early about the responsibilities of the workplace. Who knows, maybe they could end up with careers at the *Post* like he did. He had planned that for Peter. Kathy had been no exception. She had been expected to work during summer vacations, most of the time assigned in the newsroom to perform whatever tasks needed doing. San toiled in the pressroom, the heart of production of the paper, where the pressmen, who soon learned he was a Jensen, made sure he got his share of the grunt work. He came home at the end of his shift drained by the physical labor. By comparison and thanks to Evelyn's intervention, Win ended up in a soft job in display advertising where he could use his artistic talents. Evelyn did not completely share Grant's enthusiasm about the kids working at the paper at young ages, but she had to admit at the same age she had been expected to learn to operate farm equipment on her father's citrus ranch in California's San Joaquin Valley.

But summers were not all work for San and Win. Weekends were often spent crewing on the family yacht sailing to Catalina and the Channel Islands off Southern California's coast. The gorgeous, sleek yacht was a training ground for the boys to learn the various phases of sailing: navigating, manning the helm, mending lines, winching, raising and lowering sails—often in heavy winds—cleaning heads, fixing gadgetry forever in need of repair, and on and on. Grant's goal was to ready them to crew in the annual race to Ensenada, Mexico, the highlight of his sailing year. Kathy wasn't included because, when home from Georgetown, she wanted to be with her friends on weekends, not bobbing around in the ocean isolated from the action.

Events in the boys' lives caused the gulf between them to widen. San's adoption was approved and papers were filed for U.S. citizenship. His name was officially changed to Sanford Aun Jensen, the middle name being included at his request. Grant and Evelyn wanted to have a celebration, open a bottle of vintage Dom Perignon or two from the cellar, but they couldn't bring themselves to do it with Win's not being included. Consistent with Burton Isaac's advice, they decided to treat San on an equal basis with Kathy in sharing the estate. For Win they provided a flat million-dollar bequest, generous but less than a one-third interest in the estate would have provided. The amount was a compromise between Evelyn, who thought Win should have an equal share even though he was not adopted, and Grant, who insisted the amount be smaller since Win had a father, was likely to return to Burma, and would never be adopted.

Symptomatic of their dodging thorny family issues, Grant and Evelyn did not sit down with the children, as they referred to them collectively, to explain their decisions. This ignored Isaacs's observations that the worst results come from surprise, that time is needed for people to reach acceptance. Because they were uncertain about their estate decisions and changes might later be required, they decided to wait until San and Win reached twenty-one and then announce the terms to all three. They still feared Kathy would resist if they went to her for advance approval.

Nothing changed for Win. He was too tentative about his future and the relationship with his father to consider a change in citizenship. In his mind, he was seen as the inferior twin, having fewer friends and being less of an achiever than San. He had lost the one person, Kathy, who had run interference for him with girls. San had adjusted much more easily, it seemed, to life in America. All Win had to boast about was his artistic ability, recognized when one of his images was selected for the cover of the 1984 Broadmoor yearbook. Upon graduation, Win would enter the Rhode Island School of Design. San had been admitted to the University of California at Berkeley. He could have gone to multiple universities, but was drawn to Grant and Evelyn's alma mater. San and Win would be separated for the first time since they first met at St. Paul's in Rangoon when they were eight years old.

When they were younger, the boys avoided discussing the subject of the Burmese government's impact on their lives. San knew Win's father was in the military and Win knew the government supposedly killed San's parents. As time progressed, however, the two young men came to have increasingly strong views about their homeland which they expressed vocally. To San, the military government in Burma was a totalitarian regime that gorged on human rights abuses. Win, on the other hand, excused the government on the grounds that it was following a "road to democracy," which, as his father said, simply took time. The chasm between them tore at San. He couldn't disagree more with Win, but their roots were deep. They were virtual brothers. That should be more important than political disputes, he told himself. Yet the controversies continued to make lively dinner table conversation.

"They're killing people, shutting them up in hell holes, torturing them, confiscating their property," San said.

"There's no proof of that. Just because the U.S. government spouts that line and imposes economic sanctions on a desperately poor nation doesn't mean it's true. Democracy can't come overnight."

San turned to Grant, asking what he thought.

"It's a repressive regime, but it's hard to know where it's headed—democracy or not."

"The generals say they'll take steps to become more democratic," Win interjected.

"Yeah, like Hitler proclaimed to the world in the mid-thirties that he had no warlike intentions," San said.

"Hardly a fair comparison," Win almost snorted. He was tempted to end the remark by referring to San as Peter, but he would never do that in front of Grant and Evelyn; that was reserved for San alone.

"I've been comparing the *Sun* to the *Post*, Dad," San said—occasionally using Dad and Mom since the adoption —"We list Burma with a bunch of other human rights violators, like those in Latin America, but I don't see editorials devoted exclusively to developments in Burma as I do in the *Sun*."

"We're watching it. Carefully. But we've got to choose our ground. We can't be on a soapbox about every wrong perpetrated around the world."

This was more of a problem than Grant was prepared to admit. He had been under pressure from the editorial staff to do what San was suggesting, but so far he had resisted. How long he could continue to influence the situation and treat Burma less harshly than countries like Guatemala and Peru he didn't know. In a way, his was, and had been, a waiting game, hoping the regime would change its ways and deliver democracy or at least lower its profile so that it became less of a subject in the news. The topic was hot enough that he knew he couldn't avoid it for long. ⌒

FIFTEEN

Editorial Fight

I N EARLY SUMMER 1988 Bill Farley, the *Post's* editor, called Grant and asked for a meeting to discuss an issue before it was taken up by the editorial board. Grant knew it must be important because draft editorials were reviewed through established channels prior to reaching the board. He suspected he knew the reason: undoubtedly, another issue involving Burma and democracy. Waiting for Farley to walk in the door, Grant glanced at the new photo on his desk. It pictured the three children taken at a recent reunion at St. Cloud Road when everyone was back from college on summer break. A nice, happy family scene, though one would need to have the background to know that diverse group was in fact a family. The obligatory grins masked the divisions between them. Kathy and Win, being in the same time zone in the East, had visited each other and become even closer, but San was out of reach for both of them. St. Cloud Road had seemed vacant and lonely. Grant and Evelyn anticipated any opportunity to get everyone back under their wings, even though living with all the undercurrents had threatened their own relationship. Without the children, it felt to Grant uncomfortably like the cold, lost years that followed Peter's death. He knew it was the same for Evelyn.

Farley walked in and saw Grant staring at the photo. "New?"

"Yeah."

"Nice." Farley handed Grant a piece of paper, saying "Draft editorial. I knew you'd want to see this one."

The draft was headed "*Burma—Dead End Path.*"

"Let me read it," Grant said, as he thought, *What? Not again.* There had been a handful of editorials on Burma presented to him over the years, and on all he had urged moderation. He motioned Farley to a chair at the side of his cluttered desk. All the furniture had been Grant's father's. He would never consider remodeling the office, as Evelyn had once urged him to do, but new framed commendations, and photos and headlines from the *Post* were added as time passed. He was comforted by the ghosts that inhabited the space. He sped through the copy. It assailed a new law enacted by the government taking away citizenship rights of hundreds of thousands of ethnic Burmese minorities.

"I thought," Farley backed into the conversation, "because of the boys, you know . . ."

"The boys don't have a role in our editorial policy, Bill."

"I know, but it's anti-junta stuff. We've gone pretty light on these guys," he paused, "at least by comparison to most of the papers we claim as competition."

Grant had heard this before: the *Post* talks about the regime failing to follow its "path to democracy" while everybody else accuses the generals of torture, rape, jailing innocent people, and murder.

"True. They have been slow on their so-called 'path.'"

"Slow? The cart is stuck in the mud. It's been years now with no progress at all."

Grant tapped a cigarette out of a pack of Camels, then fumbled through the papers on his desk until he found his gold pocket lighter. Almost as an afterthought, he held the pack out toward Farley who declined. Grant considered his editor to be a longtime, good friend, but the age-old division in the newspaper world between the publisher's office and the editorial operation was a limitation on the friendship being very deep. Actually, Grant had few close friends. Some of his old buddies had drifted away as he rose to the pinnacle position he held, and he tended to distrust newer acquaintances in the business and social worlds. "Tell me why we should run something this tough, Bill."

Farley emitted his trademark single loud noise, something like a bellow, as if to say *it's obvious.* "Because it raises the question of whether we, the country, American business, our citizens, do business with the bums or not. The more we trade with them, operate manufacturing plants there, send American tourists roaming around, the more we help cement this corrupt regime's position."

Grant tipped back in his leather chair and stared at the red ashes about to fall from his cigarette. He knocked them into an ashtray. Smoke drifted toward the ceiling. Grant walked around the desk. "Win's headed to Burma. It's his first time back."

"I'm not sure his timing is very good with the mounting unrest there," Farley said. "What they're doing smothering student protests is horrible."

"He's decided to take some time off from RISD and go to Rangoon to study. His father apparently is in bad shape."

"You seem well enough to me."

Grant smiled. "You know what I mean, the real father."

"I didn't think they were close."

"They aren't. Win hasn't seen him since he came here. The father seems to have little interest, but I'm told they write. With the old man in the condition he's in, Win seems to be drawn back to him. Blood, I guess."

"Speaks well for the boy."

"And he has an opportunity for painting instruction from some famous Burmese painter who is affiliated with the National University there," Grant added.

"Funny about kids," Farley said. "How different two people can be. He and San." Farley was a small man but, with sleeves rolled up to expose sinuous forearms, he gave off an aura of power. The shaved head lent more authority.

"That's true in blood relationships," Grant said. "So, it shouldn't be a big surprise that it would be the case here."

"I always think of them as brothers."

"They are in some ways. Loyalty? A lot in days past. But now they fight. They're different. They have no common interests. Their goals? Like night and day. Their work ethic? Not even close. There's tension, I think jealousy, you know." Grant thought of how inseparable the boys had been when they were young, through many of their teenage years. *What had happened? Was it his fault that they had grown apart? Or Evelyn's?*

"It didn't seem to be a problem to either of them when they went their separate ways after graduation to schools on different sides of the country," Grant said as he walked past the wall lined with memorable headlines from the *Post's* history, his thoughts darting quickly to what major story's headline might be the next to grace this space. But he couldn't lose track of the boys. "We always tried to treat them equally."

Grant knew Evelyn had come to feel closer to Win, though she'd never admit it. Maybe, it was because of their common interest in the art world—she was a minor collector and a long-time docent at the art museum—or, maybe, because she always felt sorry for Win by comparison to San and tried to defend him. Grant loved both boys, but San had come to them because of Peter. Win had not. Grant recognized that he and San were more alike, with similar interests, maybe similar ambitions. He'd even begun to think it was possible San might have what it would take to succeed him as the *Post's* publisher when the time came, years down the road, as he once dreamed Peter might. That was not a consideration with Win whose interests were in art, not journalism and business, nor with Kathy, who was headed toward a career in the foreign service.

Grant returned to his desk and sat down. "What's the timing on this, Bill?

"The focus of the news is there, right now, in a big way, which usually dictates our timing, doesn't it?"

"I'll read it more carefully."

"Let's be frank about this. People feel you've had the brake on the Burma story for a long time."

"Bullshit."

"I thought I remembered that Win's father is part of the junta."

"Yes, but low enough down in the hierarchy that he managed to get himself shot in the ass by the rebels. That doesn't happen to the top guns in any army, does it?"

Farley headed toward the door. "You're running out of time, Grant. You'll be out-voted on the editorial board." He paused. "And I'll be with the majority."

Grant slumped, his frame so large he appeared to be spilling out of his chair. Grant felt confronted at every turn by people telling him what to do: *the editorial board, the fucking extended family always sticking its nose into things; these backbenchers who existed on his sweat and the dividends it produced. Fuck them.* "How much time can I buy?" he asked.

"Not much."

"I don't want this editorial to run right now. Win is supposed to be on his way in a few days. We don't know what might happen to him. Christ, he might get there and have visa problems and not be able to get back."

"The regime knows of his relationship to you, the paper?"

"It came up with the authorities in Rangoon when we first brought the boys over, but that's ten years ago." Grant had never discussed with anyone but Evelyn the Burmese lawyer's suggestion that things would go more smoothly for the boys to come to the U.S. if the newspaper were to go light on the regime. Since that time the student visas had been reissued, San had been adopted and become a citizen, and Grant convinced himself that things were not so bad as to require a strong indictment by the *Post*.

"How long is he going to be there?"

"Don't know. Depends on his father."

Farley asked, "Will you commit to the piece if I can talk the board into waiting a couple of weeks?"

"Let me think about it." He felt flushed as Farley left the room. He fought the concern, expressed by Farley, that he might be overstepping ethical standards. The editorial department had to be independent; the separation was as fundamental an underpinning of the newspaper business as any. He'd have to go along with the board as gracefully as possible. But that didn't mean he had to like it.

Grant and Evelyn often walked on the beach in Santa Monica. They would start at the Sand & Sea Club and walk to the Santa Monica pier, sometimes farther, then back, about three miles round trip. This was often where and when they discussed important developments in their lives, usually Grant's frustrations at the newspaper, particularly with the jealousies and bickering of his siblings' families, where some thought they, or their children, could do a better job as publisher than he. There were few people at the beach as the day was foggy and damp, the traditional Los Angeles June gloom. They were alone. No doorbells or telephones to interrupt. Waves crashed and seagulls yawed, yet the noise seemed muffled. They could concentrate on each other and whatever they were talking about. Their walks there after Peter's death had been endless. Walking along the beach offered a sort of catharsis.

"How many are coming tonight for Win's sendoff?" Grant asked.

"I think about twenty. A lot of his artist friends. It'll be casual."

"You mean weird, don't you?"

"Grant!"

"Those people sometimes look like they're in costumes, for Halloween or something."

"You're terrible." She stifled a half-laugh.

He glanced sideways to see if she was smiling. "Hair everywhere, earrings, tattoos, scruffy clothes. Why can't they dress more like San's friends? Or Kathy's?"

"Because they're artists. Free spirited. If they were like Kathy's or San's friends, they probably couldn't create what they do."

"That would be a plus."

"It's not their life."

Seagulls stood in rows facing up the beach, sandpipers pranced along the water's edge, pelicans dove down to snatch their prey.

Win had been doing well at RISD. The critiques he received were generally positive. He painted, in oils and acrylics, landscapes of rice paddies, fields and mountains he remembered in Burma. His work had been included in small group shows at school.

Grant started. "I got a visit from Bill Farley. They're insisting on an editorial, a tough one, on the junta in Burma. I'm not sure I can hold it off."

"Why?"

"The facts are worse than we thought." He went on to explain that the protesters, mostly students, counting in the tens of thousands, were being crushed. The military was sparing nothing to bring order—jailing, beating, shooting those who stood up against it. Thousands had died. "I can't fight the facts any longer."

Evelyn stopped. She knew that whenever the word "editorial" came up, it was smarter to avoid the subject; her husband didn't ordinarily seek her counsel in that area. "I don't think Win should go at a time like this when people are being hauled off and killed," she said.

"I agree," Grant said. "Though I don't think they'd have a reason to go after him. It's been ten years since those discussions we had with the lawyer about the regime and our editorials. Besides, his father is part of the ruling class."

"Yes, you wouldn't think they'd take it out on one of their own," Evelyn said.

Grant turned toward her, surprised. "It sounds funny to talk about Win as one of the Burmese regime. He's ours."

"Let's get him to delay the trip if he can," Evelyn said.

"Okay, but I think he's decided and he's going."

The conversation then turned to Kathy and her engagement to an Italian she met at Georgetown who was studying political science.

They had met him once and found him likeable enough, but they fretted over her following him back to Rome where she might not be able to pursue her foreign service career with an assignment at the U.S. embassy. First postings were not usually to prime spots like Rome. So far she wasn't listening to them, which was not unusual. Increasingly, it had become the same with Win, which is why they feared he wouldn't change his decision to leave for Burma. ∾

SIXTEEN

8888

WIN'S AWARENESS of the noise was vague. The phone was ringing; no it wasn't; yes it was. Finally, he pulled himself out of bed, naked, away from the warmth he'd been wedged against, and staggered toward the phone in the kitchenette of his studio apartment in Rangoon. This wasn't a time people telephoned him; it was the middle of the night. He turned on a small light on the wall shelf and picked up the receiver.

"Yes."

"Win. It's Grant."

"Are you all right?"

"Yes, of course."

"Evelyn?"

"I'm fine." She was on the speaker. "Everyone is. Sorry, we didn't mean to scare you."

"It's the middle of the night here."

"Guess we screwed up," Grant answered. "We thought it was still before midnight your time."

"No, but it's okay."

Win turned toward the woman half rising from the bed, patting her hair back from her face, surprise in her eyes. Hand covering the receiver, he whispered "no problem." She fell back and pulled up the sheets.

Grant started. "We were hoping we could talk you into coming back."

"Soon," Evelyn added.

"Why? I haven't been here long." He had paid no attention to Grant and Evelyn's earlier efforts to delay his trip to a calmer time. He felt they were overreacting.

"Things seem to be getting worse there," Grant said. "All the demonstrations, the students marching, the military using deadly force. I don't know if we're getting the real news—it's datelined Bangkok. We didn't even know if we could get through to you." Grant presented the news of the so-called 8888 Uprising as it was being reported in the U.S.—so named because it had erupted on August 8, 1988.

"It's not as bad as that. Not really much different than when I got here. The conditions are being exaggerated. I feel perfectly safe walking the streets from my apartment to school, the markets, restaurants, that kind of thing." The truth was, however, on that very day he'd been pulled along by crowds on the streets, and he had not felt safe. Win saw the military open fire on students and monks, civil servants and others who were demonstrating at City Hall. He heard that the same happened outside the many-spired Shwedagon Pagoda where Daw Aung San Suu Kyi, the leader of the democratic movement, spoke to huge crowds. Students and monks were rounded up and driven off in vans. To where or to what end, no one knew. He had tried to keep his distance from the protesters to avoid being caught in the government net. So far, he had succeeded.

"The reports are that hundreds of thousands have joined the protest and three-thousand people have been killed," Grant said.

"I doubt that. The ones in danger here are the people demonstrating against the regime. I'm not one of them," Win said with a mild tone of impatience. In fact, he figured he would always have protection through his father.

After a pause, Evelyn changed the subject. "How are your art lessons going these days?"

"Very well. I'm taking a different direction."

"Oh?"

"No more monks or temples or landscapes. I'm working with found objects."

"Explain that," Grant said.

"I take objects I find, like metal, sometimes stone, wood, glass, and assemble them into what you might think of as a wall sculpture, but it's really known as a painting."

"So, what does it depict?" Grant asked.

"It doesn't."

"Think as in abstract, Grant," Evelyn said. "You don't know what it is."

Win was relieved to hear her edgy tone in answering Grant. He had feared she would be disappointed over his new path. She had loved the ethnic focus of his painting.

"It's a matter of color, the division of space, design, right Win?" Evelyn said.

"Yes." Win still rarely used their names. Saying Grant and Evelyn seemed so distant given the closeness of the relationship that had grown between them. Yet, they weren't Mom and Dad either. When San had been adopted, they'd asked Win to use Mom and Dad, too, but he hadn't been able to bring himself to do it.

"Tell us how your father is?"

"He's still in the hospital, about the same."

"What's the situation?"

"He was badly wounded in the back. Now, there's a galloping infection the doctors are having a hard time controlling." Win had understood his father had been shot by rebels while fighting in the Shan state mountains. But once he arrived in Rangoon, he found the facts were quite different. Yes, his father had been wounded. Yes, his father was an officer in the junta. But that seemed to be in name only. Instead of being a military man, he was a drug trafficker, heading an opium-running operation in the Golden Triangle where the borders of Burma, Laos and Thailand join. The opium was used to produce heroin. He had been injured outside the town of Mong Hpayac in a raid by competing traffickers, not by rebels.

Win's father had told him of his role in the drug world with no apparent misgivings, maybe even pride. It meant he was an important person, and rich. Narcotics were a huge and lucrative business in this part of the world. His father admitted he was the subject of an investigation and possible indictment by a federal grand jury in San Francisco for his role in drug trafficking, but he scoffed at the idea that anything he did could have violated the law in such a distant country. For some reason, which wasn't discussed, he seemed to be protected by the regime. He asked his son to make contact with certain people on his behalf when he returned to Los Angeles, but he hadn't yet said who or what he wanted done. He acted as though it were a foregone conclusion that Win would do whatever he requested. The idea of any involvement scared Win, but he hadn't been able to bring himself to say no to his father. He would wait and see what the assignment involved.

Despite the many resources available to him in the newspaper business, Grant apparently had no knowledge of the grand jury proceedings, and Win wanted to keep it that way. What would the Jensens do if they learned his father was a supplier of heroin to the United States? Grant, though hardly soft on drug-users, had zero tolerance for dealers. He'd lock them up indefinitely, even worse if they supplied kids. Win was more than mildly familiar with the *Post's* resounding editorial position on this subject, the matter having been frequently discussed at the dinner table as the children were warned about the evils of drugs. It would be a catastrophic embarrassment to the Jensens should the news become public, a crusader against drugs and a trafficker in drugs connected through him. Maybe Grant could keep the news out of the papers. Win didn't know. Would it be the end of his relationship with the Jensens which had grown to be so comfortable, actually loving in many ways?

"Well, when do you think you will be able to leave?" Evelyn asked.

"I'm not really sure. It's a fluid situation. I work in the studio every day, spend some time with my teacher, and then I go to the hospital. That's my life. Not very exciting."

The woman in his bed sat up, and the sheet fell to her waist, exposing her breasts. She wiggled, putting her hand to her mouth to stifle a titter. He responded, swinging his hips side to side as she buried her face in the pillow, giggling. Having just met the woman, he wasn't certain she knew enough English to understand what he had been saying, but it didn't seem she cared.

"I'm afraid there's going to be an editorial in the paper pretty soon," Grant said. "It'll be negative on the junta's record of human rights abuses. We worry about you being there when it hits. Would they blame you somehow? Ridiculous I know, but they might. Would they refuse to let you leave?"

"When would it run?" Win asked.

"I can hold it off, maybe another couple of weeks."

"You can't stop it?" Win said.

"No, I don't have veto power."

"As I've said before, the regime is trying to adopt a democratic form of government," Win said. "But the process takes time. Demonstrations are disruptive and interfere with the path to democracy. Can't you say that?"

"Win," Grant replied, "we read about killings, jailings, torture. This is not a pathway to democracy. These are kids, like you, who are marching. Thousands of them are crossing the border into Thailand. "

"It takes time to be ready for democracy."

"The country had a solid foundation for it after all the years the British were there," Evelyn remarked.

Win wanted to point out that rule by the British was hardly democratic but realized he would get nowhere arguing the point. "We'll see. Let me try to do some planning. I'll write or call soon."

"Take care of yourself," Grant said, "and be careful."

"We love you." Evelyn added.

Win had and would struggle with the question. Yes, he wanted to go back. He knew he should complete his four years at RISD. The instruction there was better and broader than what he was getting in Rangoon. He missed having Kathy close by. Sometimes, he was even nostalgic about San, but it was more a sense of his own inferiority that dominated his thoughts about San. How could he compete with the great Sanford Jensen, beloved Peter's replacement? Now, a member of the Jensen family, San had everything. They hadn't been much in contact during their time at college, but he assumed that would change if and when they both returned to Los Angeles, San to work at the *Post* undoubtedly and he likely to join the downtown ranks of starving artists.

Could he leave his father in his present condition? Could he get back in time if he took a turn for the worse? The Jensens had been generous in making everything in America possible for him. Didn't he have to give special weight to their request?

He returned to bed and put his hand on her soft, warm belly. She didn't move. Whatever she had wanted when she wiggled a few minutes earlier was now lost to slumber, while he was left in a state of unfulfilled anticipation. He put his head on the pillow and listened to her soft humming noise. He would worry about it all later. ⌒

SEVENTEEN

The Tip

I T WAS GRANT'S fiftieth-fifth birthday and everyone was home for a celebration. Kathy had received her master's in international relations at Georgetown and started to work for the foreign service in Washington, D.C. Evelyn was terrified her daughter would end up somewhere in the African bush, a prospect that made even Nicolo Chiesa, her intended, look good. San had finished college and moved back to Los Angeles where he was working for the *Post* in what was referred to euphemistically as a "management training program." Grant's father had used the same process for Grant. After several weeks in Burma, Win had returned to finish at RISD. While a bachelor's degree was not that important in the art world, unless you wanted to teach or be a historian, which Win did not, he knew he had to collect the piece of paper to satisfy Grant and Evelyn. He owed it to them.

Evelyn had planned a bash in the garden on a warm summer night. Grant, who never minded being the center of attention, had dodged a fiftieth birthday celebration because "everybody has a fiftieth party." He wanted to be different. Now, commotion prevailed as tables, chairs, glasses, and plates were unloaded from a party rental truck in the driveway as the family sat down for breakfast. The subject then turned to Nicolo whom Win described as a "nerd."

"Thanks, Win. Anyway, you should know," Kathy said.

"Kids!" Evelyn interjected. "He could walk in any moment."

"Who ever heard of a nerdy Italian?" Kathy said. "Watch out. Maybe he'll be Ambassador to Burma from Italy one day and get your country back into the world community."

"If he can do that, I'll get down on my knees and kiss his you know what," San responded.

Win, helping himself to a second serving of scrambled eggs, declared, "They'll get there without his help."

"Oh, sure," San sneered.

"Slowly, I'm afraid. Sometimes I wonder if our editorials have a damn bit of impact," Grant said.

"They're not tough enough." Checking Grant to see his reaction and then to Win, San added, "But the last one did have the impact of getting Win back home."

"I was coming anyway. I wouldn't miss this for the world."

There was a pause in the conversation, until San asked, "Dad, do you remember Willie Chin?"

"I do," Evelyn interjected with a harrumph. "A dreadful character."

"Sure," Grant said. "We called him Willie *the* Chin."

"I remember him," Kathy said. "At the racetrack, Santa Anita, right?" She reached for a piece of toast and a dab of marmalade.

"Yes. Looked like the movie actor, Peter Lorre," Grant said. "And talked like him out of the side of his mouth in a high-pitched, raspy voice."

"I remember someone like that you'd talk to when we were on the grass in the infield," Win said.

"Exactly," Grant chuckled.

"What a place to take children, Grant. Those lowlife people who acted like they were your best friends."

"There were a few Damon Runyon characters at the track, I'd have to admit," Grant said.

Nicolo arrived at the table and sat down, his hair wet from a shower.

He apologized for being late. "Big time change from Roma, I'm afraid," he sang in his distinct accent.

"We're talking about an old-time New York newspaper man, Damon Runyon, who wrote stories about grifters and gamblers and hustlers, gangsters and even worse," Grant said. "I needed these kinds of sources when Dad had me in the newsroom on the police beat. Willie gave me inside tips. What was going on at the police station. Who they were after. You know what?"

"What?" San and Kathy said, almost in unison.

"He never gave me a bum steer. I could count on following his clues and be ahead of the competition."

"Why did he do it?" Kathy asked.

"Who knows. Probably for the kick of being underground in the news business."

"Why do you bring him up, San?" Evelyn asked.

"Oh, no reason." San hesitated. "Some of the guys in the newsroom were talking about him. I thought I recognized the name."

"He was a legend in a way. Check him out," Grant said. "If he's still around, he might be a good source on an assignment."

Evelyn pointed out the window. "They're not placing those tables in the right position. I'll have to go talk to them."

San said nothing about Chin's secret request for a meeting the following week. He had been told to "keep it under your hat."

Recently out of Berkeley and starting at the paper, Grant had been introduced by his father to Willie at Santa Anita. Willie remained in Grant's mind among all the characters he had met there because of one thing he said. Willie, had squeaked, "I went to college, too, kid." Figuring it would be a normal question to ask, Grant replied, "Where?" Willie leaned up close and whispered, "Joliet," sucking air through his gapped teeth as he laughed. Grant saw his father struggling not to smile as he looked for his son's reaction. Obviously, Willie had been an informant to Grant's father on his early stories, and it was no surprise to anyone that the Joliet he referred was the prison outside Chicago.

San had agreed to meet Willie Chin in the infield at Santa Anita at the three-eights pole fifteen minutes before post time for the third race. The man said he'd be wearing a floppy straw hat. San had no idea why Willie would ask him to meet at the track or anywhere else for that matter. It had been at least ten years since his father had introduced them and there hadn't been any contact in the interim.

San went directly to the infield, not bothering to stop at the Turf Club. He didn't have the time to spend all day on what was likely to be a wild goose chase. He opened the *Racing Form* and checked out the third race. He was rusty on how to read the *Form*, so he bought a two dollar win ticket based solely on the horse's name, Newsboy. It was not a likely winner with odds at 30-to-1.

The day was blazing hot, typical of September when the Oak Tree meeting was held. San remembered the track well. The grandstands, hoards of people, queues at the ticket windows, with many more in line to buy tickets than to collect on winners. He loved to watch the horses parade in the paddock. The tradition of it all delivered a strong sense of anticipation and excitement. There was nothing like the smell of turf, grass, the sweaty lather of horses, the leather; distinctly the scent of the track.

All Willie Chin had said when he telephoned was that they needed to meet right away and not to tell anyone. When San brought Willie's name up at breakfast, Grant's reaction convinced him this was a person he had to see. It could be an important scoop, exactly what he could use as one of the new boys in the newsroom. Or it could be nothing.

As San walked through the infield, he saw a few men wearing what could be described as straw hats, but none of them seemed old enough, or short enough, to be the Willie the Chin he remembered. San was at the rail when the call to the post was trumpeted and the horses started to make their way to the gate. The entries nervously took their post positions, the bell rang, and a voice blared from the PA system, "And there they go." San heard a sort of hissing sound behind him and turned. There was a man, lips spread, noisily gulping air through his teeth. He wore a straw hat.

"Mr. Chin?"

"Yeah, kid. That's me, Willie Chin. You remember me, huh?"

"Yes, I do." He saw the man as clearly as he had years before, but, more than anything, the whispered words floating off his tortured chin made the association undeniable. He remembered immediately how Willie the Chin would shuffle close and whisper, his crooked chin almost scratching Grant's coat. He and Win would go home and mimic this person who was so different than anyone else the Jensens seemed to know.

"Come over here, kid, and we'll talk," Willie said, tipping his head in the direction of the sparsely populated center of the infield. They walked away from the crowds at the rail.

"How's your Dad, anyways?" Willie asked.

"He's fine."

"I read about him in the *Post* sometimes." He stopped and chewed sunflower seeds from a plentiful supply in his left palm, apparently drawn from a pocket. He spit the seeds on the ground. "Why not? His paper, ain't it?"

San started to reply, but was interrupted by Willie saying, "I didn't have to ask what you'd be wearing, did I, kid?"

When Willie had offered that he'd be wearing a straw hat, San had started to identify how he'd be attired, mentioning a "red tie." But the old man had said he'd recognize him, "easy."

Of course, the younger man didn't need much identification. There weren't a lot of people out there who looked like him and would be wearing a suit with a red tie. He did come with his *Los Angeles Post* identification which he pulled from his wallet. Willie pushed it away.

"We've got a bad problem, kid. The name Grant Jensen shouldn't be connected with it in the rival rag."

"Why me, not my father?"

"He's a fine man, a real gentlemen. So was his father. Bet you didn't think anyone could be old enough to know three generations of Jensens, did you, kid? They were good to me. I don't want to see the family name hurt, that's all."

"I appreciate that."

"Anyways, you use the Jensen name, right, kid?"

"Yes, I'm legally adopted."

"What about the other brother?"

"He's not really a brother. We were raised that way, but technically we aren't. No blood. And he's not adopted."

"Hmm." Willie reached in his coat pocket. He extended a handful of sunflower seeds to San, mumbling something about a doctor having pushed them on him as a so-called substitute for cigarettes.

San said, "No, thanks," imagining what else might be lurking in that pocket. He wished Grant could stop smoking and had told him so on many occasions, but he couldn't see him spitting sunflower seeds.

"Okay. Let's get to it. Your brother's in trouble, kid, big trouble. What's his name again?"

"His Burmese name is Nyan Win. But he goes here by Win Jensen." San checked Willie, trying to assess whether this was a joke, or what.

"His father's a big time drug guy in Burma. Deals in opium that supplies the dopers here."

"I don't think so. He's an officer in the government there."

"A cover, kid, a cover."

"What?"

"He's a drug dealer. Trust me. The military guys let him operate. He probably pays 'em off, you know, lots of money."

San took his time. "So, what does that have to do with Nyan Win?"

"Your brother is laundering money here for the operation, kid, getting it into foreign bank accounts."

San frowned. "That's hard to believe," but it wasn't given Win's different lifestyle. He had wondered about Win's friends and his sources of funds, other than the money he was sure Grant and Evelyn provided. "How do you know?" he asked.

"Never give away a source. All I can say is, it's from the feds. They're investigating up in San Francisco. The father could be indicted. Win, whatever his name is, could be, too. "

"I don't know what I can do about it, Mr. Chin. Nyan Win and I aren't as close as you might think. We're from the same country, the same age, both lived with the Jensens. Otherwise, there are more differences than not."

"Anyways, kid, you gotta figure it out."

San wasn't sure what to do next. He knew Willie passed information for cash. How much should I offer him, he wondered. "I appreciate it. How much do I owe you, you know, for this?"

"Owe me? Owe me, kid? This is for your dad. You owe me nothin'."

"Well. Thank you."

"Next time, kid, when you need info, call me, then I'll charge—double. This time it's for the family." He grinned, sucking air through his teeth, his equivalent of a laugh. "Who'd you have in the third?"

"Newsboy."

"Good, he placed."

"I had him to win."

Willie paused to look at the tote board. "You could'a played him across the board, like I did. Won eighty-seven bucks. Too bad. You need to learn to cover your bets, kid."

As he drove to the office to spend a few hours, San agonized over the dilemma he faced with the information he had. He could ignore it. He had no reason to believe the story was reliable. Or, he could accept it as accurate and go to Win, which could result in an explosion but provide the opportunity of saying what he thought of this drug bullshit and its potential to hurt the family. Finally, the answer was easy. He had to tell him. The tougher question was whether he should also go to Grant and Evelyn and warn them what was out there, assuming, which he thought likely, that Win would not tell them himself. Either way, he risked someone's wrath: Win's if he told Grant and Evelyn, theirs if he didn't. He remembered Willie's comment about covering his bets. He wished it were clearer to him how to do that in this situation. ∽

EIGHTEEN

Accusation

SAN CALLED WIN on the pretext of stopping by his new downtown loft the following Saturday morning to see his latest artistic efforts. Evelyn had tried to explain the work as being composed of found metal pieces assembled together, but San had trouble visualizing the result.

The building was an old, refurbished industrial space formerly used in the garment trade. He trudged up two flights of concrete stairs and straight ahead saw a steel door with a door bell half hanging from the wall. Nyan Win was scrawled in black ink on a card in a nameplate on the door. *What's he going to do when Evelyn and Grant come to visit? Slip in a new piece of paper with the name Win Jensen? Had this even occurred to him?*

San rang the harsh bell, and the door creaked open so quickly it seemed Win must have been holding the handle, waiting. He was still in his pajamas and hadn't shaved. A soul patch below his lip was new. His long black hair trailed down his neck and over his ears, but not far enough to hide a small gold loop in his left ear lobe—a new adornment since taking up residence among the artists in the loft district. Win invited him in.

The first thing San thought was how his parents would react on seeing the new Win, an apparition almost. Grant, at first, would try and keep silent; Evelyn would attempt to enforce that silence; but eventually Grant wouldn't be able to resist saying something about Win's appearance.

And how would they feel about his new residence among artists in the loft district? San had sized it up almost immediately on entering. The room was large and appeared to contain the essentials, except a toilet and shower, which San assumed were behind the one other door in the room. A sagging double bed, unmade, was partially hidden by a couple of worn chairs and an upholstered floral couch without a full complement of legs. He recognized the chairs and other pieces of furniture from their earlier incarnation in the family's pool house. The scene there with Joan, and Win walking in, flashed by. Did Win care, even think about it, anymore? So much time had passed, and, from what San heard, Win had plenty of opportunity to catch up in the sex department.

A curtain against one wall, San supposed, covered a clothes closet. A kitchenette arrangement—hotplate, microwave, tiny refrigerator and big laundry sink—sat against another wall. Light filled the room from one long, tall window. Large canvasses leaned against upright surfaces. A smaller one was perched on an easel. Colorful metal pieces were strewn over part of the floor. What he saw appeared to be works in progress, rather than finished projects, but he couldn't always tell the difference.

San felt as though he were springing as he walked through the room. He figured it was due to what were obviously layers of dried paint matting the floor, a kaleidoscope of colors that gave in when he walked. He wondered how thick it must be. "You must have really been painting up a storm to have gotten this much paint on the floor in such a short time."

"I didn't. The last guy. And the one before him. And before him."

"You don't have to clean when you leave a place like this?"

"Nobody does. Or, at least, nobody cares."

"How long is the lease?"

"Month to month."

San had to be careful talking with Win. It seemed as though almost anything could set him off: the perception that he was here due to San's generous insistence that he join him in America when in fact it was Win's agreement to come that made it possible for San; the fact that San, the "reincarnation" of Peter, had favored status working at the *Post*, while he, Win, struggled for recognition in a dingy loft; and on and on. San hated the negativity.

San was not immune from keeping score. He wanted to ask how much Evelyn and Grant had come up with for Win's loft living, but he didn't, knowing it would provoke a sarcastic response. A monthly allowance, he was sure. In the meantime, San was paying for his own condominium and all his own expenses and hadn't asked for help from the family. Win had made it clear that he viewed it differently— San was being supported by the *Post* in lavish style.

"To what do I owe this visit?" Win asked with an exaggerated bow.

San chuckled and frowned at the same time, the usual edge, he thought. "Something important, Nyan Win."

"You want coffee? There's some in the pot."

San walked to the hot plate, grabbed a ceramic mug from a plastic drainer in the sink and helped himself. The coffee had a strong aroma and was dark, as though it had been sitting awhile. Win flopped down in a chair and pointed San to the couch.

"What have I done now?"

San had practiced how to say it again and again. If Win blew up, he wouldn't have accomplished anything. "I don't know what you've done, but here's what I've been told: your father is a drug dealer protected by the regime and you're involved in laundering money for him. There's a federal investigation going on as we speak."

"What? That's crazy. Where did you get that?" Win asked.

"I can't disclose the source."

"Then why should I pay any attention to it?"

"All I can say is I have reason to believe the information is reliable."

Win went to the window. "Don't you think you should have concrete, verifiable information before you accuse your *almost*-brother of committing a crime?" Before San could answer, Win added, "You do that fuckin' much or more before publishing stories, with at least some backup."

"You've got to put a stop to this before it makes the news, or worse. You know the *Sun's* front page warning—'If You Don't Want it Printed, Don't Let it Happen.'"

After a short pause, Win said, "You've spent your whole life hating my father for being a part of the junta. Admit it."

"Maybe I have, but that's beside the point. Apparently, his so-called military role is a cover for being a drug dealer."

Win grit his teeth. "So, what if it's true? What he does in Burma has nothing to do with me."

"The claim is that you are actively involved, laundering money for him. That's serious stuff, Nyan Win. You could end up in jail for a long time."

"I don't have any idea where his funds come from. It's not my business. I don't even know what money laundering really is. I help him invest some of his assets outside Burma because it's tough to get cash out. That can't be a crime under US law."

"You sure that's all?

"Yes

"Is he still sick?"

"Yeah. It's gotten worse since I returned here. I'll be going back again soon."

San wondered where the money was coming from that made all Win's travel possible. He was under the impression that the father did nothing for Win financially. San had discussed the information from Willie on a confidential basis with a former assistant U.S. attorney who said the situation could be serious, and Win needed to be in the hands of a criminal defense lawyer. If he left the country to see his father, he might have real difficulties gaining re-entry. There were other concerns as well, but San didn't know how much of this he wanted to tell Win. The more direct he was, the more likely it was that Win would hear nothing. San didn't believe Win was as innocent as he claimed.

"Maybe you should see a lawyer to be sure whatever you're doing won't get you in trouble or cause the immigration authorities to refuse to let you back in the country." No sooner than the words were out of his mouth, he realized it was a dumb suggestion.

"Where am I supposed to get the green to do that?"

It always came back to money with Win, his lack of it by comparison to all the other members of the family. He never focused on his choice of vocation, of course, and San realized that stating the obvious would only lead to another argument. "I don't want to see you, or Evelyn and Grant, any of us, hurt or embarrassed. You know the *Sun* would run with it, don't you? Front page stuff." He could see the *Sun's* headline, "Publisher's Charge Eyed in Drug Scheme."

"Don't worry. I'll handle it."

"But . . ."

"I don't want to talk about it anymore, Aun San."

Cut off, San moved around the room trying to find something to inspire easy conversation. "Do you like it? This place? It's different."

"You'd never live in it. Not your type."

San knew that was true. His condo in the Marina, which had a view of hundreds of moored boats, was newly redone and, compared to this, modern and clean. Win had described San's place as "uptight," and he'd offered nude paintings for the walls. Predictably, San turned him down.

"Any beautiful women hanging around these days?" San asked.

"Why do you want to know?"

"Just wondering."

"That's proprietary information. I don't need you in the competition." Win looked as though he was waiting for a reaction.

Why wasn't this over? It's been more than ten years, San thought."
Will you be at the house for dinner tomorrow?" he asked. Sunday
night dinner at home was a ritual for any of the kids who were in town.

"I'm planning on it."

As San headed for the door, he handed Win the attorney's card,
saying "Just in case. I hope you'll see him." San felt he was always
put in the position with Win of trying to help and never having that
appreciated. For his part, Win felt he was always being told what to do,
that he was dependent, and he resented it.

"You won't tell them about this, will you?"

"Grant and Evelyn?" San cast his eyes toward the floor. "I'm hoping
you'll tell them yourself."

"And if I don't?"

"I will. They can't be left exposed not knowing what you've done."

"Aun San, just stay out of my life, will you?"

"I wish I could." San pulled the creaking door closed behind him.

NINETEEN

Money Laundering

WIN RECEIVED A CALL from the doctor in Rangoon in the middle of the night notifying him his father had died. The cause was the staph infection he'd been fighting in the hospital for weeks. Win felt remorse that he had not been there for his father's last days, but he didn't cry over the news. The man had abandoned him so many years ago and had returned to his son's life only when he was wounded, ill and needed help. Then the "help" exposed Win to legal jeopardy. How serious it was he didn't know, but he was scared.

Yet, Win knew his feeling of guilt would continue until he returned to his homeland, and if he was going to do that, he had to get moving. The Burmese belief system, practiced when his mother died, was that the spirit of the dead stays around for seven days during which time the family prays to Buddha and makes donations to monasteries and the needy, ensuring a better fate for the deceased in the next life. Could he possibly get back there in seven days? Doubtful. Did he have enough money to make the trip? Not really. But who would assume the responsibility if he couldn't? The other living relatives were his father's sister and her three children, one of them an officer in the military. He doubted they would step in. The grandmother to whom he'd been sent at Inle Lake had died. He contemplated the irony of doing good works on behalf of a drug dealer whose business presumably had left many ago-nized lives behind. It was not that Win was innocent about drugs; he'd experimented fully and knew he was lucky not to have gotten hooked along the way as had a number of his friends.

One thing San said lingered in Win's mind: If he left America, he might not be permitted to return. That was a risk he couldn't afford to take, though he could argue that if the authorities were investigating his dealings on behalf of his father, perhaps the farther away he got, the better. In the few weeks since meeting with San, he hadn't been contacted by any federal investigators.

He decided to see Jason Nemore, the lawyer whose card San had given him. Win told Nemore by phone that an immediate meeting was necessary and provided some preliminary information. The young lawyer, starting his criminal defense practice, was able to schedule an appointment later in the day. His offices were Spartan, located in a grimy area of downtown Los Angeles near the federal courthouse among the sleazy storefront offices of pawn brokers and bail bonds-men who fed upon those in trouble with the law. Win cringed at the prospect of Grant walking into one of those places to post bail for him.

Nemore said that he'd had time to conduct some investigation: he'd been on line and made telephone calls to contacts in the U.S. attorney's office. Before him on the desk was a yellow, lined legal pad with notes written in pencil. The phone rang and Nemore answered the call. While he was talking, Win checked the diplomas on the wall and found that his lawyer had graduated from USC, both law school and undergraduate, which gave him some feeling of confidence. That was certainly as good as Rhode Island School of Design, he thought. Nemore finished his conversation and turned to his computer. Hands poised above the keyboard, the lawyer said, "To confirm. Your father's name was Ko Zaw Lay," which he started to spell.

Win interrupted. "That's right."

"It seems many people in your country have the same name. Is it like John Smith here?"

"Almost. At least my name is." Win felt somehow ill at ease with the lawyer referring to Burma as his country. It was, he knew, but so was the United States where he had lived for as many years as he had in his country of origin.

The lawyer continued. "Ko Zaw Lay has been under investigation for a variety of drug crimes. It looks like the feds didn't work the case hard, probably figuring that even if he were indicted, the Burmese wouldn't agree to extradite him to the U.S."

"What happens now?"

"The U.S. Attorney and the Drug Enforcement Administration won't proceed. A dead man can't be convicted of a crime."

"What about my situation?"

"I can't get much information. But I do know there is an investigation in which you're a 'person of interest.'"

"For what?" Win added, "I'm an artist," as though his role in life should be an automatic bar to indictment.

"Money laundering. For your father." Nemore walked to a small refrigerator in the corner of the room, pulled out two cokes and handed one to his guest. Win took it even though he had never grown to like fizzy drinks. "Tell me exactly what was your involvement in your father's activities?"

Win hesitated. Would what he told him get back to San? To Grant? He didn't think so, but did he have a real alternative? He'd shave the story a bit. "Not much. I would receive money from various sources with directions from my father about where to invest it. Mostly offshore in the Caribbean. He didn't want the money in Burma. There are many restrictions on getting it out of the country."

"What did you think the funds were for?"

"I didn't know, and it wasn't my business. Most of my life I'd understood him to be an officer in the junta. I thought the money had something to do with that. Graft is rampant in that world; it's the way the system works."

"How did your understanding change?"

"I came to learn that, while he had an officer's title and was protected by the government, he dealt in the poppy trade in some way."

Nemore pulled at the knot of his loose tie. "Anything change in your financial relationships with him after you learned that?"

"No, nothing."

"When was that?"

"Recently."

"To be convicted of money laundering, the U.S. Attorney would have to show you knowingly took the actions you did with intent to carry on the illegal activity. Your case doesn't sound like that. Besides, your father was the kingpin they were after; you're small stuff. Hopefully, we should be able to work something out."

Win looked out at the windows of a close-facing building, a hotel built in the early 1900's that had seen its best days. "If I am going back to Rangoon to pray for my father, it would have to be very soon."

"You've been here a long time on student visas."

"As a full-time student, yes, and now I'll be completing studies for my MFA. Of course, Mr. Jensen's contacts in Washington have been helpful in making it possible."

"Are you and San actually brothers?"

"No, not blood brothers. And we aren't adopted brothers. We came here at the same time and both lived with the Jensen family."

"He has been adopted by the Jensens, I understand. But you?"

"My father wouldn't give permission."

"I suspect this isn't what you want to hear," Nemore said, "but I'd have to advise you against returning to Burma at this time."

He was right. It was not welcome advice. Win reached toward the back pocket of his Levi's and felt his wallet. "What do I owe you for today?"

"Nothing. Your brother—I mean, San—told me if you called, he would take care of it."

Win's eyes widened in surprise.

"But he said you'd be on your own after the first meeting."

"I understand. What would the fee be?"

"I would expect a five-thousand dollar retainer upfront, and we'd agree on a flat fee once I know more about the facts. It would be fair."

Win wondered whether the gulp he tried to suppress was audible. He didn't have that amount of cash, much less the larger amount it could turn out to be. Win had told Evelyn and Grant immediately about his father's death, but hadn't asked the obvious question: Whether his father's demise could alter his relationship with the Jensens in any way? Not like a formal adoption. It was too late for that. But somehow, in a way he hadn't yet fully defined, being even more a part of the Jensen family than he had been. The way to start was not with Grant. He'd be furious over the troubles he had gotten himself into. Evelyn was the answer. He was familiar with her *modus operandi,* to work from behind to get Grant to agree to the position she favored. Win had benefited when her softer approach infiltrated Grant's tough exterior. He would ask her for a loan for the fees. It was clear he had to have legal help to get out of this mess. ⌁

TWENTY

The Family Reacts

S AN HAD ASKED for a meeting with Grant at the office, something he rarely did. When San started working for the paper, it was agreed he would have no special access to the publisher's suite, that he would be treated like anyone else in lower management. An exception was made, however, for occasional private lunches in the small dining room off Grant's office, the two of them across from one another at a square table, served by executive dining staff personnel. No one knew about these meetings, except for the private secretaries who scheduled them and the waiters who were selected for their discretion concerning confidential matters discussed in that room.

There were always members of other branches of the Jensen family who felt excluded from the newspaper, wanted jobs or influence, or sought higher dividends to support their lifestyles. Terry, Grant's half- brother, was difficult, but paled by comparison to sister Jane White, who sat on the *Post's* board of directors. They seemed to Grant to be obstructive, no matter what the issue. They griped about editorial policy. Political endorsement decisions were often contentious. As far as Jane White was concerned, there was "no goddamned editorial committee making these decisions; Grant makes them all, and conveniently ignores the conservative philosophies on which this newspaper was founded." Grant could vent his frustrations with San.

The lunch started with small talk about their sail the past weekend on the Lady, a Cal 40 yacht Grant kept moored in Marina del Rey and which San sometimes used as a party venue. Grant and San loved to sail when they could find time. Their last trip on the weekend had been special because of a school of dolphins that played in the boat's wake, a sight they'd seen before but was always exciting to encounter.

After the first course was served and the dining staff had retreated, San started. He'd heard nothing from either Grant or Evelyn about Win's legal problems. He suspected they hadn't been told. "Has Win talked to you about the trouble his father was in when he died?"

"No."

"Apparently, his father wasn't an officer in the junta."

"What? I've always heard he was. Then, what is—was—he?" Grant asked.

"A drug runner."

"No. You're kidding?" Grant said, face reddening, forehead creased.

"Narcotics. Dealt in poppies. The worst."

"How do you know?"

"He made me promise not to tell."

"He?"

"Willie the Chin."

"What?"

"Yes."

"When did this happen?"

San told Grant about the information he'd received at the track from Willie.

"The source is solid, but, still, I can't believe Win is involved," Grant said. "Have you told him?"

"Yes."

"What did he say?"

"He denied it. Admitted he received money for his father and saw to it that it was invested offshore, but claims he didn't have any idea drugs were involved."

"When was this?"

"About two weeks ago."

"Why the hell did you wait all this time to tell me?" Grant's eyes flashed.

"I hoped he would tell you himself. Now, with his father's death, the focus may turn even more in Win's direction. It could be serious for him. Obviously, it also affects the family. The *Sun* would love it."

"The *Sun*? Hell, we'd have to print it. I couldn't kill the story."

They halted the discussion briefly as the main course was served.

"He's got to have a lawyer."

"I've referred him to an ex-U.S. attorney. I know he's meeting with him."

"Jesus Christ." Grant pushed the potatoes around. "You know, when he came to the house, it seemed strange. I couldn't put my finger on it. I thought it was just me. There he was telling me—the putative father who has raised him all these years—that *his father* had died. I had a feeling I wasn't getting the whole story, that something was missing. Now, I'm wondering whether your Mother knew about Win's troubles all along."

San walked to the window, saw the traffic backed up, and was glad he wasn't in it. "I don't know about that, Dad. I haven't told her. I really thought it was your call. But it does piss me off. Money laundering. What a dumb-ass thing to get involved in. I told him that, too."

Dessert was served with coffee, and he returned to the table.

"What did he say?"

"He was mad, like he is much of the time when I'm involved."

Grant raised a question he'd struggled with for a long time. "What is it about you and Win? Here, you're from the same basket almost, thousands of miles away, you've been raised as brothers, but you don't act like it. You cut each other up. What's it about?"

"What's unusual about that? Brothers fight."

"No, there's something deeper. It goes beyond that." Grant paused. "Hell, the whole reason Win is here is because of you."

The dessert plates were cleared. San turned around to see if the waiters were still lingering in the small room. "You had to know, and I felt guilty not telling you. An indictment for money laundering with our position on drugs?"

"Are you sure this lawyer you've got is good?" Grant asked.

"He's recently out of the U.S. Attorney's office and should know what he's doing."

"How's he being paid? I mean, Win doesn't have the funds to be hiring lawyers."

"I took care of the first meeting," San said.

"He needs the best. I'll discuss it with your Mother, and we'll go from there. Thanks for telling me. I know it couldn't have been easy."

"Or for you to hear."

Grant left the room. It wouldn't be any easier laying this on Evelyn.

～

TWENTY-ONE

A Beach Walk

E VELYN LOOKED down the beach into the sun, the glare off the water barely cut by her straw hat and dark glasses. Grant walked next to her, his pants' cuffs rolled up a notch or two to avoid the water as it made its way up the beach, only to stop, then retreat. They were not touching as they often did on their beach walks.

"Evelyn, we have to talk about Win. There's a problem."

"Yes, I know."

"How?"

"He told me," Evelyn answered, "and asked for a loan to pay lawyers."

"What did you say?"

"That I'd have to talk to you, but I was sure we would help." She turned toward him. "How did you find out?"

"From San, and he's mad as hell. I wonder why they couldn't have come to both of us and laid it out. Since it's Win's problem, why didn't he?"

"Win's afraid of you, I think, because of how emphatic you are on drugs."

"You mean the paper's editorial position on dope. Well, maybe he should be. We wouldn't go light on the guy making the stuff or selling it. So, why should someone laundering the loot be treated differently? It's all part of a criminal operation."

"He didn't know it was drug money."

"That's what he says."

"You don't believe him?" Evelyn asked.

"I wouldn't say that."

"Then what?"

"He told San it was probably graft money. But is it any better to be laundering that? It's still a felony."

"At least it wouldn't involve drugs." Evelyn tried to temper her impatience while maneuvering her husband to the decision she wanted. "Grant, he *is* our son. Not technically, I know, but that's nobody's fault. If he could have been adopted, he would be in the same position as San."

They approached the Santa Monica pier, where the beach became more crowded, largely with Latino families escaping the heat of east Los Angeles. Kids ran from the beach to the water and back, squealing with glee, throwing balls, flying kites, doing everything but just sitting on the sand.

She continued. "He came here with San. They were raised together, side by side. How can we possibly treat him any differently than we would San?"

"We've got to think about the family, our name. If this comes out, the *Sun* will pounce on it. And I can't keep it out of the *Post*."

"Why not?"

"I couldn't even try. Years ago Uncle Jesse was involved in a stock scam. Dad didn't kill the story. And it was feature news in the other papers."

"If that happens, it happens. We'll face it then," Evelyn replied.

"He could be indicted, tried, even put in prison," he growled.

They stepped carefully, dodging the frolickers and the sand castles being built just above the water line.

"How realistic is that possibility?" Evelyn asked. "With Win's father gone, they've gotten rid of the person they really wanted."

"But they may very well require a plea bargain to some lesser offense," Grant said, "a misdemeanor of some sort."

"The paper has been pretty positive about the U.S. Attorney's office over the years, which should count for something, shouldn't it?" Evelyn asked.

"Yes, but not much, I'm afraid."

"What's wrong with San anyway? Instead of anger, why isn't he in there fighting to help?"

"I don't know. I can't get it out of him. Does Kathy know about this?"

"Not from me," Evelyn answered. "There isn't a thing she can do from Ghana anyway."

They reached the pier, and, as always, they touched the barnacle-encrusted pilings. It was a routine tradition as they turned to walk back. Evelyn hesitated, then said, "I was his champion all through school when he didn't exactly fit the pattern, the way San did. I can't let him down now. I want to get the best lawyers we can find. And, I think we should show our support by making the decision to include him on an equal basis with Kathy and San in our estate plan. The way Burton Isaacs recommended."

Grant turned toward Evelyn with a look of surprise. Despite the firm voice, he saw her cheeks were wet. He put his arms around her shoulders and squeezed. "I've already hired the best criminal law lawyers in the city."

They headed back, retracing their route but not their tracks which had disappeared in a rising tide.

"You know, Grant, plenty of our friends have had kids with drug problems. What about your sister?" She referred to the fact that Jane's two children had been in rehab. "It isn't the end of the world."

"Can you really blame them with a mother like that?" Grant said.

Evelyn ignored his attempt at humor. "The real question is: Do we believe in him?"

"Yes, I do," Grant answered.

"Face it. It would have been pretty hard for him to say no to his father when he was asked to help. You've had some experience with that, as you may remember," she said, looking at him over her dark glasses. "As I recall, you weren't given a lot of choice about whether you'd join the *Post* on graduation or try something else."

"That's for sure. Dad could be demanding."

They walked in silence for a long while, their bare toes digging into the wet sand along the surf line. Evelyn spoke, her mood more upbeat, "Win is getting close to being self-sustaining, I think."

"That, more than anything, would help with San and Kathy, too," Grant said. "But how is that possible? I thought we still had to give him a check every month."

Evelyn recounted Win's successes: two one-man shows in Los Angeles and a regular presence at the 212 Gallery on Robertson Boulevard. He both gave and received private instruction. His found-metal paintings seemed to be intriguing to buyers, in part because of the origins of the metal and the process he followed: He'd assemble the back of a sign, a section from a tractor door, a piece from a railroad car, then clean and oil the metal surface. Bumps, dents and scratches remained to sing the history of the piece. The work was different, Win claimed, than anyone else's.

"As for the estate plan, let's talk to Thomas and . . ."

"Just treat Win like Kathy and San." Evelyn interrupted in a tone that didn't invite further discussion.

"Seems an odd time to reward him."

"We'll have to figure out how to break the news to Kathy and San," Evelyn said.

Several months later, Grant learned from the lawyers representing Win that they had managed to avoid an indictment. Without Win's father—the real target—the U.S. Attorney's office appeared to lose interest in the money laundering charges. Apparently Win created enough doubt about his knowledge of the source of the funds that a prosecution would not be successful. Grant and Evelyn told

Win how relieved they were with the result and how they'd been sure all along his actions in helping his father were innocent.

Perhaps tougher was the sales job for the new estate plan. At a family meeting at St. Cloud Road, Grant explained the decision he and Evelyn had reached based on the advice of a family wealth expert. The announcement was greeted with silence and blank stares.

Finally, Win spoke. "That's wonderful. I can't tell you how much I appreciate the full acceptance—the love and trust it reflects."

"That is what it's meant to, Win," Evelyn said, smiling.

Kathy, who was home on leave, pushed her chair back an inch or two. "Honestly, I have some trouble with it. I love Win. Don't get me wrong, but," she turned to Win, "you're not legally a member of the family, not that it's your fault, and now it's too late, but still . . ."

"There's enough to go around, Kathy. We're lucky to be able to afford to be generous with all of you," Grant said.

"Still, it doesn't feel right," Kathy added, fumbling with the napkin on her lap.

Grant glanced at San. "What are your feelings? You're the person who's responsible for Win being here in the first place, your oldest friend, a brother for all practical purposes, I'd say."

"True, but I'm probably the last person to comment. I think I should stay out of it, except to say that the two of you have been incredibly generous through the years with all you've done for all of us."

Grant looked at Kathy, then Win, then Evelyn. His eyes asked for some expression from Evelyn who said "I agree with your father that it should all be equal."

When nothing more was forthcoming, Grant said, "Maybe it's not unanimous, but there is a consensus it seems." He laughed, "I hope nothing comes from this for many, many years."

"We can all drink to that," San said, raising his glass toward the center of the table where five glasses clinked together. ∽

TWENTY-TWO

Only One Letter Off

DURING THE NEXT FIVE YEARS, San progressed through the chairs at the *Post* in the management training program designed for him, as Grant had planned for Peter after college. He and Evelyn had often discussed the possibility that Peter might succeed him years down the road when he retired: three generations of Jensens at the helm of the *Post*. While plans for Peter had been lost with him on the Zambezi, Grant now fantasized that San might fulfill the dream.

When he entered the program, San's first assignment was in the newsroom, the heart of the newspaper operation. He worked in circulation, an area that was regarded as not so sexy despite its critical importance. Following were tours in classified advertising, then display advertising. He was exposed to management responsibilities in the many production departments, central to them all being the pressroom where the paper was printed. Ultimately, after five years in training and at almost age thirty, he became Vice President of Operations, in charge of all the production departments. San was recognized as Grant's heir apparent, and the plan was that San would be fully seasoned by the time Grant retired.

San's situation with the extended family—and, as a consequence, at the *Post*—became more complicated when his relationship with his first cousin, Michelle Jensen, began to develop beyond that of a couple of teenage cousins having fun together at Christmas parties, weddings and skiing and hiking in Aspen. Michelle's father, Terry Jensen, ran a newsprint subsidiary of the *Post*, an important position but not a plum, for it left him out of the mainstream at the paper. San and Michelle had begun dating when he was at Cal and she at Stanford. She was smart and vivacious. They commuted between Berkeley and Palo Alto on weekends to be together, and they relished irreverent thoughts about how the family would react on learning of their relationship. For a long while, they managed to keep it quiet, thinking there was already enough intrigue in the family. But the affection they demonstrated made it obvious they were serious about each other. Some in the family rebelled —"You're first cousins; first cousins don't marry"—snipped Jane White, ignoring the fact that there was no common blood. She criticized San about anything she could in order to promote her son, Craig, who was Vice President of Public Affairs for the paper. She insisted Craig, not San, should be the one in training for the top job. Finally, to avoid all the nonsense, San and Michelle eloped, much to the displeasure of Evelyn and Grant as well as the bride's family, who wanted to be included, no matter how unusual the marriage might be. Old-line, social Los Angeles howled with disappointment not to have witnessed a celebration of the union. Some suggested San had done this simply to strengthen his position at the paper.

Although outwardly Grant and Terry maintained cordial relations, Grant distrusted his siblings, feeling they were part of what he saw as a clandestine, family-wide effort to undermine him wherever they could. Jane became even more difficult once Grant's and Terry's wings of the family were united by marriage. Grant feared the possibility of a mistake on San's watch that might make San more vulnerable to efforts to undermine his position in the paper. That came on a Wednesday morning at eight when Grant was in his bedroom dressing for work and Evelyn's voice came on the intercom. "It's Kelly Wilcox. He doesn't sound happy."

Wilcox was the president of the Abbott Hotels Company, which included a location in Malibu on the water. The advertising revenues from this customer were large and its goodwill was hugely important. Wilcox was friendly with Grant, principally because of their business ties through the newspaper, but also because of their community and civic contacts. However, he was not the kind of friend Grant would expect to call at home at this hour. He picked up the receiver.

"Have you seen your fucking newspaper this morning?"

"No. What?"

"Go look for yourself. You're fired, as of today. That's FIRED, not FURRED, fucking FIRED. You understand." Wilcox hung up.

Grant zipped up his pants but didn't take time to button his shirt or find his shoes. He jumped into slippers and hustled downstairs to the driveway for the paper. As he passed through the front door, Evelyn called out: "What is it? What's wrong?"

"I don't know. He wouldn't tell me. But I guess I'm going to find out."

Grant picked up the paper in the driveway. Half the time his so-called delivery people managed to throw the paper over the gate onto the wet lawn, rather than hitting the dry driveway. If they do it like this for me, God knows what they're doing to the subscribers, he'd find himself mumbling. He opened the first section where full-page display ads appeared. The most important advertisers got first-section placement and paid dearly for it. He thumbed through the pages until he found the Abbott ad. He scanned the words and drawings. Then he saw it, in huge point type. "Jesus Christ," he yelled.

He marched into the house and threw the paper on the kitchen counter. "Look at this goddamned thing."

Evelyn checked the ad. At first it didn't register. She read it more closely. "Oh, my God. It's a 'W,' not a '3.'"

"Yeah, 'Visit Our Whores,' not 'Visit Our Shores.' You wonder why Kelly's mad? It's unfucking believable. I'm gonna' kill San."

"San?"

"Yes, San."

"It's not his fault."

"The last stop is the proofreading department. That's one of his departments, isn't it?"

"Well, *he* didn't do it. It's a mistake, that's all. Just one letter off. No one would have done it on purpose."

"Don't count on it," Grant fumed. "There are a few unhappy people around there, no matter how much we've done for them over the years. I wouldn't put it past some of those bastards."

A proofreading mistake in the newspaper normally wouldn't reach the publisher's level, but this one had, with a thud. Grant called San who was already at work, and yelled at him "go to the fucking Abbott ad in the first edition." There was silence for twenty seconds as he could hear San rummaging through the paper. He found it. "I can't believe this."

"We, and Abbott, are going to be laughing stocks. I want you to get to the bottom of it immediately and report back to me. Someone's head better roll." The phone clicked dead.

San had the error corrected for the second edition and personally undertook to find out what had happened. He identified the proofreader who was responsible, a seventeen-year employee with an average employment record. The man said, as expected, that he just missed it, no matter that it was in bold block print. He was sorry. San argued he should be given a five-day disciplinary layoff without pay. No way Grant bought that. This was sloppy work, far beneath the paper's standards, and the employee was to be fired. He didn't care if the union filed a grievance seeking to get the man's job back. Nothing short of discharge would ever be understood by the customer. Grant tried to ameliorate Wilcox's fury with a fawning personal apology and a run of free ads.

Grant insisted the experience be used as a platform for admonishing San and other managers about the importance of careful work and the enormous embarrassment that could be caused when serious mistakes like this were made. Unfortunately, the episode counted as another obstacle he had to overcome with family in his effort to position San for promotion. Jane White went ballistic, screaming over the phone, "We can't have someone with limited English skills running this newspaper. If he hadn't become your son, there's no way he'd be considered qualified for the job—and you know it." She insisted it was San who should be fired. Nevertheless, Grant's resolve that San should have the top job remained unshaken and was joined in by Evelyn who became furious when she heard Jane's crack about San's so-called "'limited English skills? "He can write and speak the language in circles around her," Evelyn said to Grant.

"She'll try to make an issue of it at the next board meeting," Grant predicted. "I'll be hard on him, but he'll have to take care of himself. I can't appear to be protecting him." ∾

TWENTY-THREE

Mayday, Mayday, Mayday

A RITUAL IN Grant Jensen's life was the annual Cinco de Mayo Newport Beach-to-Ensenada sailing regatta. The race involved hundreds of yachts in various classes sailing the distance of 125 nautical miles. He had never won in his class, but always loved the challenge. The German binoculars he carried to keep an eye on his competitors were a tangible connection to his father, who had left them to him. As a boy sailing with his father, he had been permitted to use the glasses. Now, having them in hand made him feel as though the man were right there, next to him. His father had been a tough but loving man. Grant hoped he showed as much affection to those he loved.

Grant was at the wheel preparing for the start of the 1998 race as San and Win strode down the dock, pushing a cart loaded with boxes of provisions for the boat. He stubbed out his cigarette in a sandbag ashtray and called out, "Hustle. We're late." They didn't have much time to motor from the dock to the starting line, where the engine would be turned off and the sails readied for the race. San and Win handed the cartons to the crew members on deck. At the same time San stuffed his mouth with the remainder of a hotdog he'd bought on the pier.

Over the years, in this short international race, only Grant's boat and crew had changed. Of course, these were all that counted. Grant had graduated to the Lady III, successor to the Little Lady and the Little Lady II. He dropped "Little" on round three when he acquired a Cal 40, conceding, with Evelyn's prodding, that "Little" had a ring of pretentious understatement for a boat that size. It was a forty-foot, sleek, white, fiberglass beauty, a storied racing yacht, complete with the finest fittings—lines, wenches, and electronic equipment. Its sails were white, with a colorful blue, orange and yellow spinnaker.

Grant loved the race in part because it brought San and Win together in a common effort in which they seemed equally skilled and interested. Physically they were both ready for any responsibility aboard ship, strong enough for any job. Win was five feet, ten inches and weighed 170 pounds. San was slightly taller and heavier. On the boat the two seemed more compatible, as they had been when they were younger before competitive instincts began to dominate their relationship and personality differences started drawing them apart. Grant was particularly excited to have them on board this year as they hadn't crewed together in the last two races. He hoped the experience would help bring them closer together.

In addition to the Jensens, three others were onboard that day, two of whom had crewed in the race in past years. The third had sailed the boat, though not under racing conditions. Grant began to give specific assignments to prepare for departure. As he did, he opened one of the boxes San and Win had delivered to the dock. He pulled out plastic sacks with new steel-blue wind jackets and matching baseball caps prominently emblazoned with "Lady III" in white.

"Here are the uniforms," Grant said.

"Wear 'em with pride guys." San smiled.

With the crew in their jackets, caps and life vests, the Lady was ready to head for the starting line. Once there, with the motor off, all hands helped rig the boat. She bobbed in the water, her mainsail and jib flapping in the light breeze. Grant maneuvered the boat into position, working to secure the best starting spot. The pistol sounded.

They were off. The weather was grey but dry, the wind light from the northwest. As time passed, the yachts, which had taken off so close to one another, began to spread out, some at such a distance they could only be identified with binoculars. The range of the boats in the race was mostly to the sides of the Lady, not so much in front of her.

The Lady had been provisioned with snack foods and beer in cans which could be crushed and stowed for return to land. In earlier days, Grant had used bottles which, when emptied, were shattered with a winch handle and tossed overboard. While smashing the bottles was to prevent them from floating on the surface, Evelyn had been appalled by the resultant littering of the ocean floor with glass and insisted a switch be made to cans. Grant didn't encourage drinking on the Lady during a race, but he didn't enforce strict limits either. He wanted to win and knew the ship and the crew had to be in perfect form to do that. He thought he could do well this year with San and Win crewing. Above all, he wanted to return everyone safely to land.

The day passed uneventfully. The Lady averaged about seven knots, enough to keep in range of the other yachts, a few of which now lay ahead, their sails sometimes full, sometimes flapping. At nightfall, after snacking for dinner, Grant announced the night schedule. Each watch of four hours would consist of two people on deck. They would alternate manning the wheel and standing by, while the other four crew slept belowdecks. There could be no beer on night watch. He and San would take the 4 am shift.

When the appointed time came, Grant was awake, lying in his sleeping bag on a bunk in the cabin. He could never sleep well when the boat was underway because the crew and his expensive toy were his responsibility. But it was harder than ever with the noise and motion that night as the bow slammed against the water and the wind and rain thrashed the sails, deck and sides of the vessel. Grant checked his watch, 3:55, pulled himself out of the bunk, shook San, who was asleep, and said, "Put on your foul weather gear, it's raging out there."

San took the first turn at the wheel, while Grant stood at the forward edge of the cockpit, the best vantage point to observe the sails and the water. It was a following sea, rolling from the stern, the wind from the northwest. Their speed was picking up. Swells were building, to at least ten feet, with the first signs of morning light on the far horizon. They had to yell to get their voices above the fury of the sea and wind.

"San, I'll take over." Grant glanced at his watch. "An hour at the helm is long enough in these seas."

"Okay." San unleashed the safety harness that tethered him to the vessel and held the wheel for Grant, who fully realized then how much pressure San had been handling.

While the rain was diminishing, the wind remained fierce. The sea was huge, with mountainous swells. The wind tore the crests of the waves into horizontal sheets of spray that stung the skin and nearly blinded the eyes. The vessel surfed, rising on the crest of a wave, stalling for a moment, then starting a swift descent, her bow rushing down what looked like a twelve-foot slope. Again and again.

Grant played with the mainsail, making small tightening adjustments that caused the boat to heel closer and closer to the water on its port side. He watched the log to see the boat's speed increase from nine, to ten, to eleven knots. The more he tightened the sail, the faster they moved and the more exhilarated he felt. Halyards clanged solidly against the mast. The hull smashed into the water. The Lady was reaching faster than she had ever sailed before. Surfing to this extreme degree was a new experience for Grant. It left him with the illusion of control, when in fact he had almost none. He was under the control of the sea.

"Dad, don't you think we're heeling too far to port?" San cried out. The rail was actually being buried in the water.

"I've got it." Grant knew that were he cruising, rather than racing, he would long ago have reefed the main.

"Got to go to the head," San yelled.

"Hang over the side. Be careful for Christ's sake."

"Can't. Diarrhea. Damn hotdog, I bet. Got to go below. Get that safety harness on," San shouted as he swung belowdecks.

"Sure," Grant mumbled, but San was gone. The anemometer recorded the wind velocity at twenty-five knots. He eased the sail a bit. The speed fell slightly, but then there was a wham as a sudden blast of wind caused the boat to heel over and round up into the following waves. Green water rushed over the port side. The boat was on its beam ends, its mainsail on the water. The sea began to pour into the cockpit. Yells from below deck—"Knockdown, Knockdown"—and the sound of bodies thrown from their bunks, hitting hard flooring, resounded through the rage of the wind. Grant had to right the nearly capsized boat. He backed off the wheel but lost his grip when his left leg buckled. He flew across the deck, tried to grab the lifeline, slipped and tumbled overboard into the dark pounding sea. He screamed, "Man overboard," trying to be heard over the furious noise of wind and water. He fought to keep his head up. The yacht moved forward with the swells.

San's skull hit the door to the head. Cries came from the cabin, "Fuck!" "What the shit?" "Knockdown!" He heard the pounding of bare feet scrambling to the hatch, then Win shouting, "I've got the wheel. Get on deck, now. Close the fuckin' hatch." Dazed, San pulled up his foul weather pants, not taking time to use toilet paper. He struggled up the ladder on the heels of two others.

San looked around the deck and secured the hatch. "Where's Dad?" he cried.

"Where in the fuck *is* he, Aun San?" No answer.

"You had the watch with him," Win added.

"I had to go below, to take a dump."

"What?" Win's jaw jutted forward in disbelief. "And left him alone on deck?"

"Diarrhea, I couldn't hold it." San said. "I told him to clip the safety harness on."

"What?" Win screamed. "You knew he wouldn't do that. The most he ever did was to put on a life jacket."

"He did have on a life jacket," San said.

They glared at one another. Someone had to do something. "We can't come about in this weather," San scowled. "We'll make a quick turn. Furl the sails and start the engines. We're going back."

"He can't be far," one of the crew cried out.

"We'll find him," another shouted.

Bringing in the sails was hard work and time-consuming. Precious minutes were lost. Once the sails were furled, San started the motor and brought the boat around, his arms and legs trembling beyond control. He knew he had been wrong to leave Grant, no matter what the reason or what he said. They threaded their way back, bucking waves that earlier had propelled them in the opposite direction. The swells were high, preventing them from sighting objects other than what was in the trough immediately before them or on the crest of the swell. Win was on the port side using Grant's binoculars and ready with a life line. One of the crew stood on the starboard side. Another was stationed at the mast, one hand grasping a line, the other cupped above his eyes. All prayed for a glimpse of their captain. They shivered from cold and fear, and took turns going below to put on foul-weather gear.

San stayed at the helm, straining to control his stomach. The boat approached the general vicinity where he thought the knockdown had occurred. He punched the man-overboard-button from which the exact position of the ship would be calculated by navigational instruments. The question was not only where Grant went in, but how far he had been dragged by the surging water. They moved the boat in wide circles. When nothing was sighted, San directed that the crew send up a distress flare. It was brilliant in the sky. Grant could see it. He had to see it. San fell to his knees, pounding his fists on the deck, sobbing and moaning "what have I done, what have I done."

Win dropped down into the cabin and radioed "Mayday, Mayday, Mayday." The Coast Guard replied immediately. Win's teeth were chattering so much the Coast Guard officer had to ask him to repeat his message three times. The heavy seas began to calm, the rolls were smaller, the wind reduced in velocity. The Lady continued to move in wide circles, but as time passed San grew ever more fearful they were not really close to where Grant had catapulted into the sea or been carried by the waves. There was no possible way to know. One of the crew was assigned to monitor the crackly radio, which now carried constant questions and messages about the Lady. The others tried to spy one of the boat's yellow life jackets floating in the water. They saw nothing in the early light but distant boats, large freighters which appeared, then disappeared, on the horizon as the Lady rolled with the waves.

Ninety minutes later a Coast Guard cutter pulled close, with a helicopter circling above, and an officer came onboard. San, in better control, but still in shock, explained what had happened, how he'd had to go belowdecks, what he said to Grant, and what he heard the others yelling. Win related that he was awake in his bunk when he heard a loud thump and a couple of minutes later a scream that sounded like "man overboard." He'd gotten out of his bag, sprung to the deck and found no one there. He added, "Isn't it the rule that the man on watch with the helmsman never leaves him alone?"

San lunged at Win, grabbing him around the shoulders. Both hit the deck with a thud, then scrambled to get on top of each other.

"Fuck you. Fuck you, Nyan Win. It was an accident. You know that." The officer and two of the crew pulled them apart, leaving them standing, hunched, weeping. San knew it was a universal law of the sea—and a clear understanding on this boat—that it was unthinkable to leave the deck during a watch. But Win didn't need to taunt him about it. San sat down, his head between his knees, mumbling, bound in terror.

The search continued with two more Coast Guard vessels appearing on the scene. A couple of straggling yachts from the race circled close by. The boats further ahead showed no sign of returning to help.

The officer on the first cutter took control, directing the Coast Guard personnel and equipment. Another stayed aboard the Lady, trying to help and maintain calm. The search went on, it seemed endlessly. Hours later an officer suggested that since sunset was coming, the Lady and her crew should return to port. He said there was nothing the Lady's crew could do that couldn't be done better by Coast Guard ships and helicopters. San resisted. He wanted to be there to find Grant, pull him out of the water, throw his arms around him, and start building the legend of Grant Jensen surviving the colossal seas. Finally, and reluctantly, he agreed. They proceeded under motor. All were quiet. Win sulked. San stared as if under hypnosis, wondering how he could live with it if Grant were not saved.

They arrived in San Diego, the nearest port, where Evelyn, who'd been notified by the Coast Guard, was standing on the dock with Jerry, the houseman. Her hand rested on Jerry's forearm. She was drained of color. After the lines were secured, she grabbed Win, the first off the Lady, and held him. Then San. She tried to put words together, but couldn't through her tears. The three of them hung on to one another without speaking, turning in circles, almost as if in an awkward dance and no leader. They stumbled into the Coast Guard office.

Finally, Evelyn spoke. "What happened? I don't understand."

There was no immediate answer. Finally, San got out something of an explanation. He focused on the rescue efforts. He made no mention of the fact he was not on deck at the critical time, nor did anyone else. Win added what had gone on belowdecks when the knockdown occurred and how the crew had gotten control of the vessel.

Evelyn pressed for more details, mixing sobs with occasional glances of disbelief at San and Win as the story unfolded. She began to gain some composure and asked about the possibilities:

"What is the water temperature?"

"How long can a person make it in sixty degree water?"

"Is a life jacket enough to keep him afloat?"

"Can a helicopter pilot spot that small a figure in the water?"

"Can the officers aboard ship see a person in such high seas?"

The Coast Guard personnel equivocated in answering, while sounding generally positive. "We'll do everything we can Ma'am. There's no way to know for sure, but we have a good chance. We'll resume again tomorrow at first light."

A smart woman with all the right questions, she didn't ask a thing about predators in these waters.

Evelyn, San and Win stayed at the office until 6 am, waiting for word that did not come, at which point the chief convinced them to go home, saying, as diplomatically as possible, that his officers could be more effective in the rescue operation if there were no distractions. He assured them they would be notified immediately as developments occurred. Evelyn asked to use a private office where she called *Post* editor Bill Farley to deliver the awful news and told him to keep the story out of the paper while the rescue operation was in progress. The Coast Guard was sure, she told him, that Grant would be found.

Jerry pulled up their car. Evelyn climbed in the backseat, with San and Win at her sides. Evelyn tried to be positive. "They'll find him. They have to find him." Much of what she said was garbled because of emotions, except one thing she repeated clearly: "This can't possibly be happening to us again. Not again." ⌁

TWENTY-FOUR
Searching Dark Waters

EVELYN COULDN'T SLEEP, immobilized in her bed, blankets strewn with Kleenex, her mind swirling between prayers for her husband's recovery and grotesque images of what might have happened to him. About noon, Farley phoned. He apologized for the intrusion, but sought approval for the *Post* to go public with the story in the next edition. She was angry, but came to accept the argument that the paper couldn't afford to be scooped by the *Sun*. More important, she couldn't deny Farley's argument that Grant himself would have insisted that the story run.

After getting rid of the editor, she called Kathy in Ghana. She had to leave a message with a foreign service officer for Kathy to return the call immediately, that it was important. She struggled to keep the sound of fear and anger from her voice, so that the officer wouldn't detect trouble and Kathy wouldn't be alarmed before the terrible news could be delivered directly. Next she called Farley and asked him to inform Grant's sister. Later, he reported that Jane White's reaction was complete silence, uncharacteristic based on any experience Evelyn had ever had with the woman. Michelle was asked to inform Terry.

The story ran with the headline, "Publisher Lost at Sea," and reported the knockdown and the search efforts that were on-going. The article ended with laudatory observations about Grant Jensen as a man and as a leader in the newspaper world. Even the *Sun* included a positive story about his role in the community and in the industry.

The orange, yellow glow of a Los Angeles chemical sunset began to filter through the den window. Evelyn rose to turn on the lights when she heard the doorbell rang. Shuffling feet sounded in the hall. The front door opened, then shut. Not hearing an excited greeting in Jerry's high-pitched Cantonese accent, she knew it must be a stranger. The footsteps moved toward the den. Jerry cleared his throat as he knocked on the open door. "Mrs. Jensen, two officers. See you."

"What do they want?" She turned.

"Didn't say. Come in?"

A shiver raced through her body. She nodded yes.

Two officers in white Coast Guard uniforms entered the room, one male, one female, stiff hats in one hand, identification in the other. Evelyn tried to inspect their documents, but her hands were shaking so that she couldn't. She asked if they would like to sit down, if they wanted tea, if they were cold. The female officer answered "no, Ma'am" politely to each question. Jerry started to leave, but Evelyn signaled him to stay.

"What time will you be resuming the search in the morning?" she asked.

"That's what we came to talk to you about, Ma'am," the male officer said, his head down, eyes cast on the floor. "As I said yesterday, if we were not successful in the next twenty-four hours, we would have to suspend the rescue operation. I'm afraid we're at that point. We've covered hundreds of square miles. And nothing. We'll still be on alert though."

"You can't give up." Her voice was loud, commanding.

"It's doubtful he could have survived, Mrs. Jensen."

"Of course he could have. Get out there tomorrow. I'll pay for it."

"It's not the cost. It's procedure after two days."

"Officer, do you know who my husband is?"

"Yes." There was a long pause, and the officer said, "We're very sorry, Mrs. Jensen."

She looked at them, around the room, at Jerry, then saw Peter's photo on a side table. Tears began to flow from her eyes. Everyone was motionless, unable to touch her, unable to help.

She turned her back on the officers and said, "Jerry, show them out please." They walked out of the room. She clung to the back of a leather wing chair, feeling as though she couldn't walk. Their marriage since Peter died had not always been perfect, but they had a positive relationship. She had loved Grant and respected him and he had loved and honored her. Difficult as he sometimes could be, the idea of living without him was completely incomprehensible. She didn't know how long she was there, but eventually she was able to take a deep breath, square her shoulders, and move to the phone.

After informing Kathy, San, Win and Farley that Grant was lost, Evelyn closeted herself in her bedroom for three days. The door was opened and closed for meals Jerry delivered, at which she picked. The terror of what Grant might have experienced bore into her. She couldn't break the connection between Peter's disappearance and Grant's. They appeared and reappeared. She shook her head, even hit it against the fabric-covered wall in her dressing room to erase the picture.

Finally, thoughts of the children and the newspaper began to break through. Evelyn knew a state of uncertainty couldn't be permitted, for the family or for the future of the *Post*. In many of the great newspapers, the roles of family patriarch and publisher are filled by the same person. In a few cases, it is the roles of matriarch and publisher that are joined. The health of the family is in many ways dependent on the success of the newspaper. And the health of the paper is dependent on a stable family where infighting is not permitted to rule. Grant had been a classic example, and he had done a pretty good job of holding it all together. But there was no one to step in and fill Grant's dual role. Evelyn couldn't as she wasn't from the founding family, nor was she experienced in newspaper management. But she could be the matriarch of her family, and then fight for San to become the publisher of the *Post*. To do this though there would be no time for mourning. She had to pull herself together and take control. The first step was to secure the publisher's position for San, and that wasn't going to happen until Grant's death was accepted as fact. She telephoned San and asked him to come to the house to talk with her.

He arrived unshaven, his eyes red above darkened circles. He hadn't been able to bring himself to return to the office since the accident.

Evelyn started, "San, I want to see to it that you follow your father as publisher." She hesitated, "It would be three generations of Jensens, and I know it's what he would want."

"Mom, there's something you don't understand. I was on the four o'clock watch with Dad when . . ."

"Yes, I know that," she interrupted.

"What you don't is that I had the watch, but I wasn't there. I was belowdecks getting sick when the knockdown happened."

Her eyebrows arched, "I thought . . ."

"That's right. I should have been with him." He started to pace around the small den.

Evelyn stared at him. She couldn't believe it. She had sailed enough with Grant to understand the rule. She looked away, then back at him. She didn't know whether to scream at him or envelop him in her arms.

He moved toward her, starting to sob, falling to his knees at her feet as she sat straight-backed in an upholstered chair. "I'm so sorry," his voice cracked, "so sorry. I had a horrendous stomach attack. I couldn't hold it. I told him to use the safety harness."

She stood and walked a few feet away. Finally, she said, "San, you can't blame yourself. There probably wasn't a thing you could have done even if you were on deck. It never would have happened if he'd put on the harness. "

"I tell myself that." He pulled a handkerchief from his pant's pocket, wiped his eyes and blew his nose. He sat down in a chair, hunching forward. "But it's hard to swallow. I will never be able to forgive myself."

"You're going to have to. You have a huge job to take on."

"That's the problem. It's earlier than anyone ever thought this would happen. Jane would fight me no matter what or when. Now she'll blame me, say I shouldn't get the job when I caused Dad's death."

"No one needs to know what happened."

"Everyone on the boat knows. Win knows it and was all over me. It'll be in the Coast Guard report. There's no way to hide it."

Evelyn moved to the fireplace. She turned as if to warm her back though no fire was burning. "No one's going to think you did it deliberately. And I'm surprised at Win."

"We actually fought over it."

"I will take care of him. There's not going to be any more infighting and conflict in this family. That includes both you and Win. And Jane? I don't care what she thinks. No one on her side of the family is up to the job. You're ready, trained in virtually every operation in that newspaper. Of course, we know Terry will support you for Michelle's sake. I assume you've told her what happened?"

"Yes."

Evelyn hugged him, then closed the conversation, "Kathy will be with us, and Bill Farley should be able to manage the board. You can do it. I know you can do it."

Farley came to the house. Evelyn kept him waiting on the terrace as she struggled at her dressing table to hide the effects of a night of crying. She pressed cucumber under her swollen eyes, a technique her mother showed her years before, then put on lipstick and brushed her hair. The last thing she wanted was to appear as the lost widow, helpless and hapless. She needed to show Farley she was in charge during the transition between Grant and San. If she could get through that, then she could relax, and it wouldn't make any difference. If she fell apart now, San was out as publisher. She walked downstairs and outside.

Farley hugged her, mumbling a combination of sorrow and hope that despite it all, Grant would be found. Evelyn no longer believed there was a chance, but didn't say so. She turned right to business. She wanted San to be named Grant's successor. She lined up the arguments: San's intelligence, his charisma, most of all, his experience. He'd been prepared for the job. The dynasty argument did not need to be made. Apparently, Farley was prepared for her pitch. He didn't argue for his own elevation to the post, saying he'd do everything he could to help San, and to get the board of directors and senior officers to agree. At Evelyn's request, he committed to stay on as editor for another four years to assure continuity.

Having gotten that far, Evelyn disclosed the fact that San was not on deck at the time of the knockdown.

"My God, Evelyn. How could that have happened?"

"It wasn't his fault. He had a stomach attack and had to go belowdecks. Grant didn't attach the safety harness, even though San told him to. But, my question is, can we keep that quiet?"

"I don't know. I doubt it," Farley said with an air of disapproval. "It would be in the Coast Guard report, which will be a public record."

Evelyn replied, "I want this to be clear, Bill. I do not blame San. It was not his fault, but I'm afraid he will have to live with it for the rest of his life. I am fully prepared to stand up to anyone, the board, the family, whomever, and see that he gets this job. He deserves it. Grant, no matter what, would have wanted him to have it."

"I can see you're determined. All right. I'll focus on rallying the board. You work on the family."

"Except Jane," Evelyn answered. "I can't deal with her. And she listens to you—at least as much as she listens to anyone."

Evelyn knew the challenge ahead. Jane White would fight for the job for Craig. Terry Jensen would be co-opted by Michelle from seeking the position for himself, and his two other children who worked for the paper didn't have remotely enough experience to manage the operation. There was, of course, the threat that the board might try to bring in an outsider from another newspaper. The position at the *Post* was one at which many would jump. Jane's wing of the family might opt for an outsider to keep power from Grant's family. Another newspaper might come after the company.

Two days later, Farley arrived again at St. Cloud Road. Evelyn couldn't face being seen at the office. He informed her that the board had acted in an emergency telephone conference to make the paper's general counsel the acting publisher until a board meeting could be scheduled. "You don't need to convince me," Farley said. "San is smart, experienced, attractive and has leadership ability. He's the right candidate for the job. But, some are saying it's too early, at thirty-two, for him."

"John Kennedy was elected at forty-three and he had to run the entire country," she countered.

"I'm not saying San's too young, but he's perceived to be in certain quarters. Some people, not just family members, may be looking for excuses."

"What does that mean?" Evelyn asked with a tone of annoyance.

"Frankly, San's race."

"What?"

"It will never be said openly, but there will be innuendo, 'Publisher of the venerable *Los Angeles Post*, from Burma.' Worse, 'From Myanmar. A tinhorn military dictatorship that denies freedom and democracy.'"

"They damn well better not say it in front of me. He *is* our son. He *is* a Jensen." She stood. "Let's go outside and get some fresh air." They walked out on the terrace and sat down at a wrought-iron table.

"This is a beautiful garden, Evelyn."

"Yes, but sometimes I feel it's a jungle to be tamed."

He continued, "I'm not saying they're right. But it will be implied."

"The hardest thing to beat down," she said.

"Evelyn, you know there are those who care about him, who will say he shouldn't take the job even if it were handed to him on a silver platter."

"Why?"

"Conditions in the industry. The timing is bad. It's pretty tough to succeed in today's world as a head of even a great newspaper like ours. Some say impossible." He didn't need to detail the downhill conditions for Evelyn: falling ad revenues, declining circulation, development of the Internet, piranhas circling the vulnerable, union troubles. "It's one thing to hang on during a downturn, as Grant was. It's another thing to start in the job when times are as bad as this. You have to be able to pull out of the slump and you may not be given much time to do it."

"You sound like those pessimists who argue the newspaper business is a dying industry."

"It may not be moribund, but it's getting sicker. Our stock price is a fraction of its high, as you well know. You may not be doing San a favor—put it that way."

"He'll survive." Evelyn looked out over the lawn toward the pool and tennis court. *Survival? This place, this wonderful home. How will I survive here without Grant?* She pushed the thought from her mind.

"Jane will use everything she can against him, comparing him unfavorably to Grant," Farley said.

"Yes, I know. But she never cared about Grant. If she could have gotten him out of the way, she would have. Now, she's going to play the poor, crushed sister? Please."

Evelyn felt she couldn't live through a repeat of an interminable period of grief and uncertainty. They had waited several months before officially acknowledging Peter's death, while they prayed, even fantasized, that somehow he would reappear. Perhaps he was injured and had been nursed back to health by a tribe along the river. Maybe, after having been held captive by a tribe, he was able to escape. It had been draining. She had to accept that the chances were even slimmer Grant could reappear from the vastness of the Pacific Ocean. Though she wouldn't admit it, she was on the brink of re-entering a state of active grieving for Peter she thought she'd left behind a long time ago. There had to be resolution. She had to move forward.

Upon arrival back in Los Angeles and learning what had happened, Kathy became enraged. She wasn't much of a sailor but she knew her father should not have been left alone. How could it have happened? Why didn't someone else go up on deck? Where was Win? Eventually, working through her anger, she came to accept the view that there would have been no difference in the result if San had been there. In doing this, she deferred to Evelyn's position that the family had to stick together or be overrun by the White clan. Evelyn and Kathy committed to working on Win to bring him into the fold as well.

Evelyn decided to hold a memorial service thirty days later at St. Joseph's Episcopal Church, where Peter's service had been twenty-two years before. Evelyn asked Win to speak about Grant's lighthearted side, as much as he could, poking a bit of fun at some of his idiosyncrasies, his competitiveness, his gruff tolerance of his kids' stunts. Win rose to the occasion by wearing a tie and dress shirt, but didn't otherwise tame his Bohemian all black, long hair artist appearance. Kathy spoke of Grant's great strength in supporting the family after Peter's tragedy. Other speakers included Bill Farley and the president of the Los Angeles World Affairs Council.

San was asked to deliver serious, but hopefully not somber, words. Last up, he stepped forward to speak before an audience of several hundred gathered in this high-domed church. The elite of Los Angeles from both the social and business worlds were there, men dressed conservatively in blacks and blues as expected for a memorial service in a house of worship. He couldn't help wondering how many might have whispered to their neighbors before the service about his failure on the Lady in the early morning hours of the race. He had decided not to make reference to the accident, and, in deference to Win, not to refer to Grant as Dad or father. San took a deep breath, remembering Grant's oft-repeated advice: "stand tall, be confident."

"You have heard how Grant Jensen lived his role as publisher of the *Post* and how he lived his active life in the community. I want to add some thoughts about him as a moving force in dragging home a couple of scruffy orphan boys from a faraway country that few here have probably visited, on his taking a chance on us, on his living with our antics—skate-boarding in a neighbor's swimming pool, as Win just confessed—and, finally, in fully making us members of the Jensen family. He gave us every advantage." He gestured to Grant's large black-and-white photograph to his side in the apse of the church, positioned on an easel, surrounded by white roses, Grant's favorite flower. "And with it, there was plenty of his brand of tough love. We never had to wonder about that. And we knew that Evelyn was with him all the way. We will have a challenge to live up to his role in our family."

Tears welled in Evelyn's eyes, but there was a slight smile on her face, too. Concentrate as she might, she couldn't absorb all his words. She only knew, at some vague level, he was doing what she had hoped, speaking with the kind of authority that would dispel his doubters. He appeared as a natural successor to his father, no matter that he didn't look like him.

She glanced at Win. There was no softness in his face. She knew how he felt. Her last conversation with him had ended abruptly when he said "it was wrong for San to succeed to a position his own negligence created." With uncharacteristic bluntness toward Win, she'd replied she didn't "ever want to hear those words spoken again."

The reception after the service was at St. Cloud Road where so many joyous celebrations had been held, and this, the second wake. San, who had spotted Willie Chin in the church, could not find him in the crowd at the reception. Perhaps he had not gone to the home.

The next day, Grant's temporary memorial marker was placed next to Peter's at Forest Lawn. It simply read:

GRANT ALBERT JENSEN

1935—1998

- 30 -

Only old-time newspaper people could be counted on to under-stand the " -30 -." It was engraved as well on Grant's father's grave a few steps away. In earlier days, it appeared at the end of a newspaper story to indicate "the end."

The plaque next to it read:

PETER ALBERT JENSEN

1964—1975

OUR BOY

The immediate family members were present at the internment on Inspiration Slope. They stood, heads bowed, as the minister recited the Twenty-Ninth Psalm. Evelyn wept quietly. Each of them took two white roses, placing one at Grant's marker and one at Peter's. Evelyn kissed her roses before letting them go. She prayed that Grant understood she hadn't blamed him for Peter's death—at least any more than she blamed herself—and that he realized how much it had meant to her to have San and Win enter their lives. With the boys, some of the warmth and intimacy of their earlier relationship had been restored, making it possible for them to survive Peter's loss.

On the way home, in a black limousine large enough for the imme-diate family, the matriarch issued an imperative: "I don't want anyone in this family ever setting foot on a boat again." No one was about to argue—at least not under these circumstances.

At the board meeting a week later, San was elevated to the position of acting publisher. Not a word was said about his behavior on the Lady that morning, not even by Jane. She must have decided the time wasn't right to fight for her son instead of San. Having accomplished that, and having put Grant to rest—as much as one could without a body—Evelyn collapsed, finally submitting to her emotions. She did not see or talk with anyone other than immediate family for five weeks. ⌒

TWENTY-FIVE

Succession

C ONTRARY to Evelyn's urging, San declined to move into the publisher's suite when he was appointed to the acting position. He knew he had to earn the right to be in that space, and that some, probably many, would agree he should not have the full title from the beginning. He worried that whispers as to what happened, or hadn't, on the Lady might become public knowledge and hurt the *Post* indirectly if he were the publisher. Most of all, he missed Grant and prayed for his forgiveness.

A year later the board of directors did elevate him to the top job, and he agreed it was time to move into Grant's office. His focus on the job had helped him work through the awful depression he experienced following Grant's death. The sense of blame had sometimes been so strong it immobilized him. But as far as Evelyn was concerned, he had no choice. He was responsible for the paper. She was responsible for the family. Neither one of them could escape. Grant had performed in both roles. They could at least divide what he had managed to do alone. Over time she convinced him. Now, he was ready not just to occupy the position, but to fill it. To some degree, however, he still feared being in the space. Grant and his father were always there, like ghosts, looking out from photographs and important awards bearing their names. His grandfather's countenance spoke of disapproval.

Grant's did not; it reflected kindness despite his sometimes rigid personality. Could he, San, do as good a job as they had?

While San hoped to live up to Grant's accomplishments, he disagreed with some of his editorial positions. Burma was one, a big one. Grant had soft-pedaled it; San wanted the junta exposed. Over cocktails one night, Farley told San how much pressure Grant had brought to minimize the issue in the paper. On one occasion when Win was living in Burma part-time, Grant had gone so far as to break down in front of Farley, saying he wasn't going to lose San and Win over a "goddamned editorial." Losing Peter had been enough. San didn't know but suspected Grant's stance was taken to protect Win. Now, San wanted the gloves to come off, to tell the truth about the "path to democracy" bullshit the regime spewed out. He decided the most effective way to cement a change in editorial policy was to hire an editor he knew from the *Washington Post* whose strong human rights beliefs assured his opposition to the regime. Increased in-depth coverage of Burma—the name San used—was the result, as were editorials damning the junta.

San found nearly all of Farley's dismal admonitions about the newspaper business were coming true. The core problem stemmed from declining advertising revenues and circulation. With them, everything else fell: profits, dividends, stock price, employee count, news coverage, and, of course, morale. The Internet seemed to pose the most intractable reason for the drop in circulation. Reading habits were changing. Younger people were relying on television, and more recently on the web, for news.

To cut costs, San ordered extreme steps. Sections were cut or combined with others. Salaries were frozen. A plea to employees to forgo wage increases only led to a strike by the Pressman's Union which shut the paper down for three weeks. Everyone was negative: analysts, bankers, stockholders, managers. And the family. The idea that dividends might be suspended or cut met with a hue and cry. The older generation needed the income to live on in retirement. San's generation wanted the money for expensive cars, private schools, and the like. Jane White led a campaign against San, screaming about his inability to deal with the problems facing the *Post*. Evelyn had barely been on speaking terms with Jane since Grant's death. Kathy was supportive of San from her far-flung posting abroad, but she didn't attempt to exert much influence. Win expressed no support for San, though he was not yet openly active in the opposition campaign.

The newsroom decided to do a special three-day report on Burma titled "Burmese Military Junta Stiffens Reprisals." The story was inspired by the filing of a lawsuit in the federal court in Denver on behalf of Burmese citizens against the State Peace and Development Council (SPDC), as the regime so grandly named itself, and a consortium of American companies involved in the construction of an oil pipeline in Burma. The suit was based on an exaggerated theory that forced labor, forced relocation of homes, jailing, torture, rape and murder, tactics allegedly being used by the military in connection with the project, were condoned by its American partners in violation of the Alien Tort Statute enacted in 1789.

One of the partners was Olympic Minerals Exploration whose chairman was Stephen White, Jane's husband. San had advance knowledge of the report when Farley told him family members were conniving to stifle the story.

"There's nothing I can do about it," San said. "It goes where it goes."

Farley nodded in agreement.

"Kill a story because it involves the family?" San asked, as if to convince himself. "Grant wouldn't."

"You can't, of course."

"These people drive me batshit."

Farley let out one of his trademark bellows. "Goes with the job, San. You're doing what's right. The story needs to be told. It's all the more credible when your background is considered."

San's background had been both a positive and a negative in his life. If he hadn't been Burmese, he would not have been found by Grant and Evelyn, and would never have come to the United States and become publisher of the *Los Angeles Post*. He had a uniqueness that benefited him in school and after. But he never had been fully accepted as the scion of the Jensen family, having legitimate claim to the prestigious position he held. To some he was always a product of his origins, an interloper in the broader family and in Los Angeles business and social worlds.

"I appreciate your giving me a head's up. I'll be prepared when the 'you know what hits the fan."

It did just that. An outraged Jane White called in late morning the first day the story ran.

"San."

"Hi Aunt Jane."

"Don't 'aunt' me."

"Is there a problem?"

"You know goddamned well there is."

"You mean the Burma story?"

"That's exactly what I mean."

"I've had it triple checked, and it's one hundred percent accurate."

"I don't give a shit. I want it killed. It makes my end of the family look terrible."

San was prepared for the call. He had known the coverage would upset Jane and the rest of her clan, but she was overreacting. The story didn't say Olympic was committing these appalling acts, but that Olympic and others were condoning the military in the terrible things it was doing. "I can't do that, Jane, you know that."

"What I know is that I own a hell of a lot more stock in this company than you do, and I'm telling you to kill it."

The door to San's office opened abruptly, without a knock, and Craig White stepped in. San figured Craig and his mother must have been on the phone together when her call was transferred to his office. San pushed the speaker phone button, saying to Craig, "It's your mother," as if his cousin didn't already know the voice squawking on the other end of the line. "The story isn't that negative," San said directly into the speaker. "Uncle Stephen's company is only one of several. They've all denied knowing what the military was doing. That denial is at the front of the story."

"You've got a bug up your ass because it's your country," Jane said, sounding as though she were spitting. "If it were Cambodia, you wouldn't run the story."

"Of course we would. We go where the story takes us."

Jane harrumphed, "So, the fact that your real parents supposedly disappeared at the hands of military officers doesn't have an influence?"

"I'll never be able to get my parents' deaths out of my mind. Could you? When you heard the bullet fired that killed your mother? But that isn't the point."

"You're running the paper into the ground, that's the point." Jane said halting between each word apparently for emphasis. "We can't just stand by and watch any longer. Now, you're after Burma, to vent your hatred. You're blindly trying to sell news from half way across the globe that nobody here gives a good goddamn about. I won't take it anymore." The receiver clicked.

San hit the speaker phone button. Craig, head bowed, said nothing. He usually was not vocal when issues got too controversial, a trait not surprising for someone who managed the public relations side of the business. The contrast with his mother was extraordinary. She was tough, large and manly, and had only to open her mouth to eliminate any doubt as to how ferocious she might be. Craig was tall and thin, patrician in appearance, understated in manner. "Do you agree with that crap?" San asked

"You know my mother, she can get pretty hot sometimes."

"This is beyond that."

Craig rose from his seated position at San's crowded desk. He folded his arms on his chest. "She means it. You're in trouble, San."

"You'd love to see that, wouldn't you? Happy to sit down right here behind this desk."

"Actually, no. One day, yes, I would have. Not now. All the forces are running against you. I have no desire to commit hari-kari."

San chuckled, almost under his breath. "Craig, you're a wimp. Besides, you're totally conflicted. What's best for the *Post*? Or what's best for your father?"

White turned and walked toward the door. "My father has nothing to do with it. That's not something you can say, can you?" ~

TWENTY-SIX

The Junta Strikes

WHILE SAN was building his career as publisher of the *Post*, Win struggled to heighten his reputation as an artist. With the assistance of the green card he'd been able to obtain, he gave instruction in found-metal assemblage, and he had a handful of small gallery shows in Los Angeles. He also had a minor place in Yangon's art world, with a couple of one-man shows and his studies at the National University of Arts and Culture. Win felt resentment every day for the differences between his life and San's. No matter how hard he tried, he couldn't lose it.

Win married Myint Thi, a Burmese, whom he had met when he visited an Asian tours company office in Los Angeles where she worked part-time while attending USC. She helped him with a visa problem. They were married in a Buddhist ceremony within a few months of their meeting and six months later she gave birth to Anna Marie. Evelyn hadn't tried to influence the religious ceremony, but she had pressured them for a wedding reception on St. Cloud Road. The couple sidestepped the offer, feeling the occasion was about them, not about the family's friends and business connection. Evelyn had had four children, three marriages among them, but only one major wedding event when Kathy married the Italian diplomat in a union that produced an early, messy divorce, and no children.

They had recently returned to Yangon where they rented a loft in an old office building, with walls of crumbling plaster and cracked paint. Win climbed two flights of stairs to the loft and opened the door. A breeze blowing through gauzy window coverings was a welcome, if slight, relief from the sticky afternoon heat of Yangon. A ceiling fan, buzzing softly, helped move the heavy, stale air. He called to his wife, "I'm home."

Myint Thi walked from the bathroom into the living area clutching their year-old baby in her arms. "There is a problem. It's serious." Her eyes opened wide. "Soldiers came here looking for you. They said you must go right away to the State Peace and Development Council offices. They were very mean. They scared Anna Marie. I just got her to stop crying."

"What did they want?"

"They wouldn't say. Only that it will be very bad for us if you don't go there immediately." She paused, "Are we in trouble?"

"Not that I know of."

Win took a bus to the government building that housed the Council offices. He was worried his summons there had something to do with his father's drug-running activities, a part of his family history he had never fully disclosed to Myint Thi. On arrival he was left to stew, sitting on a hard wooden bench in a long hall, while uniformed soldiers walked into and out of offices. No one seemed to pay any attention to him. After thirty minutes a soldier ushered him into a large, windowless, dingy room where three uniformed officers sat at a small table. They didn't stand or speak, but motioned him to a chair across the table. The officer in the middle leaned back and grabbed a worn piece of white paper from a desk behind him. Holding it in his shaking hand, he thrust it forward, almost in Win's face, and said, "Your newspaper."

The paper was an internet printout, bearing the name *Los Angeles Post* and a recent date. It was headed "Free Aung San Suu Kyi." Win read on: "Aung San Suu Kyi , inspirational leader, Nobel Peace Prize laureate, head of the National League for Democracy, and rightful president of Burma, now under house arrest by the governing military junta for twelve years . . ."

Win scanned enough of the rest to see an uncomplimentary reference to General Than Shwe, the powerful chairman of the State Peace and Development Council, who ruled the country with a steel-like grip. Win looked up at the officer who glowered at him.

"Well?" the man barked.

"This does not represent my view, Sir."

"Is your family's newspaper."

"No. It is not my family. It is not mine. I have no role in its management."

"Your brother is publisher and was born here."

"He is not my brother, Sir. But we were both born here and were raised together, yes."

"He is traitor."

Win did not comment. What could he say?

The officer grabbed a small stack of papers from the desk and threw them at him. They landed on his lap, spilling onto the dusty floor. "All your paper's stories. All against our government. All lies."

Win picked up the papers and thumbed through them, playing for time. They were the hard-hitting anti-junta editorials the *Post* had adopted since San had led the way.

"You stop these."

"I have no way to do that, Sir."

"You own newspaper."

"My interest is very small. I have no influence, as I said."

"You become publisher then."

The suggestion would have been laughable had it not been for the threatening nature of the confrontation. As if he'd ever had a chance to hold any important position at the paper. He'd been pigeonholed from day one as an artist and not even one needed in the newspaper's display advertising department. "I am an artist, a painter, Sir."

"We know all about that."

Win continued, "I don't have the experience or skills to manage a newspaper. I don't agree with the publisher on many things, Sir, but replace him, I couldn't."

Another officer, who wore a cap with gold scrolls and who appeared to be the senior in attendance, took over. His English was more polished. "The *Los Angeles Post* has financial problems. Your brother is being blamed. Many want to see him out. You can make that happen through your family."

Could they possibly know of the pressure he'd experienced from Jane and other extended family members to help unseat San? Even if he didn't care about San and their relationship, Evelyn would never forgive him if he participated in that effort.

The officer continued, the hum of the ceiling fan persistent in the background. "Our government has been good to you. An important art show. Few ever attain that in their entire lifetime."

"I know, Sir."

"Your work conveys anti-government sentiments."

"What?" Win asked. "I work in found metals; there is no message."

"You live here comfortably," the senior continued, as if Win had not spoken. "You come into and out of the country when you please; no one bothers you." There was a pause, as he apparently waited for confirmation. "These things can change, you know. Your editorials have changed; before they were not so negative on our government. You will need to do something to stop what is happening at the *Los Angeles Post*. Now."

Win hung his head, not knowing what to say. His legs were shaking, and he placed his hands firmly on his thighs, hoping the quiver would not be obvious to his interrogators.

"Your brother makes the claim that the government was responsible for the deaths of his parents. He is wrong. They were pocketing drugs they were supposed to be delivering," the officer who appeared to be the leader said. "They were executed by drug traffickers, not the government."

Win had never heard any suggestion of this before. If it were true, would it change San's attitude about the junta? "If it could be proved it was drug traffickers . . ."

"It was almost thirty years ago. It is too late to prove anything. Your visa expires shortly," the senior officer said. "In fact, in thirty days." Boots scuffled against the rough wooden floor.

"Yes."

"You will have to leave then. Unless you go there and stop this," he said, pointing to the papers now scattered on the table, "there will be no return. No new passport from the Home Ministry. Nothing." The officer paused and smiled, "You are married?"

Win didn't want to answer, but knew he had to. "Yes."

"And have a child?"

"Yes, Sir." He thought he saw where they were going, the bastards.

"I assume they will want to return with you?"

"Of course."

"They may not," the officer spoke in a loud and firm voice. "The problem must be solved first."

Beads of sweat from Win's underarms dripped down his sides. The assholes had him. He couldn't solve "the problem," as they put it. But there was no way to argue with them. He asked to leave, standing rigidly, hoping his legs wouldn't buckle under him. Admonished to take what had been said seriously, he backed from the room and closed the door behind him. As he walked through the corridor, he felt as though all eyes were upon him. He left the building and started down the street.

Win had worried that San's activist anti-government stance might come back to haunt him. Until now he had never been bothered by the authorities during his stays in the country. He didn't know how much of that had been attributable to the officers not connecting the dots to the *Post*. Now they had. He didn't think he could quiet San, even with the unproven news that his parents had not been killed by the regime—San was on a crusade.

He felt like his entire life had been ruled by San: San, the anointed

Peter; San, the achiever; San, the publisher. San, San, San. Fuck San. But Win still had an ace in the hole: his cousin was a colonel in the army. Maybe Kyan Se could get these dogs off his back.

Win was not able to meet with his cousin for two weeks because it took time to locate the man. When he finally did, he found him absent from the city on assignment. Win was running out of time. He learned some of his art work had been removed from the gallery show by the authorities, and he hoped his cousin might be able to help him protest the action. But in the overall scope of things, that was insignificant in comparison to making sure Myint Thi and Anna Marie would be able to leave with him.

He met with Kyan Se for lunch at a Vietnamese noodle shop down the street from the Strand Hotel. They hadn't seen each other, or even been in touch, in the many years that had passed since Win's father sent him from Rangoon to Inle Lake to live with his grand-mother. They approached one another with hesitation, took a chance and introduced themselves. They chatted about happenings in their lives and their families: schools, marriages, children, jobs, deaths. Win then explained the threats the soldiers had made at the meeting and what they had done at the gallery. He asked for Kyan Se's advice. Maybe he was imagining it, but his cousin seemed to stiffen and sud-denly appear uncomfortable.

"I have no role in that kind of thing. I am not an important person," Kyan Se said. "My assignments are mostly in the field."

"Do you think they really mean it?" Win asked. "How could I be expected to change the editorials of an American newspaper? How can my art send anti-government signals? It's ridiculous. The paint-ings they confiscated are not of anything; no monks, no prayer wheels, no temples, not even a golden Buddha. What are they going to do, stop me from making art?"

"Obviously, they mean it. You are not alone. Books are censored as well." Kyan Se slurped noodles from the bowl into his mouth. This was not considered bad manners in Burma, but Win was struck how Western he had become in his eating habits, using silverware held just so. Western table manners had been among the hardest lessons for him to learn. He smiled at the memory of Grant's fingers snapping at his elbows whenever the elbows came to rest on the dining table.

After listening to Win's story, Kyan Se said, "I will do this. I will contact my superior and explain the problem. I will try to get assurances from people in higher positions than those who met with you that your return will be assured or that your family will be permitted to join you there. But I cannot promise anything."

It was not the clean answer Win had hoped for, but it was a step forward. After lunch he started back to the loft to explain everything to Myint Thi, walking first through an enormous open-air market where vendors sat on mats on the ground selling their wares and food. The bustling life in the crowded aisles seemed so vital and normal; it left him feeling he was the one among the many hundreds milling about who was facing serious problems. If it were only his dilemma, he could deal with it. But it directly impacted his wife and child. Reluctantly, he was forced to realize that San's view of the government was more accurate than his own. Had they been arguing all these years over nothing?

He wandered from the market to the streets, next to deserted colonial buildings with crumbling facades and vines creeping through broken windows, then on under the umbrellas of shade trees lining the roads. Without intending it, he found himself at the Shwedagon Pagoda admiring at its huge gold dome, his mind being soothed by the serenity of the surroundings. Hundreds of pigeons pranced and flapped as he walked through their midst. He had to be honest with Myint Thi, but try not to scare her.

Myint Thi put Anna Marie down in her crib for the night and tiptoed toward her husband in the far corner of the loft room where he was reading under a dim bulb. He whispered to her to sit down, that he wanted to talk. It wasn't easy living in one room with a baby.

Win outlined the discussion he had at lunch with Kyan Se.

"How did he explain them taking your work out of the show?"

"He couldn't, except they do that if work expresses anti-regime sentiments. There's a risk they could close the whole show."

Myint Thi sighed.

"He didn't seem surprised that soldiers had marched into the gallery and told the director to take everything off the walls for inspection. I asked him about the one I titled "Iron." It was a sign that had marked the entry to a British Iron Works plant in Mandalay in the forties, its letters now so faded as to be hardly legible.

"The big red and black one?"

"Yes. I asked, but he couldn't explain, how that was anti-regime."

The phone rang. Win lurched for it before the noise could awaken the baby. He knew it had to be Evelyn; no one else called that late.

"Win, I'm planning a family weekend." Her voice was upbeat. "There are some things we need to discuss about the *Post*. I'm thinking in two or three weeks or so. Will that work for all of you?"

Win couldn't tell her about the threats that had been made to him. "I'm not sure it's possible on this end. What about a telephone conference?"

"No, you have to come," Evelyn answered, her tone less lighthearted. "There are a couple of personal issues, as well. If money is a problem, I'll take care of it. Besides, I want to see that grandchild of mine."

"Well, I can come. I have to return shortly anyway, but I know Myint Thi and the baby can't. It's not money. Myint Thi's mother is ill and needs her here to help."

His wife frowned, with surprise. He shook his head and held a finger to his lips.

"I'm sorry," Evelyn said in an abrupt tone that didn't reflect a lot of sympathy. "Things are not perfect here either. I'm afraid I'm going to be an old lady before I get my clutches on that little girl."

"What isn't perfect? What's the issue with the *Post*?"

"I'm not going to get into any of it until we're all together. You'll see why when you get here. But it's important to you. Someday, Win, you're going to own a big chunk of the company."

"The personal matter?" he asked.

"No previews on that either. We'll have plenty of time to deal with all of it."

The call ended. Win tried to explain to his wife. "I couldn't tell her the truth. She'd get right in the middle of it. She thinks she can solve everything. When I go back, I'll talk to San, see if I can't get him at least to tone down the rhetoric."

As he was deliberating how much to tell her about his meeting with the officers, she said, "I'm afraid you won't get back and Anna Marie and I could be held here. We wouldn't see you for a long time." He hadn't spelled out all of the warnings that had been laid on him, but instinctively she seemed to understand the possible consequences.

He cupped his arms around her shoulders and whispered in her ear, "I love you. I won't let that happen." She clung to him. They rushed, tearing off each other's clothes. Their bodies welded together. Win fought the inner terror that he would never be able to make love to Myint Thi again.

Win waited until his visa was about to expire before he left for Los Angeles. Whenever he boarded the flight to California he could almost feel the excitement and fear that accompanied his first airplane trip so long ago—to a family he barely knew in a culture and a country that were total mysteries. The thread that sustained him then was that he was going to be with his best friend. Now he knew the family and the culture, but he was leaving his wife and child not knowing when and where he would see them again. His efforts to extend his visa or obtain permission for them to join him had failed, even with cash inducements that often made the difference in this notoriously corrupt system. All he had been able to arrange was the means of getting funds to Myint Thi while they were separated. He was anxious about Evelyn's phone call. Obviously, the problems were serious or there wouldn't be a special meeting to discuss them. ∾

TWENTY-SEVEN

The Matriarch

U NLIKE WIN, San knew the reason for the meeting, at least the part concerning the *Post*. He and Evelyn had long discussions about his position being threatened. They agreed that a united front in their immediate family was essential to influence other stockholders, their family's stock holdings being far from sufficient to rule the day. Evelyn had not, however, disclosed to San the nature of the personal matter she wanted to discuss. It worried him because she was usually so open.

San was happy to see Kathy, home on leave again from Ghana. He did not feel the same about Win. The two seldom saw one another anymore, except at command performances like this, and when they did, it was awkward. But he was still drawn to Win, as though he were responsible for him and had to be his protector.

San and Kathy chatted on the terrace by the pool, drinking ice tea, when Win arrived and walked out of the living room toward them. Kathy threw her arms around him and kissed him on the cheek. He hugged her and planted a kiss on her forehead. The two men shook hands, uncomfortably, each asking about the other with no evident interest in the reply. Kathy enlivened the conversation, as she always did, with stories about foreign leaders, in this case telling about seeing the King of Tonga and trying to find a place to break through the retinue of burly bodyguards surrounding him to shake his hand. The King and his guards were impeccably dressed in Savile Row's finest, not in the sarongs and sandals she had expected. Evelyn came out to the terrace and lost no time saying that she couldn't understand how Kathy could live in such desolate places. They were fine to visit, as she had, but to live in? What man would marry a woman who moved from one Third World country to another? It's not like being assigned to Paris, Geneva, London, or Berlin. Ghana, for god's sake. She shuddered as she appeared to whenever anything was said about Africa. She decided years before she would never return to Africa and Kathy's being there had not changed her mind.

Win talked of his recent extended stay in Myanmar and the positive reception his show had received from the public and reviewers after all the trouble he encountered in getting it permitted. He hadn't told anyone in the family, other than his wife, about his encounter with the officials in Yangon and didn't intend to. He was terrified by the experience. If the authorities could shutter a gallery show of his this way, his career would be over. And then what?

Every time Win said Myanmar, instead of Burma, San seemed to hold his breath. He was quiet, knowing they would get around to his life at the *Post* soon enough, and there would be little positive to say.

Kathy broke the ice, saying, "Mom, we all know there are a couple of reasons for the meeting, so why don't we start?"

Evelyn sipped from the glass of ice tea Jerry served, not answering the question but asking, "When are Myint Thi and Anna Marie coming home, Win?"

He answered the question, "Soon, I hope, but her mother is still sick."

Evelyn shifted in her seat, then started: "I wanted to talk with all of you about this at the same time. I wish I could say, 'there's good news and bad news,' but I can't. It's hard news." Evelyn, who had appeared somewhat preoccupied at the beginning, was now openly nervous, her hand trembling as she put her glass to her lips. "I have been diagnosed with cancer, an unusual form, I'm afraid, called esophageal cancer. Obviously, it involves the esophagus."

They looked at one another, speechless. Michelle, who had arrived late because of commitments involving their children, put a comforting hand on Evelyn's shoulder. Questions started, each trying to draw out details: when and where was it diagnosed, who is the doctor, what are his qualifications, did she get a second opinion? Evelyn answered patiently. She seemed more at ease having dropped the bomb.

"I'm so sorry, Mom," San said. "What's the course of treatment the doctor's recommend?"

"Basically, there isn't much they can do. It's a type of cancer that's been at work before there are any symptoms to alert you something is wrong."

"They're finding things every day," Win said. "Surely, there is some treatment that's available."

"I've had a zillion tests: CT scans, endoscopy ultrasounds, biopsies. The prognosis isn't pretty," Evelyn added. "They can't operate. The tumor is too close to the heart. There's only a one percent chance they could get the cancer if they did operate. And I'd go through hell while trying to see if those impossible odds would pay off. It's not worth it."

Kathy got up and crouched next to her mother. She asked, "What about chemo, radiation?"

"These are things to help you, palliative is the word they use, but nothing to change the result." She looked at Kathy, San and Win, deliberately. "At age seventy I may not have reached my life expectancy, but I've had a great life. An exciting, rewarding life. Not so bad for a valley farm girl, don't you think? " Her resolve began to crack and tears started down her cheeks.

They were all quiet until San, in his take-charge role, insisted that a second opinion be obtained from the best doctors, wherever in the world they might be. Evelyn said she'd think about it, but evinced no willingness to endure more poking, needles and tests.

"My biggest worry, frankly, is the three of you, not how you'll do without me—that's not a problem, you'll do fine—but how you will be with one another. I'm distressed about the problems between the two of you," looking to San, then to Win. "Kathy, I wish you were married—this time happily. The other issue is the *Post*. You're not alone, San." Finally, the other elephant was being acknowledged, the challenge faced by the heads of all major newspaper in the country, many of whom were blamed personally for market conditions over which they have no control. "We—all of us—need to be together to support San and help him through this because there are others, and you know whom I'm talking about, who will be doing the opposite."

"Of course you can count on us, Mom," Kathy said.

Win was silent, but nodded.

"I appreciate it, Mother, but all this isn't very important given the news we've received." Evelyn didn't respond. San continued, "I welcome the support, but I don't want charity. He waved his arm at the others sitting at the table and said, "They have to believe in me."

"I'm concerned that all your father built up will be torn down," Evelyn said.

"It pains me more than you can know to have to undo anything Dad created, I promise you," San countered.

"You three have the most to gain, or lose, by what happens," Evelyn said. "You will each be inheriting the same amount, a large amount, of company stock. You have to get along together, have a common purpose, and fight for it. Above all, that's what your father wanted for you." With that pronouncement, Evelyn stood. "I'm going to have a nap. Stick around if you can and we'll have an early supper." They all rose to hug and kiss her as she walked toward the living room. The children stared at each other. What attempts there were at positive thinking were feeble. They agreed that San, given his medical connections as a member of the lay advisory board at St. Thomas Hospital, would find the best experts available on esophageal cancer.

The following Saturday, San and Win met for lunch at the Book Mark in Brentwood. Win had mentioned having lunch and San had suggested the small bistro as an artsy place, frequented by local film and TV writers and a smattering of journalists. Win arrived first and noticed there were a number of customers dressed, as he was, in trademark artists' black, so he assumed it must be a hangout for them, at least for those who could afford the fare. By contrast, San arrived in cords and a polo shirt.

They sat at a corner table. Win took a deep breath and said, "Well. . ."

"I guess it's your dime," San replied.

"Okay. When I came back," Win started, "I had something important to discuss with you. Not that it's any less important now, but with the news from Evelyn, I feel funny crowding the agenda."

"Likewise, with my problems at the *Post*. Nothing else seems very meaningful when you know she's dying. She's been my principal ally, which makes it all the tougher."

"Are we really sure nothing can be done?"

"She agreed I could talk with Dr. Rosenthal, the oncologist. It's as she said at lunch, unfortunately. Terminal and not long at that. He has an outstanding reputation. It seems nothing can be accomplished with a second opinion. And she's adamantly opposed to it."

"I don't think we should give up; there must be something that can be done," Win said.

"I'm worried about everybody's whereabouts the next few months," San said. "We really all need to be here with her."

"What about Kathy?"

"I've talked to her. She says she's been trying to get a sexy assignment for once, maybe Paris, but she'd take a temporary tour in Washington to be closer—3,000 miles—it's better than Ghana."

"And you?"

"I can cancel most of my out-of-town plans," San answered, "but there are probably a couple of Newspaper Publishers Association meetings I can't miss. Can you stay?"

"That's the issue I want to discuss. But I have to have an understanding Evelyn won't be told. I don't want to lay another problem on her."

San agreed, and Win spilled out the story about the regime's editorial demands, detaining Myint Thi and Anna Marie in Burma, and threatening Win's career as an artist there. As he related the story, he thought he saw San with a condescending "I told you so" written on his face. But San said nothing and let him continue. He paused as they ordered lunch.

"I have to ask you to lay off the Burma stuff, Aun San, until I can satisfy the officers and get my family out." He deferred by using the old name for the country, just as they both continued to use each other's Burmese name in conversation together. "I've got to remove Myint Thi, the baby, and my artwork as pawns for these guys." Actually, what he wanted to say was "these bastards," but he didn't let himself go that far. It was hard to admit he had been wrong and San had been right all along about the generals.

"It doesn't make sense for them to focus on us," San said. "We're just an independent newspaper with half a million circulation."

Win tried not to laugh. *Who do you think you're kidding? With the joint news syndication with the Washington Tribune, the Post is within reach of millions of readers and listeners every day.* "They're not dumb, you know. They completely control the press in Burma. Why not try to do it elsewhere? Second, they want to attract tourist dollars and bad publicity in the press doesn't help. Third, they hate the sanctions we impose. What better way to meet their ends than to stop the attacks—as they see it—coming from the media?"

"You know I can't turn off the editorial spigot or change the news because of a personal issue," San said.

"Why not?" People at adjacent tables turned, and San raised his index finger to his mouth. Win lowered his voice, "You turned it on when Grant died. And he had it turned off before you."

"He'd been protecting us, you, me," San replied.

"Exactly the point. They know we've done it before. Obviously, they're trying to force us to do it again. Unfortunately, their leverage is me."

"Grant built the brand and got away with a lot of things I can't. I've just inherited the brand. "

"All I'm asking is that you control the situation like he did until I can work this out."

"When Grant was running the show, Burma hadn't made Bush II's axis of bad guys list. Now, there it is right along with North Korea and Iran. Am I also supposed to ignore what's going on in those countries, too?"

Win didn't answer. Lunch was served and they began to eat, neither one with much enthusiasm. They talked about San's other problems at the *Post* and Win's experiences in Burma.

San returned to Evelyn's illness. "I don't see how you can keep this from her. She'll continue to ask when your family is coming home. She's going to think, justifiably, that they should be here, that her illness should trump whatever is wrong with Myint Thi's mother."

"Evelyn's also been my biggest supporter," Win said. "She's been there for both of us."

"Ironic, isn't it?" San replied. "The principal champion for each of us, no longer there to lean on. As I trace the past, I think it was Evelyn, not Grant, who was the real strength of the family. He was smart, had charisma, worked hard. It was almost like he was cast for the role of publisher. But she's held the family together despite, or in the face of, his tragedy. "

Win cleared his throat and placed his hands on his lap under the table so San wouldn't see they were shaking. Win had practiced his words time and time again so they'd come out as nonthreatening as possible. "There is a movement out there to replace you. Board members, investors, even some members of the family. Not Evelyn or Kathy, of course. I don't want to have to be a part of that."

"Oh, so now you're threatening me?" San shot back, dropping his napkin on the table and motioning to the waiter for a cup of coffee.

"No, I said I don't want to be involved. But I've got to do something. You must see that."

San looked out the window as an ambulance passed, siren blasting. He said, "You asked at the beginning of lunch what we can do for Evelyn."

"That's right."

"My answer," San said, "is that we can do what she begged for—our family to present a united front. We could at least take those worries off her mind. You could stay. It will only be a few months. You could even move into the house. You'd be a comfort and help to her. In the meantime, things will cool down in Burma."

"That's a joke."

"And the lawyers can find a way to get Myint Thi and Anna Marie out of the country. While I can't promise anything, I'll take more care with any Burma stories and editorials. Fair?"

"I don't know." What Win really wanted to say, however, was *Fuck you. I don't want your typical get the lawyer's solution. Besides, lawyers couldn't do a goddamned thing in Burma about this problem.*

"Tell me, Aun San, how would you feel if it were Michelle and your kids?"

"Terrible, of course, and I do for you, but there are limitations on what I can do." He looked at the ceiling for some seconds, then down. "I am not Grant. I do not have the power he had. But I will do all I can."

Win reached for the check the waiter delivered to the table.

"No, it's on me, my restaurant," San said, reaching for the bill.

"I invited you, remember. It's mine," Win's responded. He knew then he would have to do something he really didn't want to do: meet with Jane White as she had requested, no, demanded. ⌁

TWENTY-EIGHT

Skullduggery

JANE WHITE had never before asked Win for lunch alone. She didn't offer a reason for the meeting; she didn't need to. He was intimidated, as he always had been, by his aunt. She was an earthy character in a way Grant had not been. Win was also uncomfortable with the place she'd selected, the University Club. He'd not been there for years and could only remember it from starchy family gatherings during the holidays where sport coats, ties, shiny shoes and hair combed back were requirements for admission. It was one of Los Angeles's old-line, downtown clubs where the city's movers and shakers boasted membership.

Win puzzled over what to wear. He didn't own a suit. But he had an old blue blazer which, with cords, a blue shirt and an ancient rep tie, would do, he thought. He had no intention of cutting his hair to conform. Nor did he remove the small gold stud from his left earlobe. Actually, he didn't understand why his aunt wanted to have lunch there. Conformity didn't fit her rough-hewn style either. Perhaps she was making him a co-conspirator in giving the finger to the traditional conservatism that marked these rooms.

He was greeted at the front door of the club's imposing brick building by a uniformed porter who led him to his aunt. They entered a cavernous room, wood-paneled and luxuriously appointed with antiques and plein air paintings by California artists. She was deep in the middle of a large couch from which she struggled to rise by extending her hand for a lift. She planted a perfunctory kiss on his cheek. He recognized her as much by her powdery smell as by her oversized body and large facial features. She leaned on his arm for support as they walked down the hall to a spacious dining room, paneled as well in beautiful woods, where the maitre d' greeted her by name. In distinct contrast was the maître d's cool nod and "sir" to him, accompanied by a disapproving glance at his scuffed loafers. Win knew he should have shined them, but he couldn't find the polish or the shoe brush. They were led to a table for two in front of a window with a view of azaleas and greenery. Settled at the table, Jane suggested they order, then talk.

"You've wondered why I suggested lunch?"

"That's fair to say," Win answered, his voice wavering as he added, "especially here."

"Why? The price is right. I started staying here when Grant was a member and I would come to town for board meetings. Still do."

"Looks expensive to me."

"The money isn't around like it used to be. That's what I wanted to talk with you about. Under Grant the *Post* made money, lots of it. Now San is running it into the ground."

"If that's the way you feel, fine," Win said, knowing the last thing he wanted was to get into a family fight of the Whites versus the Jensens, "but I don't see how that involves me."

"What do you mean, doesn't involve you? It sure as hell involves all the members of the family. And you are a member of the family for all practical purposes, no matter that you couldn't be adopted like the other one."

"So, what are you proposing?"

"That we join together to support removing San," Jane answered. "If the family did that, it would have a huge impact on the institutional investors, whose support we need to get him out."

"My ownership interest wouldn't make a ripple."

"When a successor generation destroys a family company, people talk about the gene pool running out. Can't be said here, can it? San may have the name, but he hasn't a single Jensen gene in him," she snorted.

The "gene pool" reference pissed him off, but before he could call her on it, she continued. "You may not have a ripple yet, but you soon will when Evelyn dies. It's important the family take a united stand."

The implication of what she said hit him full force. "Aunt Jane, do you really think Evelyn ever, in a million years, would undermine San? Or that Kathy would?"

"You'll have to win them over."

"Me? No way." They were interrupted by lunch being served.

Once the waiter left the table, Jane asked, "Who are the trustees or executors under her will?"

"I don't know."

"Why not? You damn well should know," she huffed.

He shrugged.

"Do you know how the estate has been left?" she asked.

"No. I've never seen anything." He didn't mention Evelyn's recent remark that everything would be divided equally. What right did Jane have to that information?

She sipped her Chardonnay. "You see Evelyn frequently, don't you?"

"Virtually every day, and I've spent the night there when she's been agitated."

"Why don't you approach her, suggest she name you as the trustee or executor? When she dies, you will have control of the estate's interest and can vote the shares."

Win was stunned. He couldn't answer. San had been privileged to succeed Grant and then, Win thought, had done a lousy job with the responsibilities he'd been given. But, still, this was underhanded and disloyal, to Evelyn as well as to San.

"If not you for trustee or executor, then who else? Kathy is thousands of miles away. San is so busy taking care of the paper, or should be, that he doesn't have the time to deal with the estate."

"Maybe,' Win said. "But let's face it, he's the businessman, the logical one to do it; not me, a 'way-out' artist. They don't think I have a business bone in my body."

"Show them they're wrong. You can do it."

Win had as much difficulty digesting the meal as he had accepting his aunt's devious ideas. Half of the salad remained on his plate, untouched, but he threw down glass after glass of lemonade as Jane drank her Chardonnay.

"How long do they say she has?"

"We've brought hospice in. I'm afraid it won't be long."

"Actually, it's merciful in these cases if it's shorter."

"It's still hard to accept."

"Of course. You know, your mother and I have been at odds to one extent or another over the paper ever since your father died, even before that really. But I've admired and respected her. I know she was a good wife and mother." Jane's face softened, but almost as soon as it did, it hardened again. "You know this goddamned place." She thrust her arm out as if to encompass the room. "It used to be I couldn't walk in the front door, had to take a side elevator from the parking garage to the ladies dining room. I'm no feminist, but what a pile of crap."

Win had to laugh. This is the way he remembered his aunt. He couldn't begin to imagine her submitting to the club's old rule. "So, why did you do it?"

"Your dad, I guess. Didn't want to embarrass him—any more than I did by simply existing," she guffawed. "The crazy old sister from San Francisco and all that."

Win cleared his throat. "You haven't said who would replace San?"

"We don't know for sure yet. Probably your cousin Craig. That would keep it in the family. If not, I know we can attract someone good from outside. It's a plum spot."

Win wasn't surprised. Get management control of the paper for her side of the family. That was her game. He'd never been impressed by her son Craig and could hardly see how he could run the paper more effectively than San, even if San's management had been flawed.

"Think about it. I'll follow up in a couple of days," Jane said. "We don't have any time to waste."

Win walked in the direction of his loft, east of the city core. He passed Pershing Square, a pathetic answer for a city park, which was basically an underground parking garage with an ugly surface that attracted those who wanted to speak or preach to the small crowds of homeless who gathered on the park's benches. Like almost any park anywhere, it was populated more by pigeons than people. A few blocks east, he came to Spring Street—once the financial center that had housed banks and law and accounting firms that long since had migrated to the west edge of town—now increasingly home to art galleries and artists' lofts. He felt almost as uncomfortable here as he had at the University Club, wearing a blazer and loafers, though he managed to hide his tie in a pocket. Win walked the streets waiting for something in a gallery window to draw his attention. He seldom saw found-metal work like his own, which relieved him that he was not in a crowded, competitive game.

Alternatives haunted him. If he didn't acquiesce to Jane's request, he would face increasingly heavy pressure to do so. She was not one to make a suggestion and wait for the thought to germinate. On the other hand, there was Evelyn who would do anything for San and had. It was too dramatic to think Jane's plan could kill her, but Win couldn't be responsible for a downward spiral in her health. In any event, it was far from clear to him that he could influence other shareholders. San pulled within him, but not strongly. Yes, he was beholden to him, yet it could be said it was San who should be indebted to Win because San never would have come to the States without his friend. With reluctance, he decided Jane's plan to oust San was the best chance he had to be rejoined with Myint Thi and Anna Marie. ❧

TWENTY-NINE

Reading the Will

WIN SAT on a straight back chair next to Evelyn's bed, as he had for an hour or so each morning and afternoon for weeks. They talked. Occasionally she dozed. Much of the time their conversation concerned art. She had taken great joy in even the smallest development in his career, his inclusion in a group show at a local gallery being celebrated as though it were a one-man show in New York. They talked about his most recent stay in Myanmar. She could not understand why Myint Thi and Anna Marie still had not returned to the States. He skirted the question whenever it came up. How could he tell her San had to be ousted for them to be able to leave the country?

Evelyn often mentioned San and his tribulations with the *Post*. She was sympathetic, almost sorrowful, with no doubt he was doing as well as any publisher in the nation in these tough times. Her words about San were often confused as she drifted in and out. Sometimes she mentioned his name along with Grant's and the words "dark waters." Sometimes she mumbled Peter's name and smiled.

Win had moved to St. Cloud Road from his downtown loft shortly after the family meeting. He used the same bedroom he had as a child and set up an easel in San's old room. He grabbed an hour here and there to paint when Evelyn was sleeping, but he didn't feel much inspiration. He had returned to painting Burma-inspired themes from his youth, monks with flutes, oxen and carts, boats with standing fishermen dipping their nets into the water. Everything came out somber and dark. He had given up metal assemblage for the duration, except for the rare occasions when he returned to the loft for a few hours and had enough room to do that type of work.

San came by the house every Saturday and Sunday, always over Evelyn's protestations that he was too busy and needed to take care of the paper, not her. Kathy had obtained a leave and was due back soon. In addition to hospice personnel, who stopped in daily to administer the morphine drip, there were round-the-clock caregivers. The nurses were supplied by a Filipino family. Evelyn, who didn't much like people fawning over her, referred to them in a whisper as her guards.

Win had difficulty bringing himself to talk with Evelyn about financial details of the estate. He didn't know how close she thought she was to the end. The hospice people were always vague about timing. He was amazed by her fortitude. She almost never complained. The pain was deadened by morphine, but still there must be some, he thought. How does she do it?

Finally, he summoned the courage to ask. "Mom"—using the appellation at her request —"would you like to talk about how things will be taken care of when, when you're no longer here to deal with them yourself?"

"Haven't we discussed that?" Evelyn answered, "I thought we had."

"No."

"I get so confused. Maybe with San or Kathy. Sometimes I don't know what I've said or whom I've said it to."

"No, I've never known anything about the arrangements."

She struggled to pull herself up in bed, and her breathing reflected the effort. "It's very simple. Everything is divided equally between the three of you. There's a trust. I think San is the executor/trustee." She paused, then added as if an explanation were necessary, "because, you know, of his business background."

"Of course, but is that such a good idea now, do you think? Given how much he has on his plate at the paper."

"That's a point. But Kathy's never here. And," she said, "you've not seemed that interested in those affairs, my creative, artistic son, now have you?"

"I think I could handle it. I'm here and I have more time."

She looked at him without responding, then her eyes closed and she drifted off.

An hour later, Win was sitting next to the bed again, thumbing through an old issue of *Art in America* when Tina, the lead caregiver, knocked on the door. She was carrying a silver tray which held a glass of water and a small china saucer with four pills. "Time for your pills, Ma'am," she said, not looking to see whether her patient was awake or not. It was the appointed time, noon, and the pills would be taken. She nodded toward Win and said "Sir." He thought he saw her roll her eyes as she acknowledged his presence. He never knew whether the message she was sending was one of dislike or impatience. Other than the fact that she objected to preparing another meal when she was cooking for Evelyn, he didn't know what the problem was. San was a different story. Win observed that Tina always smiled and nodded to him. Probably it was because San was the one writing the weekly checks for the help. Or maybe it was because San was not there to bother her as much as he was. But it wasn't important. Why did he care?

Evelyn died seven weeks later. San and Win had been cordial to one another in Evelyn's presence, civil otherwise. Kathy had tried to add a light touch, returning them all to childhood tales of how they managed to evade Grant's house rules. Shortly before Evelyn's last breath, San thought he saw a smile on her face as they retold the story of being arrested for skateboarding in the neighbor's swimming pool.

A week after her death, San received a call at work from Tina. He couldn't remember that she had ever called him during all the time she'd been caring for Evelyn.

The voice on the phone addressed him as "Sir," which was Tina's custom. Either that or Mr. San.

"Yes, Tina."

"There is something I wanted to tell you, Mr. San . . ."

"How are you, Tina?" He interrupted. "We so appreciate everything you did for Mother."

"Thank you, Sir. She was a fine woman. It was a privilege to work for her."

"Yes, she was."

An awkward silence lingered until he asked, "What can I do for you?" She had been given a $10,000 bonus, which he felt was generous for the time she'd been on duty at St. Cloud Road. Was she calling for more, he wondered.

"It's about Mr. Win, Sir. I don't know how to say this, but I'm afraid he was trying to pressure your mother about her will, and I thought you should know."

San turned his back on the photographs of his father and grandfather that seemed increasingly to convey criticism as the *Post* moved into the doldrums. While they had faced difficulties during their tenures, nothing had happened that brought into question the very existence of the newspaper industry. Tina's news about Win wasn't a great surprise but it did disappoint him. "How do you know this?"

"The baby monitor by her bed, so she could call us or we could ask how she was." She added, in a defensive tone, "I overheard it, Mr. San. Mrs. Jensen never turned it off."

"What did he say?"

"He said he thought he should be the person to represent the estate, that you were too busy with the newspaper to have to take care of the estate as well."

"Really. What else?" San asked, fearing the answer.

"Something about the house, either that he would like it or would like to live there, it wasn't clear."

"What did Mother say?"

"She asked questions, said how much she appreciated all of you, and then would fall back into the past. I never heard her say yes or no, Sir."

San fought to remain calm. "When was this?"

"Different conversations over the last few weeks. He seemed to bring it up more and more as time passed. Then one day, somebody came, a man, I think a lawyer. I don't know. I was given the afternoon off which was unusual. After that, I didn't hear Mr. Win talk about it anymore."

San knew he had to be careful how he phrased the next question. "Is there some reason you didn't mention this to me before?"

"I was afraid he might fire me, Mr. San, and I knew it was important to your mother for me to be there with her till the end."

Damn him, San thought. Sneaking around. If he questioned the arrangements, he should have come to him as the trustee of the estate. For Christ's sake, he shouldn't have been pressuring Evelyn on her death bed. "Tina, I may ask you to sit down with the lawyers and get this all down in detail."

"Whatever is necessary, Sir."

San had not been diligent about getting the estate processes going. He knew Clyde Thomas held the will and trust in his office, signed about two years ago. San was aware of what it provided as a result of lengthy discussions with Evelyn about what she wanted. Everything was to be split equally between the three children. That was after one large charitable gift, $1,000,000 to Cal for the planned Jensen Family Wing of a new campus library.

San picked up the phone and told Thomas what he had learned. They decided to call an all hands meeting to review the will. San speculated about problems that might arise. He knew that Win had been obsessed by what he saw as an unfair advantage: that San had already received his share, millions in salary, benefits and stock awards, whereas Win was an SA, as he referred to himself, a starving artist. But San knew his rewards had not been obtained unfairly. He'd worked his ass off for years coming up in the company and finally assuming the mantle of leadership in the toughest period for newspapers in history. In the meantime, Evelyn supported Win, he was sure of that, his loft, his travels back and forth to Burma, who knows what else. Win could hardly be accused of having a disciplined work ethic.

The "reading" of the will came at a meeting at Thomas's office in Century City five days later. The offices were understated with dark green carpets, conservatively upholstered couches and chairs, antique reproductions, and Spy prints on the dark wood-paneled walls. San had told Kathy what he learned from Tina so she wouldn't be surprised. She tended to be soft on Win and had trouble believing he could have done anything so destructive to their family relationship. She thought there must be an innocent explanation for what Tina had overheard. From what she knew about baby monitors, there wasn't much of anything you could hear clearly anyway.

Everyone was seated at a conference table on which were stacked several thick files. Thomas sat at the end of the table and opened the meeting. "It's time we got the estate proceedings under way. I've been over these files. As you can imagine, they go back many years to when your grandfather was a fairly young man. The most recent documents were executed by your mother on January 6, two years ago."

"That is not the most recent will," Win interjected.

"What do you mean?" Thomas said, less as a question than a declaration.

"Here is the will she signed six weeks ago. Obviously, it's more current."

"Who prepared that will?" the lawyer asked.

"Foster Kranz. He has offices here on the west side."

"Never heard of him," Thomas sniffed.

"She wanted to see a lawyer who was 'independent,' as she put it. She asked me if I would find someone, and I did."

"You could have come to me for a referral," Thomas said.

"She worried you'd be insulted."

"Did you inform Kathy and San?"

"No."

"Why not?"

"We were under so much pressure with her illness and all. I didn't think it was time to get involved with, shall we say, the business aspects of things. There would be plenty of time later."

"Let me see the document," Thomas said, unwilling to acknowledge its status as a will.

Win handed the lawyer a sheaf of papers. The silence in the room was cut only by the sound of pages being flipped by the lawyer. Finally, after what felt like an hour, rather than minutes, he spoke. "Obviously, I've only had time to scan it, but the provisions of this document are very different from the ones I drew. First, no trust is created, meaning that the estate would have to go through the cumbersome, time-consuming and expensive process of being probated, which Mr. Kranz should well know. More fees to him, more expense to you, that way. That's not true with the will and trust I prepared. Also," he turned to San, "it makes Win the executor with full powers during the probate. Unlike the earlier trust, you do not have a role. And the will gives the family house to Win to live in as long as he is acting as executor." He hesitated, then added, "That could be a long time."

San felt like confronting Win, but Thomas had told him to keep calm no matter what happened. He was sitting at the conference table next to Kathy whose hand he felt pat him on the knee. Otherwise, she sat rigid, looking down, never at Win.

"Under what circumstances was this signed? Where, when?" Thomas glared at Win.

"I anticipated you might want to discuss that, so I brought Mr. Kranz along. He's waiting in the reception room and can answer those questions. In fact, he arranged to have the will signing videotaped. He has it here to show you. Shall I have him come in?"

San rose from his chair. "Wait a minute." His face flushed. "What the fuck do you mean, 'videotaped it? Why?"

Kathy seemed startled as though she wasn't used to her usually cool, dignified brother reacting in a charged way.

"Mr. Kranz recommended it," Win answered, "so there couldn't be any question down the road as to how the matter was handled."

"What did Mother think was going on, Win?" Kathy asked. "Was that fair to her? I really can't believe you would do this . . . after all she did for you."

San interrupted. "He did it to cover his fucking ass. That's what it amounts to." He was standing over Win, almost hyperventilating.

Thomas tried to intervene with a calm warning that everyone ought to take a deep breath. He admonished San to let him be the lawyer and ask the questions.

But San would not be stopped. "I won't watch it. Our Mother on her death bed being treated like some sort of a puppet."

"We're getting nowhere," Thomas said. "Let's end this meeting, and I'll talk with Kranz and find out what he has to say. I'll watch the video. San and Kathy, you don't need to see it, now or ever."

Win asked to be excused to talk with Kranz. Thomas, San and Kathy remained in the room. "The big problem," Kathy said, "is really less what Win has done than it is what has happened to us as a family. Thank God, Mother isn't here to see this."

"I don't buy the idea we are somehow all equally to blame. No, I'm sorry." San hit the table with the palm of his hand. "Clyde, I want to do whatever is necessary, I don't care what it costs, to fight this so-called will. What Win forgets is that the reason he's here in the first place is because I brought him here."

"Why did he want to be the executor so badly," Kathy said. "It's not his cup of tea to track business matters."

"I'll tell you why. He wants my ass out. It will give him the official standing to accomplish that."

"Even with the estate's share in the *Post*, and it's a lot, it won't give him control," Thomas said.

"No, but it's the picture he can paint. The estate and the extended family, led by the White clan of course, are against me. That could swing others over. Everybody's mad as hell about the stock price anyway." San rose and strode to the window. "There'll be a hell of a fight. Kathy. You mentioned Mom not being here to see this. I'd say double that for Dad." ∿

THIRTY

Escaping the Curse

WIN STRUGGLED over what to do about San, who had hardly spoken to him following the disclosure of the new will. He didn't *want* to undermine him, no matter what had happened between them, but it appeared he had no choice. The junta had shown how it could keep Aung San Suu Kyi from leaving to visit her terminally ill husband in London. She knew she would never be permitted to return to her country once she left. Not that his case had anything like the profile of the beloved Suu Kyi, but it did reinforce the power of the generals to curb freedom of travel. Win didn't know whether they'd change their position based solely on San being removed or whether an actual change in editorial policy would have to be demonstrated, but anyone at the paper's helm would be viewed as less strident on Myanmar than San.

Jane White, the bulldozer, wouldn't take an "I'm not sure" or "maybe" answer from Win. She wanted a commitment. She ranted about San permitting the *Post* to print the story "damning" her husband—"his own uncle, for Christ's sake"—for his company's problems in Myanmar. She claimed to represent the feelings of other, more distant members of the family who had no one employed by the newspaper, but who still could trace a bloodline to the founder. Even a handful of large shareholders—mutual funds, hedge funds, universities—were pressuring Win to join the pack of bloodhounds seeking San's ouster.

It was no answer for Win to explain that as executor he didn't have that many shares, two million, compared to many multiples of that held by others. The response came back from Jane that if he joined the clamor, there would be no one left to hold back the tide against San, and the board would have to ask him to resign.

Outwardly, San showed no weakness. He was energetic, involved, positive. But as months passed, the *Post's* situation continued to deteriorate. It became an almost intolerable environment. The bottom was falling out of the company's stock. Investors were screaming. A hostile bid for control could strike at any time.

Win decided to talk with San one more time to see if he could convince him to step down voluntarily. He knew the best way to do that was to involve Kathy. She was upset with both San and Win but was desperate to find a way to restore family unity. The idea was hers: the three of them would spend a long weekend together at their home in Aspen and talk with Burton Isaacs, who had worked with the family before. She hoped he might be able to help them understand their differences because he specialized in representing families, like theirs, of substantial wealth who continued to manage family-founded businesses. Isaacs's practice flourished because the model, where family factions were often pitted against one another, was a recipe for trouble. Aspen seemed a logical place to Kathy since they had passed many vacations there as children and Isaacs worked from his home in Aspen during the summer. San and Win acceded to her request, agreeing that a lawsuit would bring uncertain results and huge costs in attorneys' fees. But they gave their consent with hesitation, each doubting the other would move to heal the breach.

Standing in front of a picture window in the living room of the family's West End home, Isaacs laid out an agenda for their discussions. The house was comfortable but not elaborate, a vintage seventies structure built of wood and river rock. The first day was to include a morning "work" session where each member of the family was to state the concerns or interests that were getting in the way of the relationship between the three of them. This process would get those problems on the table in a calm and reasoned way. Nobody's position was a complete surprise to the lawyer, who had asked for private meetings with each in advance. This would be followed by a "mini-outward bound" type excursion in the afternoon. Isaacs knew the Jensens were frequent hikers who, he assumed, could handle the outdoor team-building part of the experience. Less clear was whether he, a relatively short man with a belly that protruded over his belt, would be up to it as well, but he was calling the shots. The second day would hopefully find the parties coming to a consensus on plans for the future.

Win went first and complained that he had been unfairly accused of having influenced Evelyn in her decisions about the estate. He resented the fact that San was fighting him on what were her decisions. "It was what she wanted at the end of her life. The videotape showed she was fully competent to make the decisions she did. She wanted me to administer the estate."

San, who had been looking out the window at the mountain on which they all had skied and hiked for so many years, slammed a yellow legal pad against his knee. "That's a lie. It's not what she wanted. It's what Nyan Win wanted. He pressured her when she was in a weakened condition. He subjected her to being videotaped."

Isaacs interrupted. "And that's the purpose of your lawsuit, to invalidate the will Kranz prepared?"

"Of course."

"And a ruling is pending?"

"Yes, and while I've been told by the lawyers not to disclose this, I can't sit here and just listen anymore. We have proof, Nyan Win, that you pressured Evelyn. Tina heard you doing it." He proceeded to explain what Tina had told him Win had said.

"She's not telling the truth," Win answered. "There were no business matters discussed in Tina's presence, ever."

"She heard it on the fucking baby monitor. Clear as a bell. And she'll testify to it." San stared at Win whose face seemed to be turning whiter.

"You see, Burton," San said, "control of the estate is not enough. From Nyan Win's newly anointed position as executor, he's maneuvering to force me out. Apparently, he doesn't want the job himself. At least he's realistic on that score. He wants an outsider whom he thinks can reverse conditions in the industry that have reduced dividends to a point that won't support his life style. Getting out and working at a real job has never been on his radar."

Win's voice cracked. "Making a living as an artist isn't easy. I can use all the help I can get. But what do I get at the *Post*? A review of my Madison Gallery show claiming I had marched backward in ignoring my found-metal paintings in favor of the 'sappy, realistic paintings of iconic Buddhist images' that I had painted before. I asked San to kill the review but he refused, saying it was a clear case of editorial independence and he couldn't interfere."

Kathy squirmed in her chair, then started to review the history from her perspective. She had opposed San and Win coming to live with them in the first instance, but didn't veto the idea in deference to her parents. She never believed the estate should be divided equally in thirds, and said so, but she was prepared to accept that division now in order to resolve the issues between them. "What I am not prepared for is for you, Win, to use your position as executor to oust San. I'm certain my mother and my father would have fought that."

Win interrupted. "Let me give an example, Burton." He pointed his finger at San. "He approves harshly worded editorials and reports critical of the regime in Myanmar. I have a wife and a child who are in that country and who are in danger because of what the *Post* writes."

"Then go there yourself and protect them," San interjected. "Obviously, I can understand your wanting to be with your family, but don't put the blame on the paper—or on me."

Glancing at Kathy, then Isaacs, San continued. "So, that's why he wants me out. If I'm not the publisher, he thinks our editorial policy on Burma could revert to its soft tone under Grant. Then he wouldn't have to worry anymore about Myint Thi and Anna Marie."

Win replied in a tough tone. "You can't make it anyway, Aun San. You have no support, so I don't feel guilty going along with the many other investors who are seeking a different answer."

"It would be unbelievable to Grant," San said, "that a member of the family would be prepared to sacrifice the principles on which the paper was founded by compromising editorial policy."

"You seem to have forgotten," Win said, "that he did that very thing to protect us."

"No. He upheld the paper's standards, always," San snapped back.

The discussion continued to circle until Isaac offered a diversion. "Some of the basic issues are on the table. We're going to break now and take a hike. Nobody has to talk but all have to take part. I've picked out Truro Lake up Independence Pass. I was there years ago, and a lot of the climb requires bushwhacking, so I've hired a guide. There's a beautiful glacial lake at the summit. You all appear to be in good enough shape to make it with no problem. We'll continue our discussion there. "

Truro Lake lay off the beaten track in the mountains east of Aspen, a long drive up Lincoln Creek Road toward Grizzly Reservoir. There had been almost nothing said as Otto, the guide, drove the Land Rover, except grumbles by the jostled passengers about the miserable condition of the bladed, bumpy dirt road where holes and rocks prevented all but SUVs from navigating the terrain. No one seemed to be

admiring the beauty of the surroundings, the flow of the creek plung-
ing over boulders next to the road, the forests, the meadows, the
fields of wildflowers. Otto parked on the side of the road beyond the
reservoir, then led the contingent across a marshy meadow toward
the mountain. They were already at 10,700 feet according to the guide.
The lake, at 12,500 feet, presented a steep hike.

They crossed the meadow, passed through willows, and started
up the mountain, making their way, sometimes on a hiking trail,
other times on animal paths, among trees, over streams, and through
deadfall in fields of yellow senecio, blue columbine, and rosy paint-
brush. Isaacs repeated claims —"I think this may be it," "Oh, I seem
to remember this"—affirmed the wisdom of having hired a guide.
The hikers spread out, each walking at his or her own pace, stopping
occasionally to sip from a water bottle or wipe a brow. Otto took the
lead, pausing from time to time like a retriever, apparently to be sure
everyone was in view. The weather was brisk, and a mild wind rustled
the aspens and whistled through the pines. Some would question
starting a hike in the high country at midday in August considering
the potential for sudden afternoon thunder and lightning storms, but
the skies were clear as they began their trek.

After a short time, they reached timberline at about 11,500 feet.
No longer were there trees for the breezes to blow through, though
gusts of winds could be heard blowing down in crevices and gullies, a
harsher sound precisely because it wasn't softened by quaking leaves
and swaying branches.

The guide came to a field of scree and boulders, rising a hundred and fifty feet up a steep slope. At the upper edge of the field
was an arch formed by warped timbers that marked the entrance to
an old mine. San, behind Otto, climbed up to explore the area. The
entrance to the abandoned mine shaft was not high, about five and
half feet, and hadn't been blocked shut. Miners in the late 1800s
were short men, and the shafts were just tall enough for them to
stand erect, at least most of the time. The hikers today would have

to duck to make their way through the narrow passage and around the logs and debris littering the floor of the dark tunnel. Otto yelled to the group below. "It's an old mine, come up and see." He had told them stories of hikers who had abruptly met bears who made their homes in these dark places.

Kathy, still at the bottom of the scree field, leaned against a large, shoulder high boulder and took a swig from her water bottle. Win, about eight feet behind her, sat on a low, flat stone and shook his head, as if to say "not for me." He asked Kathy to wait. "There's another thing. I know it's hard to understand my position when you don't have all the facts. What I can't say to him is that I will never see my wife or child again unless and until the *Post's* attacks stop."

"You didn't menton that before."

"I'm afraid to. It could result in a tirade about the injustice of the regime that would worsen matters."

"Tell him and trust him." She turned to see Win grimace.

"He won't listen," he said under his breath.

A pika chirped from its rock home warning others of intruders. Isaacs passed Kathy and Win and started up the scree, struggling to make his way through the rocks as one might expect of a New York lawyer who obviously enjoyed his food and wine. He had to plant a boot against a boulder or wedge a knee in a void between rocks and pull himself forward. In other areas, where the stones were smaller, he had to take care because they weren't firmly embedded. It was tough going, and his breathing came deep and hard. When he was within about fifteen feet of the mine entrance, he pushed his foot against a boulder, wedged one knee between two others and started to muscle himself up, straining with his arms and hands. As he braced his foot on a stone, it gave way, taking other loose rocks with it which pounded down the hill. He scrambled to grasp a secure boulder.

Kathy saw the rocks tumbling down toward them and jumped behind the boulder she'd been resting against. She yelled, "Win, move. Landslide." Win, who was sitting in the path of the rock fall, looked up, seemingly frozen until the last minute when he dove behind two boulders. The crack of rock on rock, frightening at the beginning, began to diminish. The slide rumbled to an end, leaving dust hovering in the air as the hikers made their way toward the boulders where Win had disappeared. He was just beginning to stand, dusty but not bloody. Otto looked at Win, "Are you okay?"

"I think so."

"The rest of you?" Otto asked, his eyes moving from person to person.

Everyone seemed to be untouched.

"That was a close one," Otto said. "There could still be unstable rocks here. Let's move to the clearing over there away from the scree."

The hikers did as they were told.

Isaac was the first to speak. "We're very lucky, you understand? One, or more, of us could have been wiped out by that."

"Maybe it was meant to happen this way," Kathy said, "to help us get our own problems in perspective. People go through worse things than we have."

"Worse things than loosing Grant?" Isaac asked.

"No, that's as bad as it gets," Kathy answered. "And Peter too. In neither case a body to make closure possible."

"So, Nyan Win, it appears you have avoided the Jensen family curse," San said.

"What does that mean?" Win asked, brow furrowed.

"Just that; others in the family who have been in serious accidents have died. You have been in an accident and avoided even minor injury. You are a lucky man."

"I see. I wondered whether it was intended as a comment on my position —or lack thereof—in this family."

"No. It was not."

"We should be getting back," Isaacs said. It's getting late. On our return, we need to start finding solutions." Isaacs stood and, with the rest of the contingent, followed the guide down the mountain. ∾

THIRTY-ONE

The Knife

C ONTINUING CONVERSATIONS at the house did not led to a breakthrough, and the effort ended no closer to a solution than when they arrived. Frustrated, Isaac stepped away. The fortunes of the *Post* continued to deteriorate, and a host of vocal dissidents unleashed an orgy of criticism at the man in charge. Win assumed a role in the assault, calling unhappy family members and board members whose votes would influence whether San remained. Eventually, a small delegation of the most important of the *Post's* directors asked for a meeting with San. It took place late one afternoon in January, 2006 in a large antiseptic conference room down the hall from San's office. The group was headed by Taylor Malone, the first director recruited by San and the CEO of States Bank, the largest bank still headquartered in Los Angeles. The others were chairs of three of the board's most important committees: audit, compensation, and nominating/governance. Two had first become directors during Grant's tenure.

"San, I'll be direct. We've come to ask for your resignation," Malone said, chin thrust forward giving him a look of determination.

Malone didn't offer the reason, nor did San ask. His fears about the purpose of the meeting had been confirmed. "Taylor, you're on this board because of me, remember?"

"I do."

"And the rest of you. Are you in agreement with this?"

"We are," one answered, the others exchanging glances at one another, then nodding.

"You all have your positions on this board because of me." San smirked. "Strange thing. Having selected my own executioners."

Seconds passed, feeling like minutes. San cleared his throat. "We're doing as well as other newspapers. Better than some, aren't we?"

"Yes," Malone answered.

"I saved our ass by avoiding the *Examiner* acquisition," San said, referring to a so-called expansion opportunity that, in reality, would have turned out to be a high debt trap.

"That's true, too."

"And, Taylor, you supported that acquisition, as I recall."

"Yes, I did. I was wrong as things played out."

"You couldn't predict where this business was going any better than I. Doesn't that count for anything?"

"Of course. But a majority of the board feels you haven't provided the kind of leadership needed to deal effectively with the changes wrought by the digital world."

It sounded to San as if the words had been scripted for a memorized delivery. He would make sure his weren't. "Bullshit, Taylor. Who has?" he asked.

Malone dodged the question. "You know what we're facing. In the new world of director responsibility, we can't just stand by. We're forced to act."

"Covering your ass is the conventional way to put it, I think."

Again, there was no response.

"A sacrificial offering is not required in the new world, or old," San said. "You approved every major move. Not one of you cast a dissenting vote—ever."

Malone rose and extended his hand, saying, "We are sorry, genuinely sorry. Please let me know your answer." San did not take his hand. The others fumbled, thanking San for what he had done or offering words to affirm their friendship.

As they were exiting the conference room, San asked, "Who will be my replacement?"

"Bill Farley—in a temporary capacity till a permanent replacement is found, and then he will retire."

"He's agreed?" San frowned.

"Yes." Malone closed the door quietly.

Even Farley? San leaned forward to the center of the table where a stack of yellow lined legal pads rested in a black leather box. He took one off the top and slung it side-armed across the room. The pad bounced off the window and fell to the floor. He dropped his head to the table's cold surface and spread his arms. *The sanctimonious bastards. Nobody did a goddamned thing but agree to what I proposed, ever. Never came up with ideas, no solutions, never helped us get business, pushed bad deals.*

He raised his head and looked west toward the ocean. The sun was balanced on the horizon, about to disappear. He waited for the green flash; he had never seen the phenomenon that was supposed to occur as the sun set below the horizon. Orange streaks in the clouds with grey slices at the bottom were forming. Another gorgeous Los Angeles sunset was raging through the sky. *And Farley, Grant's right hand. My mentor. Without him, there's no way to fight. Nowhere to turn. It's over, fuck it, it's over. Thank God Grant isn't here to see it.*

The rush of anger mixed with a strange feeling, almost relief. After years of fighting against the *Post's* inexorable decline, at least it was now in the open, no longer did he have to wonder where most of his directors stood. But he was left with the question of which of the directors, all of whom he counted as friends and colleagues, were still in his camp. He'd find out soon enough. Would those who still supported him take a stand and resign with him? Or sidle up to him and whisper they were in his corner all along? Every one of them had been honored to be a *Post* director. It was a prestigious corporate board anybody would want to join, at least until the paper's problems became a quagmire demanding excessive time commitments.

The story came out on the *Post's* front page, above the fold, with the bold headline reading "*Post* Scion Resigns as Publisher." No effort was made in the story to mask the resignation as a retirement. No vague plans were announced, not even that he was leaving to spend more time with family or pursue other interests. The story was about how San had succeeded his father at a young age when his father drowned at sea, how Grant Jensen had himself succeeded his father a generation before, and how San's leaving ended the family dynasty. The stories of San's unique origins and adoption and success in the business and civic worlds in Los Angeles were glowing. The disasters in the newspaper world were referenced in a way so as to portray San sympathetically as a victim of the storm pummeling the industry.

As it turned out, not a single director resigned with him. ∼

THIRTY-TWO

An Unheralded Return

WIN HESITATED as he approached immigration at the Yangon Airport. Stations on the left bore the sign "Residents," on the right "Non-Residents." He had been denied permission to return to his birth country for more than two years. Communications with Myint Thi during the interim had been restricted to letters and an occasional telephone call. Still, he guessed, he qualified as a Resident. At least he would try it; the queue was shorter. He was tense, yet excited, anticipating the reunion with his family. He advanced toward the window. The agent glumly rummaged through his new passport and visa, then clicked on the computer, hesitated, and studied him. Finally, the man began to stamp documents in rapid fire succession, a hollow thump marking each motion. He pushed the papers back, inclining his head toward the exit as if to indicate his captive was released.

Win had not been able to get over the fear that the regime would deny him permission to return, even though San had been ousted from the *Post*. There was no way to count on the junta to provide free access to him and his family. He worried that the authorities would impose some additional condition, such as an editorial lauding the junta, or, at a minimum, the passage of a certain amount of time without the paper criticizing the government, before he or his family would be permitted to travel. As it turned out, it was only typical bureaucratic red tape that had resulted in six months of delay and frustration after San was out before Win recieved permission.

Win proceeded through customs with his two carry-on bags, one with personal belongings, one with presents for his family. He had wanted to bring more, but feared it would complicate his re-entry. He submitted a customs form showing nothing to declare and exited to a public area where he spotted his wife holding their three-year-old daughter. He half-ran to thow his arms around them, kissing and holding tight. Myint Thi smiled and turned to Anna Marie to explain "this is your Daddy." The little girl looked down and said nothing. He wanted to cry. Finally, his family was at his side again.

A man in uniform stepped toward them and introduced himself by name and rank. He didn't have to give his rank; Win knew from the uniform, the ribbons and the medals, that he was a lieutenant in the military. Win wiped his eyes with his sleeve. The officer asked "Is there anything I can do for you?" Win replied, "Thank you, but no." He knew full well the officer was not there to help, but to convey the message that he'd hit the government radar and had better watch his step.

Win hailed a broken-down, vintage taxi to take them to the loft they had shared before he left Yangon and where Myint Thi and Anna Marie had lived since. The vehicle was cramped and without air-conditioning. He was struck by the dusty, rough roads, the teeming bicycles, the monks and nuns in colorful robes, and the moldy smell that flowed through the cab's open windows. It was all so different from Los Angeles, from St. Cloud Road. Not that he would ever be returning to live in that house. With Kathy's intervention, the estate issues had been settled. The home was to be sold and the proceeds, expected to be more than five million dollars, divided equally between the three, as was the rest of the estate. When they were Aspen with Isaacs, Kathy told them in no uncertain terms, "We all have to grow up and be grateful for what we have, not dwell on what we don't," words sounding as though they had been scripted by Evelyn. Burton Isaacs had also been a force in compromising the differences between the two wills. The executorship question became moot when San was substituted for Win who was leaving for Myanmar and could hardly deal with the estate from there. San and Win never had to meet with each other personally on the solution.

A screened-porch area off the main room of the loft served as Anna Marie's bedroom. Breezes and a clicking ceiling fan provided some relief from the afternoon heat. Win read a book in English to her. He kissed her on the cheek and hugged her. How many times had he imagined being able to hold his daughter this way?

As soon as Anna Marie fell asleep Win and Myint Thi tumbled into their bed and started to make up for the years they'd been separated. Win couldn't help wondering what Myint Thi had done all that time without him—without, he hoped, any man. He knew what he had done and felt shame for it, which added to his guilt for the luxurious way he had lived in Bel Air, compared to the life his wife and daughter had here.

They held each other. The years had seemed like a life-time. Now they were back together as one, as though they had never been apart. Myint Thi whispered, "I love you." He tightened his arms around her, they kissed, he thrust, they merged.

Win sat up in bed. "You'll never know how much I wanted you with me."

"Or how much I wanted to be with you. I contacted the people in the government you told me to. No one would help me."

"At least things are better now thanks to an agreement on the estate. San and I will never be close again, but we are at a place, I think, where we can have some relationship without hating each other."

Win soon found himself caught up in Yangon life. He visited the National University Museum and prowled the better galleries showing Burmese artists. Without being obvious about it, he tried to find out if the junta still censored the arts. No one would speak openly, but heads nodded and voices dropped implying it was true. Win's career was all but dead. His bi-continental life had made it almost impossible for him to function successfully either place. The political pressures in Myanmar erected barriers there. A once mildly enthusiastic following in Los Angeles had disappeared, reflecting, he feared, how important Evelyn had been to his career there. He was now only an observer, a critical one with knowledge and an eye, but he was out of the game and became seriously depressed about it. Haunting places where he had enjoyed some acclaim only deepened the darkness. He and Myint Thi talked frequently of when and how they would return to California and came closer to making the move with each passing day. ⌇

THIRTY-THREE

The Saffron Rebellion

S AN LINGERED at the breakfast table over a cup of black coffee, reading the *Post* and the *New York Times* before he headed to the office he'd set up in the guest house of his Bel Air home. The telephone rang. He picked up the receiver and heard the voice of Paul Drum, an old Berkeley fraternity brother who had, rather miraculously given his lackluster record in college, been named U.S. Deputy Secretary of State for Southeast Asia. Drum explained that the State Department wanted San to join a United Nations mission to Myanmar to observe the "Saffron Revolution," so-called because thousands of monks were suffering atrocities for marching and demonstrating in the streets against the *tatmadaw*, the military junta that ruled the country. He said reliable sources on the ground were needed to gather information and make an assessment of the situation. San was aware of the charges because of the news coming out of Thailand, as reports direct from Burma were blocked by the regime. The Internet had also been disabled.

"How many people will be on this mission?" San asked.

"Just three. One each from Italy, Japan and the U.S."

"Paul, they wouldn't take me. I'm not very popular there, to say the least."

"They have to accept the mission because of international pressure. They can't effectively refuse. We're entitled to name one person. That's you."

"Why me?"

"Obviously, it helps that you were born there and know the language. You've had a distinguished career and are highly respected. Need I say more?"

"And I look like them. What is this, really? A covert operation?"

"No, it's all open and above board. San, there are a half million monks in the country. Who knows where this could go."

"The question is whether I can be neutral. I have a long, unhappy history with the military there."

"I remember from school. Your parents."

"Yes, murdered by the regime." San never believed they were involved in drug running. "Also we've run negative editorials in the *Post*."

"You'll be fact-finding based on what you see. Apparently, the mayhem is not even debatable."

"Is it safe under these conditions?" San asked.

"You'll have U.N. security twenty-four/seven."

After discussing details as to who, when and where, San said that he would talk with his wife and call him back.

San found Michelle at her desk working on the annual fundraiser for the City of Los Angeles Art Museum. She served as board chair, a perfect position given her influence in the community and her past experience as painting curator at a New York museum. He knew he had to approach her carefully about Drum's proposal, even though she had been urging him for months to involve himself in something, get his body out of the house and his nose out of the papers. She often seemed impatient with his ranting about the newspaper world, scouring the *Post* and *New York Times* every morning to find points to criticize, anywhere from typos to editorials. She was also upset with his drinking which, she felt, had become an increasing problem since he was fired. She had urged him to stop. He didn't.

He sat on a chair across from her desk as he outlined the details of the invitation.

She frowned. "When would you go?"

"Right away."

"When we're supposed to be leaving for Aspen in two days to celebrate my birthday?"

"I'm sorry. I know it's terrible timing, but I have no control over that. We could go to Aspen as soon as I get back. In about a week."

Michelle rose from her desk and walked to the window. "San, you know I want to see you engaged, but entering a war zone is not what I had in mind."

"We'll be with U.N. people all the time."

"No one can assure you of complete protection when you've been on the government's radar the way you have."

"I feel I need to go, Michelle. These are, after all, my people. They're being slaughtered. Besides, maybe it's time Win and I talked. It can't happen by telephone."

"Where did you get that idea?" she asked.

"Kathy, mostly."

"I expected as much." Michelle had little tolerance for Win after his role in San's firing, and was not patient with Kathy's attempts to smooth over problems between the two men. "I wish she would stay out of it."

"She means well," San answered.

Michelle picked wilting tulips from a bouquet on her desk, dropping them, one by one, into a waste paper basket. "I don't like the idea of your going there. I'm worried something terrible might happen." She turned. "But I do understand it's important to you. You'll have to decide for yourself."

San had limited time to plan. He couldn't get Win off his mind: whether or not he should try to see him. He telephoned Kathy in Paris and asked her opinion. "I'm still mad about what he did to you and what he did to Mom with the videotape," she said. "Still, he is our brother, and brothers don't always act in ways that make you love them. How do you feel? You're the one who's been hurt the most."

"I keep coming back to what Mom and Dad would want me to do. They'd want us to resolve our problems. Besides, even after all these years, I can't get away from the feeling I'm responsible for him somehow."

Two days later San flew from Los Angeles to Bangkok to meet the U.N. staff and other members of the mission. A driver met him at the Bangkok airport to take him to the Oriental Hotel where he found a message from a U.N. representative. They would have to leave for Myanmar earlier in the morning than planned, as problems in Yangon were escalating by the hour.

San met his counterparts in the morning at breakfast: Paulo Calabrese from Italy and Kaoru Tanaka from Japan, providing representation from Asia, Europe and the Western Hemisphere. The U.N. representative, David Wang, briefed them and handed out more background material to read in flight. Wang advised they would travel everywhere as a group. They should not go out of their hotel unaccompanied. The U.N. was responsible for their safety. The streets were perilous with the turmoil and protests. He warned they would be followed by spies from the police Special Branch and needed to be careful what they said and did in public. Not just in public; it was entirely possible their rooms would be bugged.

The air was close and hot in the Rangoon Airport as they proceeded through immigration and customs. Swarms of people stood in long lines, their chatter subdued. San felt that some of them looked at him out of the corners of their eyes. His legs shook; his palms were sweaty. He wanted to feel excitement about returning to familiar scenes he had left almost thirty years before. Instead, he feared at every step he might be stopped. He even found himself speaking in a whisper to Tanaka and Calabrese.

Paperwork complete, the group boarded a van to the hotel. San was struck by how similar Rangoon was to what it had been when he left. The exteriors of the old colonial buildings were peeling then; they were today, though somehow the structures looked smaller to him now. Telephone and electrical wires crisscrossed above the streets in masses of confusion, which he remembered from his childhood. Riders still clung to the backs of buses. The streets were alive with people, vehicles bumping along, and bikers twisting their way through the crowds, often with riders occupying a side seat.

They arrived at the Governor's Residence Hotel. San dithered about calling Win, picking up, then replacing the phone in his room several times without completing the call. He would make contact later, he decided. The delegation started its fact finding investigation traveling at a crawl down University Avenue. Security personnel walked alongside the vehicle. A wide swath of crimson robes and shaved heads moved at a deliberate pace in the center of the street. The red tide chanted prayers for democracy, thousands of voices joining the chorus, as horns and sirens blared. People lined the potholed streets, arms locked in a human chain to protect the robed men from uniformed, helmeted military and police. Monks carried colorful flags and signs written in Burmese, one of which San understood to read "Love and kindness must win over everything." He could see love and kindness among those protecting the monks, but none among the police and soldiers who had cordoned off side streets with barbed wire and stood side by side, their grey metal shields thrust forward to form an impassable barrier. They threatened through bullhorns, waved rifles, and wielded crowbars and wooden clubs in the faces of the monks marching in the misty weather.

David Wang turned from the front passenger seat to explain the demonstrators were headed to the home of Aung San Suu Kyi—rather, he said "to her prison" where she had spent thirteen years under house arrest, without television, telephone, Internet and with few visitors. "She's a true hero to her countrymen, a symbol of the democracy they're being denied under the regime," Want declared.

"Why are the monks all carrying their bowls upside down?" San asked.

Wang answered. "They carry their bowls that way as a symbol of rejection of the food on which they're dependent. It's a protest against the regime. Having the monks involved frightens the military. It's the monks who lend what little legitimacy the junta has."

Rifle shots sounded. Wang yelled "down." The van bumped to a stop, then jerked forward. Overturned hulks of torched cars and trucks dotted the side of the road. Acrid smoke wafted from smoldering seats. Wang carefully raised his head toward the bottom of the windows. "They're shooting above the heads of the protestors to scare them, but stay down." He added "It's not all simply warning. Look, quickly, over there. The monks are tied to the utility poles. And those," he pointed to the sidewalk "are being forced to kneel with hands on the back of their heads and are beaten if they move."

San couldn't remove his eyes from the monks in ripped, bloodied robes. Then, suddenly, over all the noise, he heard one distinct, loud shot. He was in his house again, alone, his mother having been dragged into the dark street by the soldiers. He hoped she hadn't been tethered to a pole, unable to resist. He'd have wanted her to run with at least some thought she had a chance. It would have been easier that way. If death ever can be easier. But his wish was idle, he knew. She never would have run. The soldiers might then have shot him for her resistance, and she would not have risked that. Any more than she would have led them to his father— the price they had put on her life. *The inhuman bastards, still killing innocent people almost three decades later.*

A question returned San to the scene. "What will happen to the monks who are tied?" Calabrese asked.

"Shoved into trucks and hauled away." Wang answered.

"Where do they take them?" Tanaka asked.

"We don't know, but there are hundreds who've disappeared so far. They're in jails, hellholes. Some have probably fled, likely over the Thai border. It's estimated that thirty have been killed so far."

The crowd arrived at Suu Kyi's home on University Avenue, a once grand house in the embassy area on Inya Lake, now dilapidated after years of neglect. Their captive leader stood on risers behind the padlocked gates of the iron fence surrounding the villa. From there she could see, and be seen by, the mobs of people standing before her, chanting prayers, singing and crying out for "Mother Suu." Hair swept back, her trademark flowers behind her ears, she waved and smiled with warmth. But there was no way for her to be heard, and she didn't stay long. When she stepped down, the crowd began to disperse, moving in the direction of the crumbling headquarters of Suu Kyi's opposition party.

San experienced the immensity of the protest. The people, masses of them, his people, standing strong in the face of threats and violence. The conditions even worse than he had realized, the editorials too soft in light of what was happening. He felt guilty he hadn't identified more with the Burmese people over the years. Instead, he had focused on an abstraction—a country and a form of government. He wondered if he would be standing in the crowd now had Grant and Evelyn not come into his life. And what about Win? Would he be here? A monk perhaps? Or, a military officer?

One thing he knew. He would call Win. What he had seen on the streets made him wonder how much divided the two of them now, or perhaps how relatively important was what did divide them. He pondered how to approach the discussion with him. To be judgmental about the government would risk shutting down any communication. But the junta's policies had to be on his agenda. They always had represented the deepest, darkest difference between them —at least after what had happened to Grant. If they didn't talk about them now, what could they discuss? The ending of his career? The decline of Win's? The family?

On arrival at the Governor's Residence San placed a call from his room. A male voice answered. "Hello."

"Nyan Win, this is Aun San."

There was silence.

"I am here in Yangon and hope we can get together and talk."

"Yes, I think we should."

Win indicated no surprise that San could detect and no reluctance. He bet Kathy had paved the way. With no further discussion, they agreed to meet at the hotel at 10 that night, when San figured he could dodge his U.N. minders.

At dinner with the contingent in a private dining room at the hotel that evening, Wang reviewed plans for the mission for the next few days. He prepared them for the possibility that their hoped-for meeting with Aung San Suu Kyi the next day at her home would be cancelled after the day's protests and violence in the streets. He thought the scheduled visit to the American Center on Tawwin Road would still occur. There would be other places of interest to see and people to meet, with virtually all of what they were permitted to do or not do being determined arbitrarily at the last minute by the government. The last step would be for the members of the mission to meet to decide upon their findings and formulate their report.

Shortly before 10 pm San excused himself from dinner, saying he was going to turn in. He walked up the broad, carpeted stairway to his room on the second floor. The phone on the bedside table rang. "Aun San, this is Nyan Win. I'm in the lobby."

"Do you want to come up to my room?"

"No, let's meet down here," Win said.

"The bar?" San asked.

"No. In the lobby. We'll walk in the park. It's a beautiful night and," his voice lowered, "it'll be more private that way."

San found Win standing at the bottom of the stairs. They

approached each other, extended their hands to shake, but ultimately, if grudgingly, placed their arms around each other's shoulders in a stiff hug. San felt his face flush.

"This way," Win said pointing toward the doors to the garden, which was fine with San as the path avoided his U.N. keepers. They walked past diners lingering over coffee in the garden, the flames from candles on their tables flickering in the light breeze. Voices were subdued. The tinkling of coffee cups and glasses amidst quiet laughter were the loudest sounds. The scene was calm, contrasting dramatically with the chaos San had experienced in the streets earlier in the day.

They entered the park on a wide lighted walkway. Win quizzed San about his U.N. role. He answered with care, but then decided there was really nothing he need be cautious about so long as he didn't criticize the government. His mission was not clandestine; it was open and publicly stated to be an official U.N. assignment. "You seem to hesitate," Win said. "Are you worried about me?"

"No," San lied.

"Things have changed. I've experienced a lot with the regime. The way they treated me, Myint Thi, Anna Marie. You can't really compare it to how the rulers kept Aung San Suu Kyi from leaving the country to go abroad to her dying husband, but there is a similarity. My family couldn't leave to join me in the U.S., and I couldn't return here to be with my family, unless and until the *Post's* policies on Burma changed. And I've learned more about how Myint Thi's family suffered at the hands of the junta some years ago. I see the government differently now," he said, his eyes cast down, as if he were confessing error.

San was tempted to say, *What I've been telling you all along*, but restrained himself.

"I'm surprised they let you come," Win said. "When I heard it . . ."

"From Kathy?" San interrupted.

"Yes."

"I thought she might call you."

"It was too late for me to warn you," Win said, "to try and stop you."

"Why? It's not dangerous," San said, "or is it?"

"Everything here is dangerous."

San wanted to ask how, but decided to wait.

"The U.N. takes good care of us."

"What exactly are you doing, if you can tell me?"

"Just fact-finding. Then we'll make a report to the U.N." San continued with description of what he had seen on their tour that day, without attempting to characterize the government's actions, which was hardly necessary when monks were roped to street lights and beaten with crowbars. He didn't trust that Win's attitude had changed.

Some time passed before Win asked, "Are you going beyond Rangoon?"

San noticed almost everyone continued to refer to Rangoon and Burma, including now Win, as though they hadn't been renamed Yangon and Myanmar.

Win nodded and said, "Yes, but when you talk with the military or police, use the new names."

"We're not scheduled to go beyond the city, but I wish I could go back to Inle Lake while I'm here. That was home, at least for a while."

"Will they let you?"

"We don't know what they'll let us do. We're supposed to meet with Suu Kyi tomorrow."

"Ha! That would be rare. But maybe I can help on Inle Lake."

"How?" asked San.

"I need to go there. They still trust me and might be willing to let you come with me."

What did he mean "still" trust me? He must not have really broken with the regime. But surely it would be better to go with Win than to try to go alone. "Have you been back there?" San asked.

"I've gone to visit the monastery a couple of times. The same abbot, U Tha Din, is still there. I'm told he has become an influential person, has an important leadership role among the monks."

Couples holding hands and individuals strolling alone passed them as they walked. The only sign of the turmoil of the day was debris strewn through the park and overflowing trash containers. The weather was muggy by the standards of someone used to the coolness of nights in Los Angeles. Mosquitoes buzzed at their ears, not unheard of in Los Angeles either, but the numbers there didn't compete with the swarms here.

"Did the abbot remember you after so many years?"

"Yes. But the person he remembered most was Grant, 'the important publisher.'"

Suddenly, they were quiet. The mention of "publisher" left them both frozen.

Win was the first to speak. "I'm sure he would like to see you since you succeeded Grant and all."

San wanted to ask if the abbot knew of Grant's drowning. He was curious if one of the reasons Win went back to Inle Lake was to talk with the monk about Grant's death and San's role in it. He wondered about the Buddhist attitude toward death, the impermanence of life, how the monk might apply those concepts to an avoidable happening. But the subject was off limits between them, like so many others, a list that had grown ever longer over the years. Leave well enough alone, he thought. It was amazing they were speaking at all, and he knew it best to tread cautiously.

"I would like to go with you," San said. "I'll talk with my wardens about the possibility and how to approach it. Maybe I can call on you to help?"

"Yes," Win nodded.

They had not broached anything serious. That would come later. At least their first talk hadn't ended in disaster.

A few days later Win and San met again on the garden terrace at the Governor's Residence during a break from San's U.N. duties.

"There is one thing I need to tell you," Win said, his left hand playing with the napkin on his lap. "Something I've hidden all these years—even from myself."

"I probably know," San replied.

"What?"

"Your involvement in the Willie the Chin thing."

"No, more important than my alleged life in the drug underworld."

"What then?"

"It's about Grant. I think I knew he was on deck alone." Win paused, looking up into the trees where colorful paper lanterns hung from low branches, "And I didn't do anything about it."

"What do you mean?"

"I was awake; it was too rough to sleep. I heard a thud against the cabin floor, a different sound than the hull hitting the water. Like someone had jumped from the deck into the cabin. Then, the door to the head slammed shut."

He stopped when a waiter arrived with glasses of iced tea and a small plate of rice-flour cakes, then continued, his words spilling out. "I lay there thinking *get up, see what's going on, be sure everything's okay on deck*. But it was so stormy. I didn't want to get up. And I didn't— until I heard someone scream what sounded like a distant 'man overboard.' I jumped out of the bunk and up the ladder. There was no one on deck, not Grant, not you. I took the helm and yelled to the others. Then you and everyone came up."

San said nothing for a long time. Then he tipped his head and squinted at Win. "And you never told me this? You mean you let me believe all this time I was the only one responsible?"

"I didn't know until I first met with U Tha Din on my return here. We were discussing Grant and the accident. U Tha Din asked me questions, and suddenly it was there. It was clear. Like the pieces of a puzzle coming together. Actually, I didn't *know* it was Grant on deck alone. It could have been you. But either way, someone was alone. I should have been up and out of my bunk right away."

San shook his head.

Win continued. "Twice I've gone back to the monastery on the anniversary of Grant's death. Somehow, the place and talking with the old monk give me some peace. That's why I wanted you to talk to him too, for both of us to listen together to his wisdom."

San rose from his chair, his face a reddish tone, his jaw clenched, and dropped his napkin on the table. He took off toward a curving path leading into the hotel's lush gardens and lotus pools. It had been ten years of agony not knowing what Win had finally just told him. Of course, Win should have been on deck at the first sign of trouble. So, he was responsible as well. If Win had gotten his ass up and out, Grant might have been saved. Win had escaped blame by hiding what he knew. And, how was he supposed to believe Win had only recently, with the abbot's help, come to realize what had happened that morning? How could he have drummed something that important out of his mind for so many years?

San continued to walk out the driveway entrance to the hotel and along the tree-lined street. Almost as fast as he piled anger on Win, he realized the same "ifs" that applied to him did to Win, as well. No one would ever know whether Win, had he gone up on deck, would have been able to save Grant any more than San could have. This is what people said to comfort him, but which he'd always had a hard time accepting. Win's revelation didn't change his own guilt. It merely added another person who might have shared responsibility for what happened.

Thirty minutes later, after walking it off, he was back at the hotel and found Win still at the table. Win said, "I didn't have to tell, you know."

"Actually, I imagine you did. I know what it's like. It's probably easier for you to live with the consequences of telling me than with the secret."

"Yes, you are probably right."

San sat down and continued. "I have a ritual on the anniversary myself, one I perform alone. I charter a small boat to sail off the coast in the area where I think the accident occurred. I talk with Grant. I've never told anyone but Michelle. Evelyn was so opposed to any of us being on the water."

"Talk?" Win asked.

"Yeah, mostly about problems at the *Post*, ones we'd had in common. It was reassuring that he'd successfully faced them; it made me feel I could also. But, honestly, I was there to seek forgiveness. To remind him how I pulled on his shirt on the longboat that day and prevented him from sliding overboard. If only I'd been there next to him on the Lady, I could have done it again. The picture of him struggling for his footing, for something to grab, then sliding across the deck into water has never left me. And never will." He looked away, then back. "But it would have been so much easier for me had you told me years ago what happened that morning."

"I know, and I'm sorry, very sorry. I still hope you will go with me to the monastery. He could help us."

San didn't reply immediately. He got up and stood by his chair. "Yes, if only to try and understand how your memory could have revived that way." Rain began to pour and they retreated inside.

San spent four days in Rangoon before the work of the delegation concluded and the team was ready to return to the U.S. The findings and recommendations of the mission were that the government was guilty of the heinous human rights abuses described and that they must stop immediately. San did not have to worry about his lack of impartiality because the other two members were just as strong in their support of the conclusion. The only difference was that San thought Myanmar should be termed a pariah. In a bow to diplomacy, Calabreses and Tanaka thought otherwise.

David Wang resisted San's decision to stay on in the country for a short period with his brother—as San described Win—but had no way to force him to board the plane to Bangkok. Win assured Wang there would be no problem since his cousin was a colonel in the army and would approve their traveling together. Besides, there had been no reported trouble at Inle Lake, the only place they would visit. They would fly Air Bagan and be there for a couple of days.

Wang declared the U.N. could no longer be responsible; San would be on his own.

San managed to phone Michelle from the hotel to tell her his trip would be extended for a few days at Inle Lake where he and Win would be staying at the Inle Princess Resort.

"Rangoon is a civilized city," she said. "I don't care if there's supposedly no problem in Inle Lake. It's in the middle of nowhere and you're losing your U.N. security. I don't care if you're going to be spending your time in a monastery. Since when do monks carry guns that could protect you?"

"Nyan Win's cousin is a military officer. That's all we need."

"That's hardly the same. I don't want you to go."

"Michelle, I'm sorry. There may not be another chance. I know you feel he doesn't deserve it, but there's a lot of history I can't forget. And I've learned more since I've been here, which I'll tell you when I get back. You'll understand. Who knows? This may help me end the nagging feeling of responsibility I've never been able to erase." ⌇

THIRTY-FOUR

A Wise Voice

THE BOAT carrying San and Win eased into the channel, heading away from Nyaungshwe town toward the middle of the lake. They sat on a hard bench at the center, their suitcases stashed on the deck behind them. The crude, wooden, eighteen-foot craft was powered by an outboard motor, and tended by a crew of two, one at the helm, the other at the bow. The boat emerged from the channel, bouncing over calm water as its speed increased. The helmsman threaded through narrow waterways between the reeds and sometimes cut through the growth where there was no canal to follow. Tiny dwellings on wooden stilts, their walls made of bamboo and thatch, their roofs formed by palm leaves over bamboo poles, dotted the reed marshes and seemed to mark the way.

Both crewmen were dressed in thin brown pants, rolled almost to the knee, colorful short sleeve shirts, one red, one plaid, and baseball caps. Their feet were bare. San smiled when he saw their caps worn backward, surprised this style would have migrated all the way here to Inle Lake. Baseball caps had not been standard wear in their youth. Straw hats, hand woven from local grasses, had been the rule then.

San could remember having seen only a few motorboats like this on the lake when he was a boy. More often then boats were muscled through the water by rowers standing, using long wooden oars moved with their legs and feet. He hadn't thought of this curious practice for years. Had it not been for this method—which attracted the few tourists who made their way then to this remote location—the longboat race so many years before would not have taken place. Without the competition that day, his life would have been vastly different. He never would have gone to the United States. And, had he not insisted that Nyan Win join him, his life also would have remained in concrete, though he could hardly imagine the person sitting next to him spending all those years as a monk living in a monastery begging for food.

San saw a structure about one thousand yards ahead, a large center building with small bamboo cottages fanning out on either side. As a complex, there hadn't been anything of this size thirty years before. The biggest structures then had been temples built of wood, thatch and tin, which would have been dwarfed by this building. As they approached, the helmsman turned off the outboard, picked up an oar, and, with the rower at the bow, maneuvered the boat to the dock. Several hotel employees were there to greet them: one holding a tray with welcome drinks, another standing next to a luggage cart, and a third, dressed more formally in a coat as though he might be the manager. The Inle Princess Resort had been recommended as the one four-star establishment on the lake. He could see why.

After having lunch on a terrace overlooking the water, San and Win left the hotel with the same crew who had brought them there. Their craft beat through the flat water. Much at the lake seemed unchanged: fishermen with large cone-shaped nets balanced miraculously on the edges of their tiny boats, children played precariously on the meager decks extending from their huts. A strong sense of calm and quiet was fed by a light mist rising from the water.

The boat glided into the shore close to the village, where San and Win hopped off and walked down a path through rows of crops growing on man-made land. Colorfully dressed farmers bent to tend their crops—women in sarongs, men in longyi, some in pants. They stared as the two men passed, probably because with tan skin and dark eyes, they looked like them, but they were dressed like tourists in khaki pants and short sleeve shirts, wide-brimmed fabric hats shielding their faces from the sweltering mid-day sun.

They continued to walk a few hundred feet to the village, its one street bordered on both sides by small storefronts. Maybe there were a few more stores, and there was one major change: at the head of the street was the temple they had worked on, whose matchstick framing had been covered with wood, bamboo and tin. It appeared to have been there forever.

"I felt we were dragging half the river's rocks, sand and water up here to build that thing," San said. "Now, it's just another building."

"Let's go in and see."

The two removed their shoes and hats and left them at the entrance. The interior was plain. A reclining Buddha against one wall bore gold leaf only on its face, in contrast to the huge Buddha sculptures they had seen in large cities entirely gilded in gold. They left after a minute or two, gathered their things at the door and headed down the dirt road where San's uncle's house had been. They found it, a hovel with small children playing in the dirt. San walked to the door which was covered by a cloth that waved limply in the wind. He called out and a woman appeared. He spoke as best he could in Burmese—he seldom used the language anymore—and returned to the road. "They left years ago. Let's see what we can find out at the blacksmith shop."

The shop was a short distance away, a structure without walls which permitted winds to blow through and cool the blazing temperatures generated by fire and hot metal. They walked into the work area and spoke with an older man who told San his uncle had left ten years earlier. San examined the place carefully. "What if Grant and Evelyn hadn't come?" he said. "I would have been in a gold leaf factory, heaving that mallet all day, every day. I couldn't have done it."

Win pondered San's words. He said in his case, he had known on his first visit back to the monastery that he could not possibly have spent his life there.

They continued down the dusty road toward the monastery, the way they'd travelled so many times, noting again and again how little had changed. It was startling, coming from a modern world where buildings were leveled after just decades in order to make room for something new. Win hesitated at the area of shoreline that could have been the place where they skipped stones. He hadn't thought of their pastime for years. He said nothing as he sensed San start to bend to pick up a stone, then hesitate, only to continue walking forward.

Not far, at the end of the road and at the edge of the water, stood the monastery. A figure appeared at the entrance as they approached, an older man wearing glasses, his head shaved, wearing burgundy robes who held his hands together to his nose and bowed. It was as if the abbot knew exactly when they would arrive and had been waiting. Probably, a novice had seen them on the road and had run ahead to tell him two men in different clothes were on their way.

U Tha Din greeted Win with warmth, and Win in turn introduced Aun San. They entered the building, and the abbot pointed to the bamboo mats on the floor, motioning them to sit down.

"Aun San, you have changed a great deal since you were here last," U Tha Din said with a laugh, almost a giggle. "You could say the same about me, could you not?" he added.

"About all of us."

"I remember the day your parents came to visit. Of course, they were not your parents yet, but I know from Nyan Win they became so."

"Yes, in every sense. At least in my mind," San replied.

Win did not respond.

"I am sorry about your father," U Tha Din said, the smile leaving his face.

San's eyes turned to Win as if to ask how much of the story the abbot knew.

"Your parents were very generous. For years they sent books and paper, pens and pencils for the monks."

Win turned toward San. "And U Tha Din told me it stopped, at a time I would place at about Evelyn's death."

"Had we known, we would have continued," added San.

As they were talking, a sputtering military vehicle pulled up to the front of the temple. Soldiers threw sacks on the ground next to several large burlap bags already lying there. San asked what was in them.

"More rice, from the military," U Tha Din answered with a tone of frustration in his voice.

"Why? The others already on the ground haven't been opened."

"Of course. They drop bundles at monasteries for the monks, but we will not eat it in order to show our protest to the government."

"Who is 'we'?" Win asked.

"The All Burma Young Monks Union."

"You are part of the Union?" San asked.

"I am not a young monk, Aun San," he grinned. "Maybe when you were here before, but now I am old."

Win explained their hope to seek the abbot's guidance about the problems in their relationship. U Tha Din agreed he would try and help, then outlined how they might proceed. He would speak first with Aun San, then with Nyan Win, probably spending more time with Aun San because they had not talked before. That way he could understand the problems from each point of view. Then the three would meet together. The two men would move their things from the hotel and plan to spend a few days in the monastery. The discussions would start early the following morning and be broken only by time to eat and sleep and for the two of them to think and then talk together.

The next day, while San met with the abbot, Win made a nostalgic tour of the *kyoung*. The way the monks lived appeared no different than the way he had experienced it—with no privacy. Maybe it hadn't meant anything to him then, but it surely would now. Straw mats for sleeping were strewn along the edges of large dormitories. Small wooden chests for a few personal effects were placed next to the mats.

Freshly washed robes hung out the windows to dry in the sun and breezes. A musty smell pervaded the room. He strolled down to the kitchen area, remembering how much better the cooking smells were than was the food. Vegetable soup, simmering on the fire, and rice and eggplant were on the menu for the next meal. Bathing still took place on a stone terrace with the use of buckets and water from a hose. Win propelled his mind back: Had he thought he would stay a monk forever? Or in this monastery for his lifetime, like U Tha Din? Or had he been on auto pilot flying as his grandmother wished? He couldn't grab a hold of it, but he knew how lucky he'd been to have the life he had, far from perfect though it may have been.

After U Tha Din talked with both San and Win, they all met in the abbot's private room, which was less spare than the sleeping rooms. A Buddha image and a few photographs of men and boys dressed in robes hung on the wall. They sat on the floor and the old monk started the discussion.

"I would like to talk first about Peter," he said.

San and Win exchanged looks of surprise.

"You understand, we didn't know him," San said.

"Yes, but did he influence you? Tell me how."

San answered, "Sometimes I felt I was being compared to a ghost, that I had to live up to what Peter would have done, what would have been expected of him. Was I really myself, or was I Peter? Reminders of him were everywhere, photographs on the piano, living in his room, stories about his life."

"Was it always that way?" U Tha Din asked. "Did they come to accept you as you?"

"Ultimately, they did. To an extent, I felt used, used to keep Peter alive, until eventually they come to love me. Even then, I was filling what Peter's place would have been at the newspaper."

Win raised his arm as if in school waiting to be called upon. "Grant and Evelyn did treat Aun San as though he were Peter. They never saw me that way, so I didn't feel I had to live up to him. But I was along for the ride so that Aun San could be there. I would have come back home, but he didn't want to. Eventually, I think Evelyn came to care deeply for me. I'm not sure that could be said of Grant, at least not the 'deeply' part."

U Tha Din looked at Win. "But did you want really to be Aun San," he asked, "and, in that way, be seen as Peter, too, as Aun San was?"

"I think he did," San interrupted.

"Then it is interesting," the abbot said. "You, Nyan Win, are jealous of Aun San's role, which is one he didn't want in the first place. Is that possible?"

Neither man responded or appeared to know how to answer. One of the abbot's robes, drying in the window, blew into the room and flapped against the sill. He took the robe down, folded it and continued. "Nyan Win, did you show compassion toward Aun San for the pressure he felt to live the life of another person?"

"And, Aun San," the abbot continued without waiting for an answer, "I ask you, did you show compassion toward your brother for his feelings of being left out?"

They answered almost simultaneously. They had never talked about it; they hadn't known.

"It is not for me to say what either of you should have done, but it is important to put yourself in the place of the other person, to know what he believes, and then examine your own motivations." He paused. "I want you both to think about this—about compassion for each other. Then, you should talk together before we meet again."

At their next meeting together U Tha Din started the conversation. "I want to talk now about Mr. Jensen, if that is alright. This was a very sad happening. It affected you both deeply."

"It was a terrible accident," San said. "The last thing I said to him was to clip on the safety harness."

Win stared straight ahead.

San continued. "I should have hooked him into it, I suppose; he didn't like to do it. It was a great mistake on my part. I live with it every day."

"But, U Tha Din, I've told Aun San that it wasn't only his mistake," Win said. "I've told him about our discussions."

San went on. "I could have made sure the watch was covered by getting Nyan Win up and on deck, and I didn't. The thing that hurt me the most is Nyan Win suggesting I made my job as publisher; in other words, got rid of Grant so the job would be there for me to take."

Win jumped in, "I didn't intend it that way. What I meant is that people were saying you were set up for it, the heir apparent, trained in all the roles, nobody else was considered."

"Whatever you meant, you resented the fact that I had the job. So much so that you fought to force me out of it."

"I knew I couldn't do the job, didn't really have an interest in it anyway. I was an artist. But, let's face it. To do what I did was the only way I had a chance to get Myint Thi and Anna Marie back. I'm not proud of it." He glanced away, then added, "They will be returning with me to Los Angeles shortly."

U Tha Din turned toward Win, "Do you blame Aun San for the accident?"

"It was an accident. I understand that now. I'm sorry, I didn't always."

"Nyan Win, did you show compassion for Aun San's actions when this happened?"

"I wanted to. I tried. The grief, the emotion was sometimes too much, I'm afraid. I was angry then. I understand everybody's role in it now, including my own, that I should have gone on deck when I first thought there might be a problem on the watch."

U Tha Din removed his clouded glasses and wiped his face. It was a hot and humid day. San and Win were sweating profusely, despite their cross-ventilation hiking shirts. The abbot replaced his glasses and said, "I think they call what happened to Nyan Win a 'repressed memory,' where someone's memory of a traumatic experience is blocked for years, then spontaneously comes back. Can you accept that, Aun San?"

"I've thought about it a great deal since he told me." He spoke softly, almost in a whisper as if he were exhausted. "I would like to have known what happened, earlier. But, no matter that he blames himself, I know I am the one who had the responsibility."

"Maybe neither of you is to blame," U Tha Din offered.

In this vein, the conversations continued for more than two days. The parting words were U Tha Din's: "Another thing to think about is resentment. There has been so much in your lives. Where did it start? What was its cause? Nyan Win, you got the opportunity to go to America because of Aun San. But do you thank him for this? Or do you resent him for it? Dependence breeds resentment. Each of us wants to be independent, and we resent it when we're not. That could explain a lot."

The abbot continued. "There have been awful events in your family, too many accidents, too much sadness. But suffering is an inevitable part of all of our lives, as is the impermanence of life itself. When you think of Peter—where all of this began—remember these words of the Dalai Lama: 'Some people sweet and attractive, strong and healthy happen to die young. They are masters in disguise teaching us about impermanence."

San walked to the Buddha at the wall. "How different it might have been for Grant and Evelyn had they be able to think of Peter in that way?" he said. "How different for all of us? None of this might have happened."

"And, who knows whether that would have been better or worse," Win added.

"Think about this and you will understand," the abbot said. He smiled at the two men. "This is enough for now. You know as much as a poor, old monk's brain has to offer. Hopefully, all has become clearer over these few days. Go forward and let your lives be guided by compassion. And come back to see me again someday—together."

That night the two men slept next to each other in the dormitory, as they had as boys when they were facing the exciting, frightening possibility of leaving their homeland and going to a foreign world. What was ahead of them now was not frightening but exciting. They had been given a challenge: much to understand about themselves and each other; much to forgive, but only after forgiving oneself; and much for which to feel compassion. Think of the other, not yourself, had been the repetitive chord. In the darkened room they whispered:

"Aun San, can you forgive me?"

"We are brothers, Nyan Win. I'll try to forgive."

"I was too hard," Nyan Win said.

"As was I. We both were. Can you forgive me?"

"I will try also. I think so."

Nothing more was said. San knew that because of Win's bringing them together here, they could finally rebuild a relationship. Somehow his brother's honesty relieved San of the oppressive feeling of guilt he had borne for so many years. Win's hand came to rest on San's arm. Win fell asleep. San soon followed. ∿

THIRTY-FIVE

Flight By Water

A T DAYBREAK, San was awakened by what sounded like the creaking of floorboards. He opened his eyes and could barely make out shadowy figures slipping through the dark room. Clearer was the sound of their murmuring and the rush of air as they passed by in their robes. These must be the bodies that had been snoring around him as he tried to sleep through the night. Unlike Win, he wasn't used to sleeping in a room full of people.

Soon there was quiet again. San leaned up on one elbow and looked to his side where Win had bedded down the night before. He could see a body curled there. Apparently Win had slept through the commotion. San tried to go back to sleep. It was too early to get up. He hadn't realized that monks got started at this hour.

After a few minutes, another figure entered the room and peered in San's direction, calling out, "Nyan Win, Aun San" in a low voice.

"Yes," San whispered.

"We must talk, now." It sounded like U Tha Din's voice.

"U Tha Din?"

"Yes. Is Nyan Win awake?"

"I don't think so."

The abbot started to shake the blanketed figure next to him. "Nyan Win, wake up."

"What?"

"We must talk."

Win mumbled, "Isn't it too early to talk again?"

"It's not about that," U Tha Din answered. "There is no time to waste."

Win sat up and turned to the old man.

"Soldiers are outside; their trucks are blocking the road. They allowed the monks to pass with their alms bowls. One of the monks returned and said the captain wanted me to come out. I'm not sure if they know I have two visitors."

"Why do they want you?" San asked.

"You remember that I told you about the All Burma Young Monks Union?"

"Yes."

"They are saying I'm the leader of it."

"Are you?" Win asked.

"I do have a role, that of an elder guiding younger charges."

"What would they do to you?" said San.

"As long as I don't go out, they must come in to get me. Even the junta is reluctant to do that, but, ultimately, if they have to . . . well, a few days ago, they did enter a monastery in Mandalay, pulled the monks out, shoved them in vans and drove away. We don't know what has happened to them."

Light was just beginning to filter into the room. San and Win looked at each other, their eyes reflecting uncertainty.

"You must leave. I'm afraid anyone found with me will be thrown in jail—or worse."

"We couldn't leave without you," Win said. He moved toward the window, standing far enough back to be sure he was not visible. Soldiers were milling, their boots scuffling in the dirt, cigarettes glowed, an occasional word could be heard, even a muffled laugh. It was hard to tell but there appeared to be eight of them. San crept forward to see what was going on outside.

San turned to Win, "What about your cousin in the army?"

"I don't really trust him. Can we get help through the U.N.?"

"They told me I was on my own if I left Rangoon and came here."

"You must leave, but not through the soldiers," the abbot said. "There is a small boat at the edge of the lake in the reeds in back of the monastery. You can go out through the kitchen. I don't believe there are any soldiers there. They probably think the only access is from the road in front. You can crawl through the reeds to the boat, then row close to the edge of the lake. About fifteen hundred meters from here, you will find a small shack standing alone. Go there. I will give you a note and the man who lives there will take you to Rangoon."

"You must come with us," Win said.

"I cannot leave the monastery."

"You know where the boat is, how to go, the people who will be there to take us," San said. "We could have trouble without you."

The abbot hesitated, appearing to debate what to do. Finally he said, "I will take you to the shack if you wish, but I must come right back to the *kyoung* to be here when the monks return. Come, I will show you the way." He led them down squeaky stairs and through the kitchen to the rear of the building, where he opened the door and peered out in both directions. "They are not here." He pointed toward the right to a small tree among the reeds at the edge of the lake. He started to walk, crouching, toward the tree, motioning them to stay low and follow. The growth was high enough to hide their bodies, but there was no way to prevent the reeds from rustling as they passed. It was becoming lighter. They reached the tree, where an old wooden boat with two long oars was tied with a frayed rope.

U Tha Din grabbed a battered bucket from the bottom of the boat and started to bail the water standing in the hull. San extended a hand, "Here, let me do that."

"No, I will," the abbot answered. "Unfortunately, I'm used to it. When I finish, you two climb in. I will push until it gets too deep, then you lift me in. Aun San, you and I will row. It will be hard because the oars are long for standing which we cannot do. Nyan Win, you will keep bailing after we get moving. It's constant in this old boat."

When most of the water had been bailed overboard, U Tha Din motioned to San who struggled with both arms to pull himself into the boat. He then, in turn, extended his hands to Win to tug him aboard. After three attempts Win ended up face down on his belly, his feet hanging over the side. He was finally able to scramble his full length into the boat.

"I'm losing my footing, I've got to get in," U Tha Din whispered. San told him to turn his back to the side of the boat, where he grabbed under the abbot's arm pits and hoisted him over the side. The boat wobbled to which Win said, firmly, yet quietly, "be careful."

San picked up one of the oars. U Tha Din took the second one and handed Win the bucket. They glided through the reeds, using the oars as best they could from a sitting or kneeling stance. Win scooped the water that was rapidly rising in the hull. San heard birds squawking and saw several ibis flying above them. He wished the birds would leave, fearing they might signal the presence of something in the water.

After a few minutes, the abbot said, "I think we are far enough now that we can stand. We can row faster that way. Aun San, do you think you can still do it?"

"It's like biking, I suppose."

"You see the small building there in the distance?" the abbot said, pointing to the water's edge beyond a soft bend in the shoreline. "We have to make it there."

San looked back in the direction of the monastery. "There's a motorboat, way off. It could be coming this way. See, there," he said, directing his hand to a distant object.

"It could be anyone," the abbot said, "but keep at it, we can make it."

A few minutes later, they could hear a man's voice from across the water, apparently magnified by a bullhorn: the words, spoken in Burmese, then repeated, used U Tha Din's name.

The abbot came as close as he could to a yell: "Keep going. Row as fast as you can. Row."

The noise of the motorboat echoed over the water. The bullhorn announced again "*Tha Din. Yuh! Makho pee psi meh!* Stop. Shoot."

"There's another one coming from the other side. We'll never make it," San said. Two soldiers stood in the center of the deck of the first vessel as it came closer, their rifles focused on the little oar boat. A barrage of bullets rang out slicing into the water on the side of the boat and splintering the hull, letting water gush in.

Win said, "Aun San, get down, duck."

"We have to row." As San said this, another round of fire was released. Win grunted, dropped the bucket and fell forward on the side of the boat. Blood spouted from the back of his neck. The water turned red and roiled with a frenzy of fish, appearing as if on cue. San reached for the back of Win's shirt to keep his mouth above water and tried to pull him back into the boat. He cried, "Nyan Win, Nyan Win."

More shots rang out as the motorboat bore down on the craft, one striking U Tha Din in the middle of the back, knocking him to the deck. The first military boat slowed as it approached, the four soldiers aboard jabbering in Burmese. The order from the bullhorn now was "Surrender." San tried to stabilize himself, standing, feet far apart, as the wake from the on-coming boats rumbled the oar boat. He raised his arms. What he couldn't stabilize were his emotions, screaming, "Bastards, you shot my brother. If you've killed him, I'll . . . You fuckers, fucking bastards."

The captain commanded, "*Lehn eh cha!* Surrender!" then spit "Or you'll be fish meat, too."

San lurched at him, falling over U Tha Din's body which lay in the bottom of the boat, apparently lifeless until it emitted a groan. "And you've shot a holy man."

"A leader of the rebellion. A traitor," the officer shouted.

"Fuckers," San yelled hysterically, shaking as he was pulled onboard the military craft, swinging at his captors. The captain cried out at him to shut up and slapped him across the face, knocking him to the deck. Grudgingly, San knew he had no way to fight.

Win's motionless body was pulled into the soldiers' boat and covered with a canvas. U Tha Din was also dragged onboard and his wound was examined as they motored back toward the monastery. On off-loading, the captain pummeled San with questions about his role in the rebellion: "Why are you here? Why was your brother here? Why are you with the abbot?"

San mumbled answers: "Here with brother trying to work out family problems. With help of abbot. Nothing to do with rebellion."

San felt the spike of a boot in his side. "Liar. Why are you support- ing the rebellion?" the captain demanded.

"Not. Here with U.N. That's all."

The captain pushed the butt of his rifle into his captive's chest.

San cried, "You, terrible mistake. Here on a United Nations mis- sion. My brother, there, related to Colonel Kyan Se, assigned to head- quarters in Yangon." The monastery was now engulfed in a mass of flame and smoke. San stared at the abbot who lay unconscious on the pier. At least he didn't have to see his beloved monastery being torched. Then, looking at Win, he said, "My brother, he is Christian, I want him. My brother, brother . . ." With that, everything turned black for San, and he rolled to his side. ∽

q

H E WAS never able to conjure the memory of what happened after he passed out at Inle Lake and before the soft touch of a nurse's hand in a hospital in Rangoon. He had no memory of how he got there or who took him. The doctors said it was the result of shock, a partial amnesia that blocked his memory. They had no explanation why it hadn't also blocked the events on the water just before, the memories of which tortured him. It would have been more merciful had it all disappeared. At least he could now better understand how it had taken years for Win to remember what had happened when Grant was lost overboard.

The authorities had apparently decided there was no reason for him to be in a hospital, and he was hauled off to a dingy jail occupied mostly by monks in dirty, flowing robes. Not until a week of interrogation had ended, leaving him with wounds and burns over his body, was he released to a U.N. officer who had been trying to convince the regime that Sanford Jensen had nothing to do with the rebellion, and that incarcerating and torturing U.N. personnel could result in even tougher sanctions being imposed on the country by the international community. Unfortunately, San remembered every minute of the interrogation.

Once released, he tried to obtain information about U Tha Din's condition and whereabouts. Only sometime later did he learn the abbot had escaped his military captors while being transported to Rangoon. After weeks in which he hid in a farmer's barn and grew his hair and a beard, he had fled the country at Mae Sot, a Thai city on the border, posing as a conductor on the bus of a friendly driver.

Win's body was cremated in Burma and his ashes eventually interred at Forest Lawn next to Evelyn, and to Grant's and Peter's empty graves. A lengthy obituary ran in the *Post* relating the unusual circumstances of two Burmese boys being brought to the United States to live with the newspaper publishing family. It told the story of how Sanford Jensen had succeeded his father when Grant Jensen was lost at sea, mentioning for the first time in that paper that no one had been on deck when he went overboard.

San returned to Los Angeles and made it his primary life's work to advance the interests of the National League for Democracy and the international fight against the use of torture. He also helped support the "Saffron Monks" in exile in the United States, which included U Tha Din. After leading the rebellion and fleeing for their lives, these holy men made their way to a temple and monastery established for them in a row house in Brooklyn. San and the abbot were in frequent contact.

While San and Michelle lived a short distance from Myint Thi and Anna Marie in Bel Air, they did not see one another often as Myint Thi blamed San for leading her husband back to Inle Lake. Kathy retired from the foreign service and lived in Paris, seeing her brother when she returned to Los Angeles once a year. San continued to read the *Post* daily until it was acquired by a national chain of newspapers and stripped of its uniqueness. No member of the extended Jensen family ever served in the senior executive ranks of the paper again.

Hardly a day passed that San did not think of Win. He knew from the abbot's teachings that he had to learn to forgive himself before he could forgive his brother, yet he found it easier to do the latter than the former. He was grateful for the last days of resolution they had together at Inle Lake, but he would never understand fully why their relationship had travelled such a rocky course. One thing he could comprehend, ultimately, was the paradox of Win wanting to be him all the while he did not want to be Peter.

When Sanford Jensen died two decades later, the *Post* ran an obituary that was largely an adaptation of the one it published on Win's death. Always the newspaper man, San had left instructions that his obituary was to close with "-30-," the same legend that appeared on his father's and his grandfather's grave stones. It did not. The obit department at the *Post* ignored the request, the paper having not used "-30-" at the end of stories in many years. ∾

ACKNOWLEDGMENTS

I AM INDEBTED TO MY WIFE, Linda Vaughn, for her editorial assistance, her patience, and her constant encouragement; to Marcella Larsen and Catherine Lutz who saw the story grow from the beginning; to Adrienne Brodeur for her guidance throughout; to Hensley Peterson, and Justine Cook, Beth Slattery and Sara Garton for their editorial comments.

I received infusions of knowledge and ideas from many, first and foremost from the Saffron Monks, U Pyinya Zawta, U Gawsita and U Agga Nyana, and Carol Keeley and Peter Poppick who made my time with the monks possible. Others to whom my deep thanks go include Tom Bernard, Dr. Archer Bishop, Daryl Buffenstein, Tom Congdon, Ross Haberman, Jay Hughes, Michael Kader, Anne Porath, Al Slaight, Lloyd Schermer, Dick Scully, Tom Van Stratton, my brother Bill Vaughn, and Diane Young.

Finally, I want to thank Aspen Words, a program of the Aspen Institute, whose Summer Words events permitted me to work shop various chapters of the manuscript with wonderful writers and teachers. ∼

CPSIA information can be obtained
at www.ICGtesting.com
Printed in the USA
FSHW02n1951240718
50878FS

9 780996 445450